FUELED: CHANGING LANES
Book Two

by
BRITTANY SHANNON

ISBN-13
978-0-9986007-5-8
ISBN-10:
099860075X

Prologue

They stumbled into the bar and right into a cluster of beautiful people. The mid-twenty-something men were all looking up and down Ayden. They tilted their pints, full to the brim, in the air. It wasn't her fault her clothing was too tight. She hadn't purchased the outfit herself. A plain, gray shirt, form-fitting jeans, and a pair of antique cowboy boots. She hadn't gotten the opportunity to change, do her hair, make a phone call. Not even the decency to object as to where she was going. Now, the country clad ensmeble was garnering quite a bit of male attention.

But Ayden didn't care for that. She was glaring at the scantily clad women that were part of the bar crowd. All sparkly tops and stilettos, mid-drifts and daisy dukes, gaping openly at the blue-eyed specimen next to Ayden. Chet was regaining his composure at her side. Donning his usual black attire and nonchalance, his piercing eyes were magnificently bold against the dark of his hair. It didn't matter that he'd vaulted through the entrance of the bar with *her*. Every female in a ten mile radius was swooning.

The bravest of them touched Chet's sleeve, angling into his tattooed arm and making a suggestive remark. Ayden couldn't help herself.

"He has an STD," she scoffed.

Chet grabbed Ayden's elbow roughly, turning around and stepping away from the doorway.

"Have you met my schizophrenic sister?" he asked a spectating male, glancing at Ayden. "This is Ayden. Or is it Lucy today, sis? Please don't cut me."

Scornful, Ayden tried to wrestle free. Chet took hold of her other elbow. The pressure of his fingers was crushing. Forcing her ahead of him, he steered her further into the bar. Ayden was sputtering under her breath, struggling against Chet's grip, and kicking out at his heels. He wrapped his other arm tightly around her waist. After knocking into a few tables, he'd had enough of her antics. He released her and kicked an abandoned stool from the bar out into her path. She doubled over it with a grunt.

Growling, Ayden shoved the stool aside and flipped Chet the middle finger. He ignored her, grinning errantly as he searched for an empty table. Ayden jumped at the opportunity. She sidled over to the nearest eligible looking bachelor, grabbed the collar of his shirt, and wrenched his face toward hers.

"Hi, I'm Lucy. You are?"

Chet's head spun on his shoulders.

Ayden's admirer smiled slickly. He reached a hand out to rest his palm on her waist, gloating at his buddies. They were all drinking martinis. Chet rolled his eyes.

"Are you from around here?" the man asked.

She traced the rim of his martini glass. "I am."

"No, she isn't." Chet grabbed the front of Ayden's shirt. He ripped her clear of the ground, heaving her around and setting her down behind him, away from those high-class perverts.

"Careful, I'll cut you," Ayden told Chet.

Chet frowned down at her.

"Cut me," he said above the noise of the bar, "a deal. Truce?"

Ayden grabbed a full shot glass off a passing tray and tossed it at Chet's face. He gracefully dodged the flying ounce of liquid, stealing a shot for himself off the same tray before the cocktail waitress noticed.

"You've got it quite wrong," he told Ayden with a raise of his eyebrows that said, "See?" With a cock of his head, he drank the shot and produced the empty glass before Ayden's nose before slamming it down on the closest table. "Much more useful when ingested."

Ayden stared at Chet slit-eyed. "I thought you didn't drink?"

"You've reduced me to desperation."

Grasping her shoulder firmly, Chet dragged Ayden a few more feet and then plunked her down in a wobbly, wooden chair at an empty table near the karaoke stage. Someone was singing a very inebriated version of Margaritaville. Sitting across from her, Chet ran a hand down his hair and dared a conceited smile.

"Having fun yet?"

"I've learned to tolerate your company," Ayden quipped.

4

"How hard can it be?"

"I know how hard it isn't," he mumbled.

"Oh, ouch!" She pretended to have a heart attack, groping her chest. "That one really hurt."

"Do you need me to make you feel better?" He slipped his fingers beneath the table to stroke her knee. "There's a bathroom just around the corner—"

"Sorry," Ayden sneered. "I choke on small bones."

Chet smiled slyly at her. She hadn't smacked his hand away.

Leaning forward so his elbows disappeared below the table, he let his hand skate up her thigh. Her cheeks darkened to a shade of dusted rose

"You're deliriously sensual when you're mad."

"I don't want to know what you find sensual," Ayden snapped, finally shoving his hand away. "It indicates you've had enough practice to know what you *don't* find sensual."

"And you don't?" he countered lazily.

"No."

"Mitchell?"

"Husband." Her expression held more contempt than he'd ever seen on her pretty face. She glanced at the bar. "The one and only."

"What about Craig?"

Ayden gritted her teeth as she replied, "Unlike *some people,* Craig wasn't into high-speed car chases and guns and sensuality. He was a proper gentleman. We didn't really get passed the classic, old-fashioned dating."

Chet allowed one of his eyebrows to arch. He sat back in his chair, linking his hands behind his head and muttering under his breath, "Point two for Chet."

"You're so infuriating!" Ayden squalled, but her shrillness was not heard above the clamor of the bar and karaoke singers.

"I offered to make it up to you," Chet grinned sideways as he kicked his chair back onto its hind legs. It gave her a teasing glimpse of his tongue ring.

Ayden crossed her arms over her chest and averted her gaze.

After a moment, Chet returned his chair to its natural position and asked, "What about me?"

A wave of hurt flared in her gaze before she squelched it.

"Our time together hardly qualifies as 'passed dating,'" she answered. "You've brought me into this catastrophe, with no way out. It's the single biggest mistake of my life."

He knew she was ticked off. Her feelings had been radically jarred. Her safety compromised. Her life in upheaval. *Good*, he thought to himself. His feelings were in disarray, too. It was about time she felt the weight of the situation the way he did. Her running to Craig was about the stupidest thing she could have ever done, and because of that they had a bigger mess on their hands.

Ayden was thinking back to several days before also. Her frown was downcast as she tried to force memories of being in Chet's arms from her mind. His lips, his body, his smell. Then, agony, tears, heartache. To think so much had transpired since then, she wasn't even sure it really happened. For a moment, the crowded room of social drunkards dissolved. The music diminished until numbness rang in her ears. She was back at the estate, on the ground. . . alone.

1

Ayden had exhausted her body of any and all emotion. She was standing in the entryway of the estate, unaccompanied, staring bleary-eyed at the cell phone in her hand. In the other, she held the picture of Chet that she'd found in the closet. The one that had been taken on the day he'd described as *the day his life changed forever*. The boy staring back at her looked lost and lonely, forlorn and unloved. It reminded her so much of that day in the grocery aisle, and the reason she had felt like striking up a conversation with him in the first place.

Since day one, Ayden wanted to take Chet's hurt away.

But maybe Chet wasn't hurting as bad as she thought. Maybe he was just so lost in his own selfishness. He lacked hindsight and basic human sentiment. He caused *her* hurt.

Both Ayden's hands were shaking, despite the spreading numbness she felt. When she opened her fingers, the photograph fluttered to the ground. Her body ached, too depleted to produce even a single more tear. That's what happens when you love bad men, she figured out. You run out of tears. Chet had taken what she'd given him. Like all men. Now, he was gone.

There was no "see you soon, toots" or "wait for me, I'll come back" while he drove away from her.

How could she be so stupid?

Wasn't it enough when she learned of Starla? If that was the kind of woman Chet liked to get involved with, Ayden should have known better. *She* let this happen again. It was her own fault and this colossal debacle was her punishment. She deserved every measure of pain she felt. Swallowing her guilt, she turned to glare around the estate.

Chet was good, alright—better than Mitchell—for coaxing her in, charming her with false acts of kindness and charisma. Ayden followed her feet into the house, down the hall to the master suite. Dialing a number, she lifted her cell to her ear.

"Ayden?"

"Craig…" Her voice broke off just hearing him.

He sounded as if he still cared, still had feelings for her. If he did—and she desperately hoped he did—he would come get her.

Chet took off in the Mustang, and she wasn't about to attempt to drive the beastly motorcycle. The estate was far enough away that she wasn't comfortable calling a cab or any of the girls she'd worked with at the salon. Besides, she wasn't supposed to have *any* connections. This was chancy enough.

Taking a ragged breath, Ayden said, "I need a huge favor."

"Are you okay?" Craig asked anxiously. "You don't sound too good."

"No, I'm not." Ayden pinched her eyes shut, then paced into the bathroom to grab some essentials. "The truth is…"

Craig was quiet while she searched for the right words.

"The truth is I want to tell you the truth. I do. And I will. But right now, I need a ride. Are you busy? Is there any way you could come get me?"

"Is it that guy?" Craig asked with obvious despise.

"I do not want to talk about *that guy*, okay?" she responded. "Can you come get me or not?"

"Where are you?"

***

Craig's Acura pulled into the circular driveway. Ayden stood outside, carrying a duffel bag stuffed full of everything she could fit in it. She'd changed out of her skirt into jeans, throwing on some basic flats. Her hair was pulled back in a lazy ponytail. In her hand was her cell phone. The rest of her belongings would have to be replaced. Everything was replaceable, she had decided. Even men. Even love.

Craig was dressed in his business suit. His hair was cropped neatly, and she knew he'd had someone else cut it last by the height of the fade. He smelled of the musky cologne she remembered, and he looked pleasant and handsome when he smiled. He helped her load the bag into the backseat and then got into the driver's side. Ayden slumped into the passenger's seat, quickly turning off the radio that was set to a station destined to undo her. She couldn't handle country music right now. Not when most of the songs were written specifically about her life.

Ayden gripped her cell with both hands as Craig pulled away from the estate. Cranking her neck around, she watched the large house grow smaller and smaller while he drove back toward the freeway. Memories lived within those walls, and pieces of her soul she was sure she'd never get back. If she broke into any more fragments, she didn't know how she'd remain upright. She pictured her head on a stick, with two sock feet, like a puppet. She'd been a puppet these past few days. . . maybe even the past few years.

Maybe all her life.

Ayden hadn't even brought the key to the front door with her. It was on the ground on the doorstep. There was no way she was going to return to that place. Sighing, she faced forward and lifted a palm to her head.

"I suppose I owe you an explanation."

Craig stretched one elbow out, resting his palm on his steering wheel. His car smelled like polish and was pristinely clean. Ayden wondered just what plans he'd dropped, or what scheduled engagements had been rearranged, so he could come pick her up. It was six in the evening. The day was practically over, but what did Craig do in his free time? Perhaps he was missing a game of golf, or a mini series on TV to catch up on. It was Sunday. There was likely a singles ward fireside.

She was just glad he'd come to get her. He was reliable. That meant something.

Shifting her gaze across the car, Ayden saw Craig scrutinizing her.

"I want to tell you the whole truth," she said.

"You look like you've been crying," he muttered, glancing back at the road.

She watched the scenery pass, remembering how beautiful she thought the hills looked the first time Chet had driven her out here. The winery was like a dream come true.

"I met Chet when I was seventeen. . ." Ayden began. "A couple years before that, if you want to get technical."

Her story continued, detail for detail, through her marriage, through Las Vegas, all the way up until the very breath she took in the car now. Craig stole a nervous glimpse over at her. They were parked in his driveway, had been for some time, and he motioned toward the digital clock.

"Come inside, and I'll make you some dinner," he said. "I need a moment to think."

Ayden nodded.

Craig carried her bag into his house and went toward the kitchen with a vague comment about her making herself comfortable. She'd never been in his house before. Wandering down the halls, she discovered it was much like the house Chet had let her live in before the big shoot out that took place in it. The day she shot and killed two men using a shotgun. What had become of that house? It was completely peppered with bullet holes last Ayden saw it. Did the police run it down, or turn it over to Nogo Saucedo?

Craig's residence was small and quaint in a nice neighborhood of Fresno, California, with a red, tiled roof and palm trees in the yard. It had three bedrooms and one bathroom in the hall. There was a living room connected to the kitchen, where Craig was standing. The makings of a chicken casserole lay out on the counter. His furniture was modern and stylish, not eccentric, but not drab either. Wall hangings were displayed in the hallway, a large clock ticked over the fireplace in the living room, and red appliances completed the kitchen décor.

"Need any help?" Ayden offered.

Craig shook his head. "Take a seat. Want something to drink?"

She strode toward the fridge. "I'll get it."

Opening the fridge, Ayden found that he had quite the assortment of beverages. She chose a canned juice and took a seat in the living room.

"I didn't mean to bother you by calling," she mumbled, picking at her nails.

Craig stopped for a minute, staring at her. He'd been reticent since she got into his car, but she guessed she deserved the remoteness. Ever since he helped her pack her belongings from the salon into Chet's Mustang, Craig must have had misgivings about her. It made Ayden feel guilty and confused, because she wasn't sure herself if she'd led Craig on. Feelings, though undecided, had been brewing between her and Chet. Still, there were fond feelings for Craig inside of her as well, and it rankled her that she'd hurt him.

"You aren't bothering me," Craig said at last. "I'm just…" He scratched the back of his head, "…confused."

"You and I both," Ayden said, taking a drink.

Okay, maybe she'd left out *some* details in her account Chet the Enigmatic Black Bird Singing in the Dead of Night. She'd left out their kiss, and the fact that Chet told her he loved her, and she told him she loved him. *Mi ami?* How ironic that only one of them meant it. That's probably why Chet had it tattooed on his chest, right below his heart. He wanted to know if all the women he seduced loved him.

Craig didn't need to know *those* niceties. In fact, Ayden hated that she couldn't get them out of her mind. She kept seeing Chet's face light up, and the sweet smile that brightened the blue of his eyes as he sat in church with her. She could feel his tongue, the metal stud, skimming across her lips. His voice, mellow and raspy, in her ear.

When the food was finished cooking, Craig brought over two plates for himself and Ayden. They sat at the kitchen table eating in mostly companionable silence, until Craig reached over and took one of Ayden's hands in his. It startled her, and she dropped her fork on the ground. She didn't know if being touched by a male was something she wanted to endure for a very long time. First Mitchell…then Chet…did men only want one thing?

She and Craig might not be in love, but there was something—a familiarity—that made the line between friendship or more dangerously thin.

When Ayden bent to pick the fork up, Craig stopped her. She looked into his deep, coffee-brown eyes, afraid of what she saw in there. He obviously still had feelings for her. Romantic feelings.

"Ayden," he stated. "I couldn't help but think—while you were gone with him—there was something I could do to make you see. If I did anything wrong, anything to offend you during the time we were dating each other, I'm sorry. I only wanted us to work out. You're the first person in a long time I could see myself having a relationship with."

Relationship?

That's exactly what Ayden wanted. A relationship. Someone she could call and tell about her bad day. Someone who she could come home to on a regular basis, and trust to be there. Someone who wanted her company and no one else's. Someone who would call her just to hear her voice. Craig would be that normal guy. Theirs would be a normal relationship. There would be no lying, no crying, no hiding. No drugs and mafia problems. This was what she needed.

"Tell me what you're thinking," Craig said quietly.

Ayden continued to watch his large palm smothering hers. "I'm having a hard time thinking, Craig," she answered.

He gave her a wan smile. "I guess I should understand that. But will you at least stay here? Stay the night. You have nowhere else to go and…and…tomorrow, when you've had some time to think, we can talk more about us."

Us?

Why was everything coming out of his mouth grating to her bones?

She knew she really didn't have anywhere to go, especially with Saucedo's men on the lookout, but staying here with Craig made her uneasy.

"I need another fork," she said, standing to retrieve one from the kitchen. When she returned, Craig lifted a hand to stroke her back a few times, and then returned his attention to his dinner.

It was eight-thirty, and they cleared the dishes together. It reminded Ayden of the night she and Chet had cooked dinner together. Afterward, Craig pulled out a heavy-duty blanket from his storage closet and let her use one of the pillows from his bed. She was setting up camp on the couch, when her cell phone started to ring somewhere. Craig was waltzing into the kitchen, and he glanced at her expectantly. She was frozen, hands suspended with the blanket clutched in her fingers, staring at the couch.

"You've got a call coming in," Craig said over his shoulder.

It was not a call. It was a demon.

Ayden knew that ringtone. *Burnin' Love.* It was assigned to one person in particular. And what in the world would he want now?

"Let it go to voicemail," Ayden demanded, huffing as she bundled up beneath the blanket and sank down onto the couch.

Craig came back, carrying her cell in his hand.

"Here," he said dropping it in her lap. She wondered if he had peeked at the caller ID, but he didn't mention anything. He said simply, "I'll get a movie from my room, and we can watch it out here. Is that okay?"

"Fine."

Ayden stared at the screen of her phone. She had one missed call.

Chet.

"Selfish fool," she murmured and then instantly felt ashamed. How could she say Chet was selfish when he'd given her everything he had? He was the kindest person she'd ever met, the most giving, the most gentle. Somehow, he was also the most unpredictable and dangerous. He'd hurt her more than Mitchell.

She put her cell on silent. Tossing her hair, she let it drop to the ground beside the couch. With a second thought, she kicked it with her toe.

Craig returned, holding up an action film Ayden had never seen. "It's a new release. I got in special delivery."

"Fine," she responded again.

When the movie started, Craig took his position on the couch beside Ayden. Their shoulders would have been touching if it weren't for the enormous blanket she'd wrapped around herself. Still, Craig wouldn't be deflected by mere inches of fleece. He raised one arm and wrapped it around her shoulders, tugging until she leaned into him. Ayden hoped she hid the scowl from her face. Her angst had nothing to do with Craig. Friends could be friendly with a side-arm-hug. He was a decent man. *A good man*, she told herself resolutely.

He was such a good man, that he sat almost stock still the entire movie. Even during the times when Ayden's cell buzzed obnoxiously from the floor, Craig hadn't so much as glanced over at her. He must have been deathly curious about who was insistent upon reaching her. She kind of was herself, but her brain was hay-wire and nothing would matter until the morning, when she could think clearly. Then she and Craig could have an adult to adult talk, and discuss their future.

Future?

She meant predicament. Goals needed to be set. Resolutions put into place.

Ayden yawned when the credits started rolling, realizing she hadn't paid attention to a minute of the movie. Her body was extremely negated of energy. It had been a draining day, and she felt like her reservoir of emotion had been utterly emptied. Nothing and no one could improve her mood. Food tasted like cardboard. She was so tired she didn't even want to sleep.

Craig stood, stretched, and then switched the TV off. He was acting stiff and reserved, but then again Ayden wasn't exactly herself either. The atmosphere was as gauche as their first date.

"I've got to get to bed," Craig stated. "Early morning work."

Ayden nodded. It was dark outside, and only the lamplight illuminated the room. Craig had removed his suit coat, and was now loosening his tie. She watched his hands work, envisioning them doing other things. Nothing remarkable happened. Her mind didn't muse, her stomach didn't flutter. She wasn't even worried about spending the night under the same roof as him, at least not for the reasons she should be. It made her uneasy because someone might find out.

Eventually, Craig pulled his tie loose and bent to kiss the top of Ayden's head. "Are you sure you're alright?"

"I never said I was," she replied. "I'm sorry. Sorry. It has been an awful day. I just need to sleep. I'll feel better tomorrow."

"Okay," Craig whispered, touching her shoulder. "We'll talk more tomorrow. Sleep good."

"You, too," Ayden said as he disappeared down the hall.

It was horrible, her treatment of him. He sensed it as well, but she prayed he was mature and knowledgeable enough to realize what a fiasco she'd gotten herself into. Even though she'd told Craig the truth about Chet's business, she'd left out how important of a role he played in Fresno's drug territory, and also just how powerful his boss, Nogo Saucedo, was…and that Ayden was on the man's list of wanted individuals. At least none of Saucedo's men knew about Craig, or where Craig lived. A solid night's rest was all she needed to regenerate. Tomorrow, she would spend quality time recovering. No tribulation could be quite as devastating as her divorce. She was prepared to start over.

The house fell quiet and dark. Craig had turned the lamp off upon exiting the room, and now just a sliver of moonlight shone through the curtains. Ayden curled up on the couch, staring at the wall blankly. She would not cry. Not ever. She would never be the victim again. After a quick and begrudging prayer, she tucked the blankets tightly beneath her chin.

Her eyes were beginning to droop when her cell phone buzzed once more. It was short. Just a text message. She didn't care to look, but snuggled deeper into the couch. All around her, the fluff felt soft and secure. Like she was enveloped in serenity. It was sure to keep her warm, and that thought made her smile erroneously. Craig would keep her warm. His house was safe. *He* was safe.

2

The incessant vibrating of Ayden's cell phone woke her up a few hours later. She hadn't realized she'd fallen asleep until she blinked at the clock on the DVD player across the room. Her vision was blurry, but after it settled she could make out the time. *2:40am.* Disoriented, she wriggled beneath the blanket and groaned. Her head was still in a slumberous haze, even throbbing slightly with fatigue. She wanted nothing more than to swallow a dozen sleeping pills and go dormant for a week.

The *bzzzt bzzzt* reverberated on the ground again, confirming Ayden's suspicions that her cell had indeed been the cause of her awakening. The room was full of night shadows, but a small glow from the phone's screen beamed upwards from the floor. She draped an arm over the edge of the couch in an agitated search for it. A few seconds later, her fingers closed around the vibrating device. She held it up to her eyes and glowered menacingly at the screen.

27 missed calls!

Chet is worried, was Ayden's first thought.

She brushed that thought aside immediately. He was not worried about her. He did not care about her. He'd made that abundantly clear.

She checked her inbox and found one new text message. From Chet, of course. Angrily, she read the words.

Chet
10:46pm: where are you

It was so much like the texts Mitchell used to send her, she almost threw her phone across the room. Her face heated as her blood boiled with fury. How dare Chet! She wanted to scream at him, to cuss him out, to treat him like the vile criminal that he was. Her chance came seconds later, when her phone started buzzing in her hand with the twenty-eighth incoming call. Chet was trying to reach her again. *Obsessive little spy.* Did he think he owned her? Claimed some right to her?

It was time. With shaking hands and a quiver in her voice, Ayden answered the phone and held it up to her ear.

"You lying little—"

"Ayden!" Chet's voice was strident and not at all his own. "Tell me you're alive. Where are you? What have they done—"

"You have no right to know anything," Ayden shouted, forgetting that Craig was asleep down the hall. She fumbled out of the blankets and scrambled to her feet.

"Wh-what?" Chet gasped. He sounded like he'd been running, but she could hear the roar of the Mustang engine in the background. He was driving, wherever he was.

"You listen to me," Ayden barked, "you no good, lying, drug-dealing—"

"Oh, God," he bemoaned.

It was a sickening, heart-wrenching wail. Ayden's innards tightened painfully in response, a twinge piercing her gut. She heard the shift of gears and the fuel being gunned. Her hands were shaking, and a sweat had broken out across the back of her neck. Even her shirt felt stuck to her spine. She'd never been so livid. Never. But when she opened her mouth, Chet's terror-stricken voice came through the receiver.

"Tell me where you are, Ayden. *Please*, for all of heaven and earth. *Just tell me!* I've been driving all night—"

"You are the one who left!" Ayden shrieked into the receiver. "You left. *You* left *me*. Don't you remember? You are the one who took off!"

"I-I-I had to," he stuttered.

He didn't sound quite right. Something was terribly wrong. She didn't care. She forced herself not to care.

"I was going to come back," he panted. "Ayden, I will always come back. It took me forever to return from Chico, but I went over a hundred the whole way, I swear. I saw the key on the doorstep. And you weren't inside. And I thought for sure they had you..."

Chico? Ayden was royally dumbstruck.

A light flicked on in the living room, and Ayden whirled around to find a very dazed and baffled Craig. He was shirtless, wearing only flannel pajama bottoms, and rubbing his eyes wearily.

"What's going on?" Craig asked Ayden.

She cradled the phone against her shoulder, suddenly embarrassed. "Nothing."

He raised an inquisitive eyebrow.

"Well, something," she amended.

Craig nodded with a roll of his eyes that said, "Yeah, I know," and rubbed at his jaw.

She whispered, "I'll tell you everything, I just—"

"Ayden?" It was Chet, on the phone. "Ayden, who is that? Who are you with? Where are you?"

"It is none of your business," she hissed into the cell.

"Is it that guy again?" Craig asked, stepping through the room and coming to a stop at her side.

Ayden momentarily stared at Craig's broad chest and the cavernous lines that were his abdomen. The deep tan. The patch of chest hair. He was huge. Bigger than Mitchell, but whereas Mitchell had been husky, Craig was well built.

"Ayden…" Chet's voice was a trembling warning.

She'd never heard Chet sound so frantic. Not even during their most dire times together. Nervously, she sent a sympathetic smile to Craig but spoke into the phone, "I have to go now, Chet. Thanks for checking up on me."

And she disconnected the call.

Craig held out a hand, and Ayden took it, dropping the phone onto the couch behind her.

"What was that all about?" he inquired.

She shook her head, finding herself leaning into him for a hug. "Can we talk about it in the morning? I'm just so, *so* tired."

"Sure," Craig murmured to the top of her head.

He didn't sound too convinced, but Ayden didn't have the strength or the will to deal with it. She was glad Craig didn't pressure her. He didn't make her feel terrified, or alarmed, or in danger. She let him lead her down the hall to the bedroom.

"Will it make you feel better to sleep in here?" he asked.

She nodded, crawling under the covers that he held back for her. It was already warmed.

"Thank you," she yawned, totally exhausted.

But to her astonishment, Craig slipped in the other side of

18

the bed. The lights were off, but as her eyes adjusted she saw him on his side, facing her. She'd assumed when he'd offered her his bed that it meant he'd be sleeping on the couch. This was an unexpected situation.

Craig blinked rapidly and then smiled a little. Ayden tucked the pillow up under her head and smiled back. No harm done. They would just sleep side-by-side, platonically. Craig wasn't thinking the same thing. His breathing seemed to increase. She couldn't be sure, in the dark, but she thought he'd inched loser. When he reached out and touched her face, she was positive he had. Her first instinct was to stop him, but then…she wanted to see something… needed to experiment. If there was a way to get over Chet, to move beyond the hurt he'd caused, this might be the way to find out. Or, better than that, this might be a way to figure out if all men were really after one thing.

Craig's fingers wove into her hair, gliding out through the ends.

"I didn't invite you in here for this, you know," he said cautiously.

Ayden nodded, but she didn't believe him.

Craig grabbed hold of one of her wrists. "If you don't want me to kiss you, you should tell me."

Ayden didn't particularly want to kiss him—not in her heart of hearts. For a fleeting second, she stared across the pillows at his dark eyes. They looked black with the lack of light. His thick lashes and eyebrows were set in an expression of hope. The whole time they'd dated, they'd only kissed. They'd shared some long, intricate kisses, but only once did his hands stray from her waist. Not once did she allow him inside her home, into her bed. They're shared religion forbade those intimacies until marraige. At the moment, she sensed he desired intimacy.

Craig sat up a bit and met Ayden halfway, their lips brushing. The kiss accelerated Craig's breathing, and he almost came back for more. Ayden looked down for a second, trying to sort through her feelings. She couldn't understand what she felt. She kissed him again, and this time, Craig pulled her roughly against him. She ended up diagonally across the bed, with her chest on top of his. Frightened, intimacy ran through her mind, synonymously with torture.

Her suspicions were correct. She did not love Craig in a romantic way. Kissing him brought her no pleasure. It disgusted her that she couldn't care for one of the few decent men left in the world. Her heart ached for the tattooed guy who'd left her stranded and broken. She didn't want to go back to Chet. Not after what he'd done. Not after what he'd said.

Chet loved Keeley. He loved another woman. He left Ayden for her.

The only reason Ayden would want to talk to Chet would be to ask him why he'd taken advantage of her, but even that wasn't worth it. His voice stirred too many undesired emotions within her. Emotions and feelings that she had sworn she would never feel again. It was too painful. Mitchell abused and used her, now this? She couldn't bear it. She wanted something normal—a normal man and a normal life—that might not be as entirely exciting, but it wouldn't be as entirely tormenting either.

"Wait," Ayden rasped, breaking their elongated kiss to pull away. She sat up and scooted a safe distance away. "We can't do this."

Craig was looking up at her, arguable prepared to *do it*. She'd never allowed things to get this far physically with him before. It shocked her. Here he was, ready and willing. Despite their religious beliefs. She turned away from Craig as she placed a hand over her pounding heart. It wasn't racing out of a hormonal reaction to her activities. She didn't know what was happening, but this was *not* what she wanted. No matter how hard she tried to convince herself, this normal relationship with Craig was just never going to happen. To make matters worse, she knew he would compromise his integrity in a moment of passion.

What was she thinking? How was she supposed to tell him that moral obligation was a deal breaker? Groaning, she covered her face with her hands.

"Do you want to talk about us?" Craig asked behind her. He was still lying down, though he was tickling her back with his fingertips.

Ayden shook her head.

"I'm so messed up right now," she responded lowly. *And*

humiliated.

She needed to repent as quickly as possible.

To her surprise, Craig chuckled. He pulled on her shoulder until she fell back on the pillow beside him. He didn't try to kiss her anymore, simply held her hand and spoke kindly.

"You've been through enough to warrant the messed-up way you feel," he stated. "But that will all go away. Ultimately, it will all be behind you."

"Behind me?" she repeated wryly.

"Yes, behind you. And—"

A sudden pounding on the front door had both Ayden and Craig sitting bolt upright in bed. Craig leaned over to the lamp on the nightstand, clicking it on urgently. Ayden heard another exploding blow to the front door, strong enough to crack it. Craig reached for her arm. His face was carved with dread, and he was frozen solid. Ayden became consumed with aggravateion, not just at his lack of ability to react to what could possibly be a hazardous break-in, but because she knew it was not just a hazardous break-in. She knew it was useless. There was no point in hiding. Her problems were not going to be behind her anytime soon.

With a final *bang*, she heard the front door to Craig's house burst open and plummet to the floor.

Seconds later, her problem was standing directly *in front* of her.

"You." Chet pointed first at Craig, though his eyes were trained on Ayden. "Keep your rear anchored right there."

Nobody could glower quite as fiercely as Chet. Not even Mitchell. Ayden's ex-husband was devoid of human feelings, and he was ruthless, but he lacked the powerful eminence that Chet had. Chet demanded submission and, at times, respect. The look Chet flung at Ayden now kept her stunned and speechless.

Craig was halfway from standing up off the bed, still bare-chested in his flannel pajamas. He looked aghast, torn between covering his face with his hands and dragging Ayden behind him. Or would he hide behind her? She thought Craig would call the police at his earliest convenience. Now that Craig knew a bit of Chet's indiscretions, and his and Ayden's history together, she wouldn't put it past Craig to act rash. But, to her surprise, Craig straightened and leveled a gaze at Chet.

Ayden glanced between the two of them, horrified. Chet was wearing his go-to all black, with his black hair spiked up, and his blue eyes striking through the dark. He definitely looked like he'd been driving all night. And running. Maybe swimming in a triathalon. At least he wasn't donning a ski mask and wielding a led pipe. Some small miracle. The room was only lit by the lamp on the nightstand, and with all the shadows dancing around the room Chet was beginning to look like a phantom. He seemed every bit as wild and frantic as he had on the phone, which made Ayden quiver, and Craig shrink.

Lethal misfortune was impending.

"Ayden," Chet turned squarely to her, pointing a long, slender finger in her direction, "come with me."

And he crooked that finger toward himself.

"Ah—I will not—you can't just come in here!"

As Ayden shot off the bed, Craig leapt up to her other side. She knew he was tall, broad, and looming over her shoulder, but it was only a minor comfort compared the apprehension gripping her. How on earth did Chet know *everything*? Where did he get directions to Craig's house? Was there no privacy in her life?

Craig slipped an arm around Ayden's waist. She knew he was glaring at Chet, but it didn't have the desired effect. Chet inclined his head to one side, his eyes rabid. His evaluation of Craig's manuever resulted in a challenge only a seasoned Chess player could anticipate. Check.

Craig might be about the same height, glowering at Chet from above six feet tall, but his frame was also close to twice the size of Chet's. What Ayden had, was a standoff. And she was right in the middle of it. Craig was the knight, crossing the board according to the rules. Craig didn't know Chet was not one skilled piece, but all of them combined, that Chet played by no rules, that Chet was not guarding a king, but Ayden, and that Chet would kill his own queen himself if she stood in the way.

"You're that guy," Craig barked over the top of Ayden's head.

"Pleased to see you again," Chet stated with a curt bow, figurativley tossing the chessboard. "Sorry to be doing this to you all the time, but I'm here to take her away again."

Chet reached for Ayden's arm, closing his fingers tightly around her bicep.

"I'm not going with you," she sputtered.

"Nice seeing you, Craig," Chet called out with a tilt of his chin, spinning toward the open bedroom door.

"No!" Ayden spit through gritted teeth, jerking her arm back. Chet would not release her, and now Craig was advancing straight on them, from knight to rook. Ayden put a hand up to Craig's wide chest to halt his momentum and turned a pleading stare back to Chet. "I don't want to go. Leave us alone. We don't want any trouble."

Chet let out a short, burst of a laugh. "God almighty, Ayden. You sound like I'm kidnapping you."

"You *are* kidnapping her," Craig countered in a low, threatening voice. With one step, he was up in Chet's face.

Chet stood motionless, his grip on Ayden's arm firm. "She wants to come with me. Don't you, toots?"

"I'm not letting her out of my sight," Craig stated forcefully.

"Do you love her?"

"What?" both Ayden and Craig asked together.

"Do you love her?" Chet demanded, gesturing toward Ayden.

Craig was tongue-tied, offering little more than inspired gibberish for a response. Chet impishly reset his board. He smirked. Check. Mate. He turned his cryptic stare on Ayden.

"That's what I thought. Point one for Chet."

"Get out of my house," Craig bellowed, "or I will call the cops!"

"Be my guest," Chet replied dryly. "Tell them I said hi—"

Ayden was being hauled in two different directions, mentally and physically. Flustered, she cried out, "Craig, Chet, I'd appreciate it if you'd both just—"

A flying fist collided into the side of Chet's face. Momentarily stunned, Chet relinquished his grasp on Ayden and stumbled back. A look of blind perplexity crossed his face. Ayden let out a yelp. Craig was cocking his arm a second time, when Ayden lurched forward to clasp her hands around his wrist.

"Please, don't!" she shrieked. Craig sent her a look of alarmed treachery. "Don't fight him, Craig. Please."

A vision of a bloodied Grayson on the floor of the nightclub popped into her mind.

But Craig shook her off, turning just in time to catch Chet as he came barreling across the room. The two men flew backward, falling onto the bed. Chet had Craig in a headlock, and they were wrestling around the room, knocking objects off the shelves, sending the clock crashing to the floor. The lamp tipped over, and the shade fell onto the bed. A picture frame on the wall cracked and clattered to the ground as Craig rammed Chet's body into it. Ayden squealed, diving for the two of them and trying to find an appropriate time to intervene. She didn't want to get accidentally hit.

Knuckles were cracking on impact, ribs were resounding with odd noises as each man struck the other. They sounded like a hog pen. All she could think about was the men Chet had hurt in his life—killed, even. Chet was volatile in an outrage. When the brawl broke apart for just a breath, Ayden jumped between them.

"Stop this! Right now!"

She had one hand flat against Craig's sternum, and the other seizing Chet's sleeve. Craig skewered her with an angry glare, shaking his torso once to dismantle her. Chet was smiling triumphantly. He licked his bottom lip. His piercing twinkled with such fun.

"Knock it off, Chet," Ayden warned.

"Is there a problem?" he rebuked. "I believe I am acting in self-defense."

"Yeah," Craig bristled from behind Ayden. The expanse of his chest was inflating and deflating enormously. "Let me finish what I started."

"No, you two."

The sound of a car door slamming shut somewhere beyond the windows caused Chet to lose his cool. His smile waned, his attention diverted away from his adversary. He instead turned a listening ear toward the hallway. Craig took the opportunity to charge, swinging an arm as he stormed passed Ayden. She grabbed Craig's elbow, but her efforts did nothing to thwart his powerful punch. He spun her around with him.

Chet ducked aside in a simple movement, missing Craig's punch completely. He strode purposefully toward the bedroom door as if nothing had happened. Ayden thumped into the wall. Craig grunted, whirling around for a second attempt, but Chet held up a finger.

"Shh!"

There was the sound of another car door shutting, quieter this time.

"What is it?" Ayden whispered.

Chet met her gaze across the room, before he slid his eyes over to Craig. "Do you have a gun?"

"A gun?" Craig asked baffled. "I would never own something so atrocious."

Chet looked absolutely offended, but he shook his head and held a hand out toward Ayden. "I'm going to need you to come with me. Now."

"Why?" she questioned, although her body began to move.

Chet took a step toward her and lowered his voice. The deep, sapphire shade of his eyes simmered with intensity, causing visuals of laughter and happiness and the beach and damp skin to flash before her eyes. His high cheekbones shone in the lamplight, connected to his angular jaw, and then his creamy neck. His tattoos crawled under his muscles. Did she really tell him she *loved* him?

"Bad things are about to happen," Chet murmured. "Now leave the hurt bunny look over there and *come with me!*"

There was the sound of footsteps on shattered wood coming from the front of the house. Chet moved speedily across the room, not leaving his orders open for negotiation. He grabbed Ayden around the waist as he flew toward the window facing the backyard, more determined than before. Craig still looked aghast, but started to catch on to what was happening. Someone was in his house—someone even Chet didn't like. The sound of the intruder echoed as the feet stepped carefully over the fallen door.

"Craig," Chet hissed, "get a weapon and be prepared."

"I do not own any weapons," Craig stated under his breath.

He was appalled at the idea.

Chet granted him well-deserved, two-second long, impatience before withdrawing a small pistol from the back of his shirt. Craig reeled backward, repulsed.

"Then get a broom," Chet ordered. "A mop. Your electric razor. Something to launch projectiles." He pushed Ayden against the window. "They're coming."

"Who are *they*?" Craig demanded, panic-stricken.

Following the sound of his voice was an almost indistinguishable chirp. Ayden squeaked, groping Chet's arm as he whipped to shelter her from view. At the same time, he aimed his pistol at the bedroom door. Ayden had been hiding her face in between Chet's shoulder blades, but she poked and eye out and followed the aim of his arm, spying a masked impostor standing under the doorframe. The unknown assailant was pointing another gun with a silencer…at Craig. Without pause, Chet fired one bullet, and the masked man fell to the ground.

Behind Ayden, the window Chet had began to open shattered with a deafening *crack*. She jumped aside as glass sprayed out all around her. Chet turned his gun toward the broken window and fired two rounds into the darkness. Simultaneously, Ayden tripped, her feet entangling in the sheets that were strewn across the floor from Craig and Chet's scuffle. She hit the ground, staring at the dead face next to hers.

Craig.

"Craig!" Ayden screeched, reaching a hand out to touch his face.

She rushed to her knees, crawling over his head. His eyes were wide open, his mouth hanging slack. A trickle of blood streamed down his temple and cheek, dripping into a pool below his chin. When did he fall? She hadn't seen him drop, hadn't heard a sound come out of his mouth.

Chet knelt down at Ayden's side, still holding his gun in one hand. With the other, he grabbed both her wrists and yanked her to her feet. She clung to his collar, but he tore her away.

"Come on," he commanded. "We have to move."

Just then, someone else entered through the bedroom door. Another man, clothed in black and anonymous in the night. Chet took aim and shot the man in less than a second. Ayden flinched, covering her ears with her hands. Chet stole one of her hands away and gripped it in his while he took two steps back toward the window. But a third masked man was already crawling through it. Chet fired two bullets into the man, who slumped over the windowsill. Ayden cowered behind Chet's shoulder, peeping behind her at the bedroom door where she could hear sounds of more footsteps.

"Chet!" she pled desperately.

He turned her around so their backs were pressed up against one another's. They were spinning in the center of the bedroom, Ayden in a crouched position, and Chet with his arms outstretched supporting his gun. But there were too many others. Several men piled in through the bedroom door, and another handful crept agilely through the window. Chet ran out of ammo, dropping his gun with a curse. It hit the ground with an ugly thud.

Ayden thought she was going to faint. The scent of blood and gun smoke was sickly strong. Her head felt dizzy. The room was fuzzy.

Chet had engaged in a fistfight with one of the masked men. Once incapacitated, Chet tossed his opponent into an incoming insurgent. Someone punched Chet in the side, and he winced, but whirled around to snap the neck of his attacker. It seemed endless, the violence. For a moment, Chet was succeeding. He'd killed three more of them without a weapon. They might have a chance for escape.

But there were just too many. Ayden cried out as the disguised trespassers took Chet down, hitting him again and again until he collapsed to one knee. Though Chet fought back, one of the men eventually had him in a Full Nelson, and the others continued to throw blows at his stomach and face. Chet's eyes were starting to swell shut. Blood dripped from his nose. Veins bulged in his neck as he let out a strangled howl.

One male tore the front of Chet's shirt, stepped back, then kicked him savagely in the ribs. Chet's mouth fell open, though no sound escaped. His eyes rolled in silent agony, his hair flopping to one side and sticking in a stream of fluid by his ear. After a particularly brutal punch to the side of his face, his head fell limply sideways.

Still, the beating did not stop.

Ayden lunged for Chet, wanting to help, *needing* to, but one man grabbed hold of both her arms. A large, clammy hand came up around her nose and mouth. It smelled like cigarettes and sweat.

"Chet!" Ayden screamed into the sweaty palm as she was dragged from the bedroom. "Chet! No! Help!"

She kept her eyes on his body until it was no longer possible. Her cries were smothered as she was detained and forced out of the house. Everything twirled before her vision, even the stars above. The night was dark and eerie. None of the neighbors had lights on in their homes. Ayden wondered how on earth they hadn't heard all the racket in the middle of the night, and silently begged someone to wake up and come to their assistance. She couldn't stop visualizing Chet. The man she thought of as fearless and undefeatable, unconscious on the ground.

A stabbing ache clenched her heart.

At the end of the driveway, there were two SUVs parked at the curb. Both had tinted windows so black she couldn't see a thing inside. The rims were also black, with huge, menacing wheels. The cars were running, though nearly silently. No sound came from inside Craig's house. She wondered if the silencers had concealed the sound of bullets popping. If no one knew what was happening, no one could come to their aid.

One of the doors to the backseat the nearest SUVs opened, and the rough hands on Ayden's body folded her inside.

In a flash, there was a cloth bag over her face, and the car door slammed shut.

4

For the fourth time, a man named Rocco held a sodden towel over Ayden's face. Armando poured a bucket of water over the towel, as Ayden coughed and spluttered against it. She heaved, inhaling much of the liquid that was seeping through the towel asphyxiating her. The water entered her lungs, burning as she felt the suffocation stealing her life. Air. She needed air.

Rocco removed the towel, holding it aside while Armando lifted the chair into its upright position. Ayden fell into her restraints when the chair lurched and settled. Spitting, she regurgitated the water inhabiting her lungs. The dirt floor spun in her vision, the chains dangling from the wooden beams above swaying. The solid, concrete walls surrounding her were pulsating behind her blurred eyesight. Bile dribbled down her chin.

"Tell me," Rocco stated darkly, leaning over Ayden with a hand on either armrest. "Where *is* he?"

"I-I d-don't know," Ayden gasped, spewing hot water and bile from her lips.

The liquid streamed down her face and neck, to her already soaked shirt. She didn't know how long she'd been kept in this imprisonment. It could have been hours. Days. There were no windows, no sunlight, no way to tell time. Just the single panel of electricity that whirred cyclically overhead. It was heavily crusted and covered in cobwebs. The whole room was dank and dusty. The only thing Ayden knew for sure, was this torture the men kept up every couple hours was going to kill her. Soon.

"You're a liar, Mrs. Harper," Rocco glowered down at her. He nodded his chin sharply at Armando, who left her feild of vision to refill the bucket.

"I'm not," Ayden slobbered, "lying."

Rocco grabbed the back of her hair, pulling until she was forced to look up at him. He was extremely built, not quite as tall as Chet yet every bit as fearsome. A fury of embers simmered in his glare. She remembered him from the nightclub. He was one of the men enjoying Starla's spectacle. He'd approached Chet, after Chet had disemboweled Grayson. Chet chose not to fight Rocco.

Ayden had felt worse pain, and was only thankful these

men had yet to physically beat her with their hands. The water and towel would kill her, she knew, but it also wasn't as intimately brutal at Mitchell's beatings. These men hadn't sexually assaulted her yet, either. They obviously wanted information out of her, so she prayed they wouldn't kill her until they received it.

"I'm going to ask you again," Rocco said as Armando reentered her perspective. She could hear the water in the bucket sloshing. "Where is Chet?"

"I don't know!" Ayden hollered, pulling against the restraints on her arms and legs. The ties were digging into her flesh, causing the raw soreness to produce little beads of blood. She shook her head, her terror heightening to berserk. "I don't know! I don't know! I don't—"

Armando titled the chair back. Rocco throttled Ayden's ranting with the sopping towel. Armando poured and poured, while she writhed beneath the cascading water. It filled her nostrils with stinging pain, getting sucked into her airway and down into her windpipe with each pilfered gulp for air. Memories flitted through Ayden's mind—smiles and gemstone blue eyes. She didn't get to say goodbye. She thought of her parents, her sister in Russia, the sweet, old ladies in Relief Society at the ward she'd barely begun attending.

By the time the bucket was empty, she was flopping lifelessly to one side of the chair. Rocco swore under his breath, demanding Armando resuscitate Ayden. Armando flung the dirty bucket aside and smacked a hand hard against Ayden's back. She fell forward in the chair, her head hanging down toward her knees while the restraints kept her at an awkward position. Armando pounded her back again, but she still wouldn't breathe.

"Cut her loose," he told Rocco. "I'm going to have to give her mouth-to-mouth."

Reluctantly, Rocco retrieved a knife from his back pocket and cut the ties on Ayden's ankles and wrists. She tumbled instantly to the floor. Armando nudged her arm with the toe of his boot, and she rolled unresponsively onto her back, sprawled at unnatural angles. He took a moment to stare down at her.

"Hurry," Rocco grunted.

"Si," Armando replied, kneeling down beside her head.

A few minutes later, Ayden coughed catastrophically. Her stomach emptied all the contents within it. She curled to one side. The throbbing in her skull was overwhelming, and such an intense feeling encompassed her—her lungs, her heart. Death. She thought surely she was dying. But before she could welcome it, Rocco hoisted her to her feet. With no gentle shove, she collapsed back into the chair.

Ayden was too weak to fight back, to try and flee. Her body was exhausted and hollow, the slithering grips of death waiting greedily to seize her. The pain was dulled as unconsciousness toyed with her coherence. She let her head fall and stared helplessly at the two men standing over her.

"No se," Armando told Rocco in broken English. "I don't think she knows where he is."

Rocco tilted his head to one side, examining Ayden. "Don't be telling boss that just yet. I have a feeling she knows something. She's Chet's girl. He taught her well. Give me an hour in here alone with her, and I'll get her to talk."

"No," Armando countered. "Those weren't our orders."

Rocco spit out a curse in Spanish. They were talking as if she wasn't even in the same room with them. "I'll speak to Saucedo after we get the information out of her. He wants to find Chet. No matter what."

Ayden's mind was reeling. They didn't have Chet?

The last she saw him, he was surrounded by men, lying on the floor being beaten…

"Give me twenty minutes," Rocco negotiated, shifting his shoes against the gravel on the ground. His fixation turned to Ayden's body.

"Fine," Armando grumbled. "But I'm not taking the fall for this one, too."

A few seconds later, Ayden heard a door somewhere in the back of the room open and close. She blinked up at Rocco. They were alone, and he now looked like he very much wanted to sexually assault her. He clasped his hands in front of his belt, watching her closely. It wasn't the crazed evil in his expression she'd seen in Mitchell so many times, but he was bad. And wrong. And dangerous. He wanted her to live through whatever he had planned.

Rocco walked out of her sight and was fidgeting at a table in the back of the room. Ayden tried to twist her neck around to see, but it was in vain. She was no longer bound, but she was robbed of all strength. Her muscles contracted of their own accord, flexing in spasms as her brain sent orders to her lungs to keep breathing. The pulse of her heart was unhurried. She burst into a fit of heaves again as Rocco strutted back around in front of her. He waited calmly, not offering assistance as she choked in the chair.

After cajoling her heart into a steady rhythm, Ayden glanced up. In his hands, Rocco had a small case. It looked like a case for sunglasses. When he flipped it open, she saw the tip of a syringe.

"Do you know what this is?" he asked, regarding Ayden thoughtfully.

He was arranging the syringe and other implements, talking more to himself than to her.

"This is heroin," he stated with what she gleaned as affection.

Ayden was shivering. She'd rather die than have that drug in her body.

Rocco flicked the prepared needle twice and then seized Ayden's arm so strongly she winced from the pain. He held her bicep in his iron grip, staring savagely into her eyes. He waited until she locked gazes with his.

"All of Saucedo's women follow a strict regimen. You might learn to really like this. If you're anything like your boyfriend, you're going to like this."

He smiled then. A thin, sinister smile, and suddenly Ayden couldn't help but think of the syringe she found on the floor of Chet's Mustang.

A vein had started to bulge at her elbow.

"Did you know," Rocco stated thoughtfully, "your…lover, Chet, used to rob liquor stores as a kid to pay for his weekly fix?"

Ayden closed her eyes, willing her ears to mute the sound of Rocco's voice. It didn't work.

"He used to…take little old ladies' purses to satiate his need. Hurt anyone who stood in his way. Stone-cold," Rocco carried on. "Chet was so hooked, he started boosting cars to sell for parts, burglarizing muchachas who wore fine jewelry. It was all outside of the business, but it drew attention. He was so strung out, Saucedo sent him to rehab. A junky is a liability in this business. You never know when they might ruin a deal and take the money—or drugs—for themselves. Like last weekend."

"No," Ayden exhaled. Her voice was so weak it was scarcely audible. "Chet—didn't—he doesn't—anymore—"

"You're wrong," Rocco replied coolly. "Do you think someone who has been shooting up their whole life would decide to give it up just because a pretty senorita came into their life? Let me tell you something, girl. You're not the first woman to catch Chet's attention. You're not even the first pretty one. He wants the same thing from you that he wanted from them. His first love is his drug."

"Motorcycle," Ayden drooled.

"Chet cleaned himself up enough to earn his rank at Saucedo's right hand. If you haven't learned already, Chet can be quite persuasive. There is no feeling in his soul. The only reason he's still alive is because Boss…well, Boss fancies Chet like a son. Chet's screwed with the business many times, but this is betrayal. Do you know what the punishment is for a traitor?"

He waited, then proceeded before Ayden could respond. "No? Saucedo kills everyone—everyone—who conspires against him. He breaks their legs, hangs them from the bridge, and then kills everyone they love. Many times is was Chet who volunteered to inflict the penalty on Saucedo's traitors. I've seen him pour gasoline over bodies and watch them burn. Alive. He's one of the best in this business, your Chet. Which is why he's one of Boss's favorites."

Rocco paused a second time, sniffed, swiveling the syringe in his fingers. Ayden watched in horror as Rocco pointed the tip of the syringe to her skin and burrowed the needle into her vein. He pressed down on the head, and the injection flowed into her blood with surprising speed. Ayden felt the cooling spread, engulfing, soaring, increasing her shivers unlike anything she'd ever felt. Her mouth fell open. Even as she was flying, she fell into the darkest hell she'd ever known.

Rocco observed her with amused devilment in his eyes. "I

thought so."

Ayden didn't see him stand or put the case away, wherever he'd stashed it. She wasn't looking at anything. Her eyes rolled back into her head as she felt her body being lifted, moved, dragged, raised, buried, imprisoned. Though, she hadn't even left the room. Any and all motor function was lost. Everywhere, her limbs felt tingly and light—free but incarcerated. The walls closed in around her until she was surrounded by nothing but darkness. And then she couldn't breathe.

Again and again, she tried to scream for help. No matter how much she told herself to shout, to move, to take in a deeper breath so that her heart would not stop beating, her brain ceased to respond. Rocco had exited the room long ago, leaving her in solitude as she sank haphazardly in the chair. She couldn't even think of Chet, or the fact that he'd escaped the men Saucedo had sent to lift him. The whole world, all matter of life, any entity or being or spirit, everything faded away. Ayden, and her soul, was lost in the midst of it.

5

Days had passed. Rocco returned to Ayden's room. Twice a day, to her knowledge, to keep her under the influence. It was two weeks total since her capture. She had no idea. To her it was merely time, time spent in a negligent abyss, with hardly anything to eat or drink, and the only face she would see was either Armando's or Rocco's, sticking a needle in her body. At least there'd been no more threat of drowning. She never wanted to taste water again, so long as she lived, and that would most likely not be long.

Ayden was now on the floor next to the chair, convulsing. There wasn't a need to keep her restrained. Rocco shook his head, went straight for the case of drugs, and moved back to her side. Flipping her over, he saw no signs of a seizure. Her fingers were icy and her lips an odd shade of blue, but her airway was free of obstruction. He forced her eyelids open, checking first one and then the other pupil. Her symptoms revealed an overdose.

"How much have you been giving her?" he asked Armando, who stood in the door.

Taking out the syringe, Rocco gave her a dose of narcan. They still hadn't extracted the information Saucedo needed out of her. Rocco was ready to hand her over. Vlad was in need of some new staff, and Ayden had desirable looks. She'd already be "trained".

"Drink," Ayden gurgled. Her face was smashed against the dirty floor. She coughed. "Drink?"

Rocco grumbled a concession, finishing with the needle and returning it to the case. Ayden stilled, her muscles twitching and relaxing. He stood and walked to the door.

"When is Saucedo supposed to be here?" Armando questioned, eyeing Ayden.

"Morning," Rocco confirmed. Checking the time on his cell phone, he saw that it was already 5:00am. "We have a few hours. She'll talk by then."

"And if not?" Armando demanded.

"She'll talk."

***

Ayden came to for a minute, blinking against her fish-eye view of the room. Everything was bubbling or caving in. She tried to crawl away from the enclosing walls, attempting a scream, but all that escaped her lips was a dry moan. Her body ached from where she lay crumpled on the ground. Lifting a hand took dexterous effort, but she managed to grab hold of one of the chair legs. Her fingers were chapped, her cuticles bleeding. Her skin was so dry everywhere it looked like a crocodile hide. After a few agonizing minutes, she had herself in a sitting position.

Her mind was still in a phase of inebriation, but she remembered where she was and what she was doing there. Chet was missing. Saucedo and his men were looking for him, and they had *her* as leverage. She finally realized that the men who had abducted her from Craig's house hadn't shot at her or Chet. They'd all been armed, but they hadn't tried to kill her or Chet. So they wanted them alive. For what? For how long?

For a mournful moment, Ayden wondered if Chet was going to come for her. Would he abandon her? Again? Did it matter?

She tried to imagine Chet escaping those men who had beaten him into the ground. Those men had nearly killed him. She truly thought they had. If he got away from Saucedo's men, did that mean Ayden had been incarcerated long? The idea of being in this moist, putrid room, drugged with the poison that was ruining her life, for any length of time, made her queasy.

Suddenly, the image of Craig's dead face flashed before her eyes.

"No," Ayden mumbled, shaking her head. "No."

Craig was dead. He'd been shot.

"Father in Heaven," she mewled, "forgive me."

She wasn't sure how much time had gone by, but loud voices arguing beyond the walls caused her to stir. She raised her head, finding she'd fallen asleep with her arms draped over the seat of the chair. Her hair was a matted, sticky mess. The rest of her didn't look much better.

"I didn't want her killed, and I don't want her doped up," came a smooth voice somewhere outside the door.

"She hasn't talked."

Ayden recognized that as Armando's voice.

"Rocco said you could toss her into work with Vlad," Armando added.

"It's a thoughtful and tempting idea," the first man continued. "I don't think it will work if I'm going to bribe Chet."

Rocco joined the conversation. "Who said we were bribing him?"

"I did."

Nogo Saucedo. That's who was speaking with Armando and Rocco outside the door. It was *the* Nogo Saucedo. Chet's boss was just here.

"I told Armando to let me have my way with her," Rocco growled in broken English.

"You know better than that," Saucedo replied. "Chet's already taken out dozens of our top men in the county. What do you think he'd do if he found out you'd had your way with his woman?"

"He'll come for her," Rocco pointed out spitefully. "Whether or not!"

"And no harm will come to Chet when he does. Not until we find my money. Find my money first, then we'll deal with these two."

Armando replied in Spanish.

"If you want to keep you head, keep your hands off her," Saucedo stated. "Is she lucid? Good."

At once, the door at the back of the room opened, and all three men stepped inside. From where Ayden was hunched over the chair on the floor, she could now see the doorway they'd been entering and exiting from. A single, rusty metal door with a thick lock. A streak of light shone through the open passage, and she craved to see real sunlight. Yearned for the warm prickle on her flesh, and the scent of grass and flowers and coastal breezes. Rocco and Armando stayed near the back, where a fold out table was stationed. They both glared at her, with Rocco repeatedly baring his teeth. The heroin case rested on top of the table, along with a pair of weathered work gloves, the bucket, and the soiled towel.

Nogo Saucedo, a shorter, Hispanic male dressed impeccably in a navy, pinstriped suit complete with a red scarf, paced over to the back of the chair. Looking down his nose at Ayden, he said, "Do you know where Chet is?"

She shook her head. It took a second for her eyes to regain focus.

"I believe you," Saucedo said.

He was every bit as terrifying as Ayden envisioned him to be. She'd thought of the movie The Godfather, and all the other films she'd seen about the mafia or cartel. He most definitely fit the role.

The domineering man turned to his employees and asked, "How long has it been now?"

"Two weeks," Rocco answered.

"Keep her here," Saucedo told them, glancing once more at Ayden. "Have you eaten?"

She didn't feel hungry. She didn't feel anything.

"Bring her some water and something to eat," Saucedo said. "Let's get Chet in here, and then I can sit down with him and have a little chat. Notify me when he arrives."

The three men exited the room, leaving Ayden alone on the cold ground. Her shudders were coming stronger now, and she chanced a glimpse down at her elbow. There was a red circle the size of a quarter on her inner flesh, and what looked like strings of sea-green wove out from it, down to her wrist. It had been a while since her last dose. She felt sick, dizzy, and nauseated. Pressing the back of her hand to her mouth, she slumped over the chair and prayed.

She prayed like she'd never prayed before. First, for Chet. And second, if it be God's will, that she remain alive.

For reasons she didn't understand, Ayden's mind traveled back in time to a memory of her and her family. She was a soph-omore in high school, and her parents drove her and her sister Rainee up to Yellowstone National Park for a summer vacation. Ayden could remember with clarity how the geysers exploded up into the sky. Steam swirled like a ghostly mist around the hot pots. The smell wasn't as bad as she thought it would be. The sulfur wasn't all that potent, or maybe she was just more fascinated that God could create something so beautiful. Beautiful and dangerous.

Everywhere they walked on those tiny, shabby looking wooden paths that led around the geysers, there were signs of caution warning not to get too close to the edge, not to step off the trails, and not to touch *anything*. How tempting it had been for Ayden to reach down and feel the bubbling water just to see for herself if it really was as scorching hot as it looked. Why was it people didn't question the innumerable galaxies in the stars above, but when they were told not to touch something because of its calculated risk of being skin-meltingly hot, people were inclined to stupidity?

The air had been a little brisk on the day her family visited Old Faithful, and she recalled waiting around for thirty minutes with Rainee and their parents for the famed geyser to finally burst. It was glorious, the whole production. God had created this world, and he had created the geysers. Yet, what logic was there to devising a land with such perilous dangers? Surely, God meant for mankind to enjoy the splendor of the world He'd created. He must have known that the loveliness was such an attraction to the human race. But wouldn't He understand the depth of temptation involved? Many visitors had lost their lives due to the boiling temperatures of the geysers, as well as the copious wild life roaming the mountains of Yellowstone.

It was an odd memory to relive in such circumstances. Without much by way of concentration, Ayden didn't care to analyze why in particular she was daydreaming about Yellowstone or geysers or beautiful dangers when today very well could be her last day on earth. Perhaps it was the beauty of the back country, in conjunction with the danger those fantastic geysers portrayed, that could be relevant to her current crisis. All her life, she'd been drawn to beautiful disasters. The more beautiful, the more disastrous.

She thought then of Chet, as she'd first seem him at Pismo Beach over seven years ago. How attracted she'd been to him that day—all six feet of his bronzed, summer skin, the hue of his blue-glass eyes, the way his long, blonde, hair hung disheveled over half of his face, his motorcycle, his smile. He was intriguing, mysterious, gorgeous. The skinny body had morphed over the years, transforming a youthful, lanky beach bum into a toned, muscular heathen. If only she'd known it was Chet behind her at the Craps table in Las Vegas, when he'd surprised her in the casino…what would she have done? Would she have acted any differently? When she'd refused his advances and told him she was married, there had been an obvious look of disbelief in his eyes. She knew now, there was also disappointment.

It was kind of loony to fantasize about such things, but Ayden had always been such a movie buff that she basically compared everyday life to Hollywood scenarios. She was aware it wasn't the most sensible, and seldom did real life imitate film, but every once and awhile something crazy would happen. A hero would come to her relief.

That hero always wore Chet's face. He was her champion—whether by default or choice or predetermined by a higher power—and though a part of her wanted to fall into the river of love with him, and let it wash over her entirely, sometimes she felt more like she was swept away in the oceanic current of chaos.

The river of love turned black, the white caps now the color of oil, crashing with cruel vengeance while the undertow sucked her under, into the freezing depths of despair. She could scarcely breathe. She could not swim. The weight of the water crushed her chest, iced her blood. There was nothing to do but let the unforgiving tide wash her away and drown her consciousness with numb misery.

6

Ayden felt herself wakening from a frigid doze. Her bones protested when she tried to stretch. As she peeled her lids open, her eyes came to rest on the link of chains hanging from the ceiling a few feet away. The room. The bucket. The water. The heroin. Was she condemned here forever? Saucedo was certain Chet would come, but it had been two weeks. Or was it three now? He was missing—he could be dead. If she could find a way to scratch tags into the wall, at least she could count her days. Wasn't that what people in prison did?

She crawled over to the chains, unsure of what exactly she was going to do. It took enormous effort, and she collapsed almost every inch she moved, but still she pressed on. A strong prompting came to grab hold of the chains, and just when she reached them, that's exactly what she did. Hoisting herself into a sitting position, she reclined her back against the cold wall. Her lungs labored for air. Her limbs shook. Spots fluttered in her vision, cajoling her into the cataleptic slumber Rocco and Armando forced her to endure. But she withstood. She felt the need to bang the chain links against the concrete wall.

Taking a deep breath, Ayden mustered up all her strength and swung. The chains sounded with a clank against the wall as she smacked them into it once, and then a second time. Her bicep burned with the effort, so she took a minute to rest. She felt hollow, like she hadn't eaten in days. She felt worthless. Catching her breath, she let her heart calm and then summoned the muscle to do it again. The chains clobbered into the side of the wall. Once. Twice.

In the next instant, the door at the other side of the room crashed open, and Armando flew inside. He looked first at the empty chair, and then located Ayden where she cowered against the wall feebly, the chains in her hand.

"Callate," Armando bellowed, crossing the room to her in three giant steps. He stunk like beer. Bending, he ripped the chains from her hands. "You're making too much noise!"

Ayden fell back, her head hitting the concrete wall. The

throbbing spread through her skull, but she made no attempts to move. She had no energy left to lift the chains even one more time. Armando spit a curse and took hold of her ankles. With a derogatory insult, he started dragging her back to the chair she'd been tied to during her torture. At that point, Rocco ran into the room. Armando temporarily dropped Ayden in the middle of the floor, looking up at his associate.

"What is going on in here?" Rocco shouted.

"She was banging the chains," Armando replied.

Rocco stared ferociously at Armando, and then spun his scowl on Ayden. "I can hear that noise outside. Don't let it happen again."

Ayden was shuddering. Her body hungered for something neither food nor beverage. Feined for it. She glimpsed up at Armando, mumbling and tapping the inside of her elbow.

Armando shook his head sharply, his gaze raking up to Rocco. But Rocco was not watching them. He was half turned toward the open doorway, a crinkle in his brow. Armando set to tying up Ayden, rearranging the chair. Her wrists were still chafed and scabbed, with crusted blood that had dripped down her wrists. She'd soiled herself too, and that contributed to the foul stench of the room. Hardly embarrassed, she lifted a hand to her hair. It was almost rigid with filth.

Watching Armando with the chair, Ayden wondered how much time Chet had spent interacting with these men. He must know them well, as their superior. It was obvious everyone knew how Saucedo favored Chet. These men resented him, which meant others did, too. If he was alive, Chet was probably running for his life. He may have left town, or left the state, or left the country. That would be the smart thing to do.

"Connections are liabilities," Chet once told her.

She lumped herself into that category.

Ayden felt so alone, with what little of her could feel. It was the one thing the drug didn't diminish, but instead heightened. Loneliness. The solitary confinement was rotting her from the inside out. She knew it was repulsive to want the drug, but the idea of forgetting where she was and the predicament she was in appealed to her. It wiped her thoughts, ebbed her pain. Her body was pining for it, shaking.

Armando returned to hoist Ayden into the chair, when Rocco suddenly hollered a word in Spanish. Armando froze, and Ayden slid from his grasp to the concrete floor. He said something back to Rocco, and the two shared a couple of sentences in their native language, before Rocco hushed Armando. They stared hawk-eyed at one another, as Ayden slumped into a rumpled heap on the ground.

Take me away, she dreamt.

All of the sudden, the familiar *pop* of gunfire detonated outside the walls. Ayden turned her head on the dirt-covered concrete—ignoring the shrieking pain that seared through her neck and skull— enough to watch Armando and Rocco sprint toward the open door and slam it shut. One of them flicked the lock, then both of them withdrew guns from the back of their pants. All three of them were now enclosed inside Ayden's torture chamber. The two men vigilantly glared at the door, and then at one another, shifting their weight anxiously.

"Who is that?" Rocco asked in a strained voice.

Bullets continued to pepper the exterior walls around them. Ayden still didn't know where she was being kept, but she surmised the room was far away from traffic and onlookers. If Saucedo's subordinates were keeping her hostage, it wouldn't be someplace very public. No doubt they wouldn't want others to know what was going on in this kind of enslaved establishment, especially considering the dope they had. Besides, she'd not heard any cars, airplanes, trains, perceived the sounds of any outward civilization the few weeks she'd been there. This building must be out of city limits, Ayden was sure.

Armando pointed his loaded weapon at the door. "Diedrich?"

"What about Al?" Rocco questioned with a panicked expression. "Chong? They were guarding the outside doors."

Armando shook his head, perplexed. Rocco double checked the lock on the door.

Ayden let a smile pull on her lips as she blubbered, "That isn't going to stop him."

Rocco cut a glance over at her. "What was that?"

"The lock." She coughed a deep, asthmatic noise. "It won't

hold."

"Chet?" Armando asked sternly. "Are you talking about Chet?"

Ayden turned her face heavenward, closing her eyes.

"Yellowstone," she whispered.

Her body was so feeble she didn't think she'd be able to walk for months, and there was a constant churning in her blood that she couldn't categorize as upsetting or exhilarating. Often she felt chilled, and other times feverish. Her body convulsed at random, reminding her bones of where they ached most. She'd forgotten what clean air smelled like, how the hot sun dazzled on her bare skin, the comfort of a plush bed with pillows, what buttery popcorn tasted like, how savory chicken made her mouth water.

The locked door shook with a violent *bang*. Rocco and Armando both aimed their weapons at the door as it continued to wobble. *Bang. Bang. Bang.* The two men exchanged grimaces, gripping their guns. They weren't expecting visitors, and it sounded as if an entire army was at the brink of war. With each resounding blast on the door, particles of moldy dust were disrupted and floated purposelessly around the room. It was like church bells on Sunday. Pounding, vibrating, ricocheting.

Hallelujah.

Ayden opened her eyes and grinned.

The door exploded open, hitting Armando first. Ayden managed to crane her neck enough to watch as Rocco fired his gun into the open doorframe until the clip clicked out of bullets. Armando struggled to regain his footing, throwing the broken door off him, but Rocco snatched the gun from right out of Armando's hands. With a mania in his eyes, Rocco shot every last bullet out of Armando's gun through the doorway until the room fell quiet again.

Rocco's shoes scraped across the gravel as he took a step toward the open door. He hesitated, still holding the useless firearm out in front of him like a flashlight. Armando was staggering to his feet, brushing his hands off on his pants. They were both thunderstruck, unprepared, frenzied. For a second, there was only silence and heavy breathing. No one was shooting.

In a heartbeat's time, Ayden saw a fist fly through the doorway and hit Rocco in the face. A loud *tink* reverberated as Rocco sagged unconsciously to the ground. Armando stood immobile facing the incoming assailant, and had raised both his hands in an act of surrender. But that didn't save him. The charging man in all black, clad with a face mask, surged into the room carrying a led pipe.

Ayden knew it was him. He'd come for her.

Chet bludgeoned Armando across the head until the ugly man who'd so tortured her fell to his knees and begged Chet to spare his life. Chet clubbed him one last time across the jaw. Armando fell to the floor, unmoving.

There was stillness only for a breath. The only sound was that of Chet's feet as he whirled around and sought Ayden on the ground. Swifter than the speed of light, he lunged across the room to where Ayden was still incapacitated on the floor. Dropping the pipe at his feet, he knelt near her head. Similar to the day when he'd rescued her from Mitchell, Chet removed his face mask and stared down at her with feral, blue eyes. Something resembling regret lurked in his gaze, but an angry vein protruded at his temple, hammering against his skin with vigor. He was vicious. Impulsive. Deathly. Lethal.

Chet's throat constricted and dropped as he swallowed heavily, reaching a hand out to brace the back of Ayden's neck. His fingers flexed carefully to cradle her head, his eyes skimming her body, perceiving her marred inner elbow. His regret was immortalized.

Ayden smirked senselessly as she gazed up at him and slurred, "And the maker of the door rolls over in his grave."

7

Chet had Ayden situated in the passenger's seat of his Mustang. They were squealing down the one and only road that led to and from the abandoned warehouse, leaving all those that had stood guard over her in the course of her capture behind. Ayden was still discombobulated and affected by the drug coursing through her system, but she managed to look over at Chet. He drove like a madman. He was wearing brass knuckles, and the pipe was in the back seat. The interior of the car smelled like gun smoke, metal, and grease. Ayden thought it smelled divine.

The headlights were off to conceal their escape, but Ayden could see Chet's face in glimpses. He kept his eyes on the road. The glowing dash illuminated his skin in a neon hue. His jaw was clamped shut, his teeth working back and forth. The lips she loved, so sweet, pinched and then opened as he took in a frayed breath. His tongue prodded the corner of his mouth as he stole a glance in the rearview mirror. Gripping the steering wheel, he cursed and nearly ripped it away from the dash.

"Who is she?" Ayden asked quietly.

Her voice sounded raw and stripped, quiet and distant, like a breeze.

"Who?" Chet asked coarsely, checking his rearview mirror for the millionth time.

Ayden didn't know why he kept doing that. After all, there was nothing back there buan empty, dirty building. With a bucket and soiled towel. And a heroin needle. She looked down at the inside of her elbow hoping what she saw wasn't permanent. She swung a glance at Chet.

"Who is Keeley?" she questioned.

It was an appropriate time as any.

Chet snapped his face over to Ayden's a brief moment, and then melted the tar on the road with his glare. She knew what she saw there. Pain. Rampage. Revenge.

They neared a paved street. The sun was just cresting the horizon, sending coral rays across the desert valley. She had no idea where they were, but at least they didn't have to worry about the headlights anymore. With the rest of the world awake, they would soon hit traffic. Traffic meant blending in. Blending in meant disappearing.

Chet shifted gears and stomped on the gas. They wouldn't blend in very well.

"You said you wouldn't lie to me," Ayden reminded him.

"She's someone I met in rehab," he grunted, shifting again.

Ayden was genuinely suspicious. "Rehab?"

"Yes, rehab. Are you okay? What have they done to you?"

She let her chin drop wobbly to her chest, inspecting her attire. Her clothes were a real sight for sore eyes. She couldn't remember what color her shirt had originally been. The scraggly hair hanging down her shoulders was no better. Muck was caked in little half moons beneath her fingernails. The smell came from…all of her. Her head…didn't feel right.

"They tortured me. I think," Ayden stated.

"They tortured you?" Chet asked, looking over to her. His eyes widened with ire. "You stupid, stupid girl!"

His fist pounded against the steering wheel as he completed a sharp turn and ended up on a barren stretch of highway. The car drifted a degree and then righted as Chet fueled the gas, changing lanes. Ayden jumped at his sudden outburst, but shriveled back into the seat as he continued yelling. *Old Faithful.*

"Why did you run?" Chet fumed. "Why did you have to go to Craig? He is dead because of you. Do you get that? His blood is on your hands, Ayden. Now, you get to live with the guilt."

"I didn't think—I didn't know—how was I supposed to know?" Ayden stumbled through her flummoxed thought process. "Where was I supposed to go?"

"You were supposed to stay put!" Chet roared. "I just had to take care of something up north. I needed to fix some things. Saucedo has Keeley—" His voice cut off, choked was more like it. "As collateral and…I am responsible for her. I had no idea he'd ever use Keeley against me. But he had a deal go bad. On my territory. Because I wasn't there. I was with you. I was set up by someone. Saucedo thinks I stole the money and the drugs, and was going to flee the country. When he called, he said he had Keeley and…I had no choice. But I was going to come back for you. You left the estate. I can't believe you left. You went to him? How long did it take? Five hours? Six? When did you decide to get in bed with him?"

Ayden's heart had begun to pound rapidly. A sweat broke out along her forehead and chest. There was a bitter, metallic taste on her tongue she couldn't get rid of. "Don't say that...don't say those things, Chet. I needed someone, like how you needed Starla."

"What about *me*?"

His voice was vociferous. She did her best to mimic it.

"You left for Keeley. You won't even tell me who she is, or why you are responsible for her. All you said was you love her. Did you expect that not to break my heart? Because it did, Chet. You broke my heart."

Chet slammed on the breaks in the middle of the lane. Smoke poured out from beneath the car as the Mustang came to a screeching halt. Ayden flew toward the dash, not catching herself quite in time. Even though Chet had secured her with a seatbelt, her wrists buckled on impact with the glove box. She groaned. He shoved the stick shift into neutral, kicked down on the parking break, and turned his whole chest toward her. She saw the venom in his face, the hard line of his mouth, the coldness in his eyes. Fatal. Beautifully disastrous.

"I will not talk about Keeley," Chet said in a low octave. "Not today. If you're ready to handle it someday—and I'll be the judge of that—then I will tell you about her. But as of right now, we need to formulate a plan. That won't happen with you acting like a deranged madwoman"

Ayden's brain felt too heavy, and her stomach roiled within her. She shook the arm that had suffered the injections at him. Her voice sounded drugged.

"Your friends Rocco and Armando nearly suffocated me to death. They held a soaking wet towel over my face and...poured... water over it. Over. And over. And Over." She made the motions with her hands. "I had to be resuscitated a couple times. I guess it became boring, because then they doped me up on...heroin...I think. Rocco wanted to violate me."

For a second, Ayden saw something close to horror sweep across Chet's features. It morphed murderously.

"Did he?" he asked.

"Nope."

The heated breath he inhaled and exhaled downwards was loudly done so. Even though her body felt immeasurably weak, she felt surprisingly fearless. Chet's anger didn't even scare her. He put his hand back on the stick shift, readying it for first gear. She shook her head.

"Don't go anywhere until you explain to me what happened at Craig's house," she said. "How did you get away from all those men? I saw you lying on the ground. Where have you been for the last several weeks?"

Her last question was clearly an accusation.

Why didn't you come for me sooner?

Chet gripped the stick shift until his fingers cracked. "For your information, I escaped. I'm quite good at it. But they took you, even after I slaughtered the men who had Keeley. Saucedo is being stubborn. He offered not to kill you—or me—if I can get him the money and the drugs that went missing. I said I would, even though I didn't take them, and have no idea where they are, but I demanded he release you first. Saucedo wouldn't. I decided to rescue you, and risk being shot in the process."

"You—" Ayden lost her train of thought. It veered to Rocco's Tales of the Teenage Chet. "*Did* you steal his money?"

Chet's calmness was returning. "No. No, Ayden. I am telling the truth."

Ayden wet her lips. She saw no signs of the brutal suffering he faced in Craig's house. His cheeks weren't bruised or swollen. There was only one minor scratch above his right eyebrow. It must have been a huge gash, but it was healed to the point of a thin, pink line.

Ayden asked, "Where have you been for the last several weeks?"

Chet sighed frustrated. "I told you once before, Ayden. I've been jumping through hoops left and right. I've been traversing all over California, up north and down south again. I've been diving constantly, and fighting even more. I will not let Saucedo get to you. You are too…too…"

"Stupid?"

He flashed her a menacing look. "That's not what I meant

to say."

Ayden felt incredibly sick to her stomach, and all the arguing was making it worse. She reached for the handle on the car door and pushed as she fell out onto the pavement. Air—she gulped at it. What she wanted was wind in her face, the rising sun on her skin, all the things she'd been deprived of. She forced her churning stomach to settle, considered sitting down, but her instincts took over when she hit the pavement. She suddenly wanted to flee.

Stumbling to her feet, she took off at a hectic run, limping into the sand and cacti beyond the highway. Ankles unsteady, hands shaking, she didn't make it very far without crumpling to one knee.

Chet was out of the car, chasing after her. He caught one of her hands, jolting her back toward him. She lurched, falling into his chest as she heaved a dry sob.

"Where do you think you're going?" Chet snarled down at her.

Ayden tried to keep her voice fixed. "I want to get away from this life. You were right all along, Chet. I can't be a part of this. It's too much. I can't take it."

She was on a come down. Her thirst and hunger for the drug fulminated in her mind. She wanted it more than she wanted him.

Chet's jewel-blue eyes moved from one of her hazel eyes to the other. For several long seconds, he gripped her shoulders and glared emotionlessly into her face. She thought of Las Vegas, when he was Nolan, the man who wouldn't smile. She was so frightened of him back then. Even though she knew she should be currently, she wasn't anything but tired. That weariness shown on her face. His gaze softened the tiniest bit, and he lessened his grasp on her arms.

"Get in the car," he ordered softly. "Come with me to the motel. Let's get you bathed. I will call Saucedo. He just wants his money. And me. If you truly want to be out of my life...I can help you vanish."

What she wanted was back in the warehouse, in a syringe. She was ready to fist-fight Chet for it.

Ayden glanced past Chet's shoulder to the Mustang still running in the middle of the vacant highway. The red paint glistened in the mist as dawn approached. The color of blood. She felt like a ship, lost at sea, without a lighthouse. That is what it felt like to be drugged—lost at sea.

"I want to vanish," she whispered, biting back the brimming of tears.

They went away on cue. She'd sworn not to cry over Chet.

"Ayden."

He lifted her chin with his knuckles, grazing her cheek with his thumb.

"No," she snapped, swatting his hand away and nearly falling over in the process.

Chet snaked an arm around her waist and heaved her upright. She wanted to shove him off but lost all motivation.

"Don't start with the 'Ayden' now," she slurred. "You left me. *You hurt me.*"

Chet gave a short, exasperated shake of his head but didn't relinquish his hold on her. "And you went running straight into Craig's bed."

Her temperament blew up. She stretched onto her tiptoes and hollered directly into his face.

"What do you care? It doesn't matter whose bed I climb into if you're not going to be around. Remember when you went to Starla? Remember how you have a list of women, while you've been keeping me on the side? Keeley. Lina. Do you expect me to be one of them? End up just another name in ink on your skin?"

Chet was breathing raggedly. Her comment was an arrow in his heart. It appeared he very much wanted her name inked on him, which ink would be considerably honorable. He was demented. She could see the flame in his eyes. He did well to disguise it, but she was learning which blue went with which emotion. Instead of calming the tides, he took hold of her middle with both hands and threw her over his shoulder.

"You don't know what you're talking about," he hissed, marching back toward the Mustang. Because the passenger door was still open, he dumped Ayden inside. "You are coming with me."

He shut the door, but as he raced around to the driver's side Ayden was trying to climb out again. Reaching across the car, he clutched a fistful of her shirt and yanked her back into the car. Slamming the car into gear, the Mustang shot forward, and he turned the wheel with a jerk so that her door crashed shut. Keeping the pedal to the floor, he sped forward into daybreak.

Ayden remained as far away from Chet as she could, even looking out the window into the nothingness. The nothingness of her soul that pined to be lost at sea.

8

Ayden fought Chet all the way into the motel room. She was frail and decrepit, but her determination to survive was kicking in. The drug was wearing off. Her need for more accelerated. Chet added miminal commentary to the spectacle, for deep inside he knew and empathized with Ayden's torment.

It was a miracle nobody saw, or nobody had the guts to intervene. She scratched his forearms mercilessly while he dragged her behind door number *12*. The second the door was shut, Ayden sprang toward the phone. It was still disconnected, she ought to have remembered, though it took a second to figure that out. She threw her hands up in the air, grabbed a pillow off the bed, and hurled it at Chet.

"How is this place going to be safe?" she demanded.

Chet's eyelids lowered, his gaze sweeping to a sawed-off shotgun on the dresser.

"This is my town," he said simply.

It wasn't going to be the best of best evenings, but they didn't have much of a choice. Ayden opened the drawer in the nightsand and searched the closet. Chet watched and waited patiently until Ayden was done having her fit of lunacy. It was clear how drugged she'd been. She was malnourished, dehydrated, and would more than likely contract some illness from the filthy confines she'd endured, if she hadn't already. She looked like a total wreck.

Eventually, Ayden gave up and fell onto the bed in surrender. It ought to have felt like a victory for Chet. It didn't.

Her fingers were quivering. "You're going to make this go away, right?"

"Ayden..."

"You have the stuff, right? Chet, give me the stuff!"

He took a step toward her. "You're not the one I'm here to fight."

She wiggled back and forth horizontally on the bed, cinching the top bed sheet into her hands and curling away from him, moaning with despair. It hurt him to see her in such desolation. He knew this agony. He wanted to place the blame on her, to ease his burdens. If she'd stayed at the estate, he could've come back to her before Saucedo found them. Craig was dead, dozens more were dead all over the state. Chet had spent several weeks getting rid of his boss's top men, including those who were holding Keeley and Ayden. It was time Chet gained Ayden's confidence. They needed to work together.

With a shake of his head, Chet crossed the remaining space between them and sat beside her. Ayden inched away toward the headboard.

"Listen, okay?" he whispered.

She was shaking her head, clutching a pillow and smashing it down over her ears.

"Can I say something?"

She struggled to maintain ownership of the pillow, but it didn't last long. Chet tore it from her fingers and tossed it aside. She scrambled away, but he caught her by her hips and tugged her back down beside him. This time, she didn't fight, but stared hopelessly up at him with big, fearful eyes. It was the look of ultimate surrender. The way she'd probably looked at Mitchell a myriad of times. It cut him up inside, sending a searing pain straight through his heart. She didn't have the black soul that he did, and the torture she'd endured because of her associaton with him...

"I'm sorry," Chet murmured. "And that is the most inadequate expression there is."

Ayden didn't reply.

"I'm so sorry for everything you've been through. You deserve to hate me. If you do, I understand. But please, *please*, I need you to let me help you and protect you. I can take care of you, at least until I help you disappear. If that's really what you want."

Ayden was relaxing in his hold, her eyes straying down to his lips. He wondered if he should kiss her. That's most likely what would happen in the movies she often spoke of.

He forced his gaze back to her eyes, staring into the depths of the sorrow he'd caused her. How many times did he wish he could go back in time? Just looking at her made him detest himself. She might be safe whenever she was with him, but what about when she went out into the world? Would he keep her locked in an estate for the rest of her life?

Chet released Ayden even though she hadn't asked him to, and rolled off the bed.

In his heart, he had hoped she would reach out to him, pull him back against her, maybe say something to keep him from going. She wasn't the only one that needed comfort. When she didn't, he sighed with resignation.

"They didn't touch you, did they?" he questioned from the window.

Ayden knew what he was referring to, and though she'd anticipated it from Rocco on several occasions, she could truthfully answer, "No."

The tension in Chet's shoulders decreased. "All I ask, is that you let me protect you," he said with his back to her. "I can't do that if you run off."

Ayden didn't respond.

Chet assumed she probably didn't believe him after his failures.

"Can you promise me you won't run away?" he asked, still not looking at her face. He couldn't bear it. The pain was so tangible it would have caused him to weep. Tears hadn't threatened Chet since he was a teen. "Can you promise not to go anywhere without me, not to call the police, or contact anyone other than me? Until I can guarantee Saucedo has been squared away, and we can safely leave this town?"

"Fine," Ayden mumbled. "Will you promise me something in return?"

Chet turned, willing himself not to crawl across the bed and wrap himself in her arms.

Gulping, he answered, "I will promise you anything."

Ayden was sitting on the edge of the bed, gaze downcast, fingers knotted together. She looked like the disheveled woman in ruins she'd been when he'd taken her away from Mitchell. She looked like he did the day he'd been forced into rehab.

"Promise me," Ayden spoke gingerly, "promise me you won't kill anyone anymore."

"What?" he gasped.

She peered up for just a bit and then back down. "I don't like it when you kill people."

Chet sank down onto his heels in front of the bed so that they were eye level with each other. "Ayden, I only kill people when I have to. Just to save others like yourself. I'm not some bloodthirsty, murderer…"

She lifted one shoulder but didn't look up. The stories Rocco shared with her proved otherwise.

"It's hard for me to see people die," she added.

He tried to ignore the waxen look of her skin as she spoke. Worse, he knew her body was accustomed to the high. She was going to suffer regaining full sobriety. Tremendously.

"It's even harder when I'm watching you be the killer," Ayden continued. "I don't want you to be the killer."

"How am I supposed to protect you?" he asked, his hands flattened on his knees.

"I don't know," she exhaled. She shifted her chin sideways, away from his face. "Isn't there a way without killing people?"

No. He couldn't think of any.

Chet contemplated hard for a minute, then lifted a palm to her leg. When she didn't shove it away, he traced a circle around her knee. He loved her knees. Feeling them under his fingertips reminded him of the first time he'd seen her bare legs at the beach when she was only seventeen. How she'd captured his heart all those years ago. Her face was etched with such fright now, lacking the glow and brilliance he'd fallen for, her clothes in tatters, her hair mangled.

He found himself saying, "I promise not to kill anyone."

Ayden was holding her breath. She exhaled through trembling lips.

"Okay."

"Hey, smile."

Ayden attempted a crooked, anything but pretty smile that made Chet cringe.

"That'a girl, toots," he said bleakly.

She glanced at the clock, her shudders wracking her body. "One more thing."

"Alright."

"Find me a church. I'm going to church."

It was an unfathomable request. He stared unblinking a

long moment. Yet, he could see the vacant ache in her chest, the need to return to her light—her God—and find some peace and comfort. There were churches throughout California. He'd researched them on the internet after first learning about her religion. He'd find her one and take her himself to ensure her safety.

"A church," he confirmed with a nod.

Ayden closed her eyes. "Thank you."

"You're cold," Chet stated, moving to turn the thermostat up.

She didn't answer.

"In the morning, we're going to go someplace," he told her. "I have an old friend, someone I haven't seen in many years, but I don't know who else to go to. Nogo Saucedo has gone to extremes over this deal, and I want you far away from Fresno while I close him out. My friend in Tahoe will know what to do. He's…he's gotten out before."

"He used to work for Saucedo, too." There was an obvious question mark at the end of Ayden's statement, and Chet gave an introspective gesture.

"More or less," he replied. "It's a long story, one he should tell you himself. If anyone can help you disappear, it will be him."

"What about you?"

Chet flicked on the television, not looking back at her. "What about me?"

Ayden sat up against the headboard once more and swallowed. Her hands shook nervously. "Don't you want to disappear?"

"There's not really a point, is there? If you're not going to be around for me to enjoy my life with."

Chet pinched his eyes shut at the ridiculous desperation of his tone. He kept his expression made of stone.

Ayden stared at his back. He'd removed the brass knuckles and tucked them away in his car so she wouldn't have to see them. The led pipe remained in the back seat. Weapons gave her excessive anxiety, but he kept the sawed-off shotgun on the dresser. After washing his hands and arms in the bathroom, he'd offered to help her bathe, but she had strictly refused. It didn't seem weird, not having belongings and a cell phone. Would he purchase her more clothes? A clean outfit and money didn't matter as much as her means for communication. What would happen if she and Chet got separated again? The idea made her panic.

"Breathe," Chet whispered, scooting closer to the bedside.

Ayden didn't realize she was losing consciousness, flopping forward off the bed.

"Ayden?"

She fell into his arms.

Her torture took its toll as she slipped involuntarily into a nightmare.

***

During sparse moments of consciousness, Ayden heard voices. One of them was Chet's. He wasn't speaking to her, and the replying voice came through distorted and harsh. Cell phone, she realized. She fell into a fitful sleep, tossing and turning, while arguing voices pierced the blackness surrounding her. Every time she woke it was like exiting one dream only to sink seamlessly into another.

Drink up.

You need more rest.

I'll be back.

Don't leave me.

You need to eat something.

What if they come for me? Are they going to come for me?

I will protect you.

Writhing. Vomiting. Bawling. Sweating.

Sweating, sweating, sweating.

There was a chair—the chair Ayden had been tied to when Rocco and Armando tortured her. She felt the prick of a needle and the seductive cooling of the drug siphoning through her veins. All sensory nerves and motor function dissipated as she fell, hitting her head on the cold, dank floor. And then she was being driven around, her head flaccidly rolling from side to side. Elvis was blaring through the radio. Her head was pounding. She was sweating, sweating, sweating.

The Mustang sprung forward into the night, galloping down the barren stretch of road at speeds that sent her mind spiraling inhumanly out of control. Starla was in the back seat, cackling. No one was driving the car, and when Craig's body materialized in the headlights, they slammed right into him.

An indeterminable amount of time passed, and Ayden could only hope that when she opened her eyes, it would have all been part of the nightmare.

***

She woke up to the rhythmic humming of spraying water. The shower was running. Blinking sleepily, Ayden looked around the dimly lit room. The curtains were drawn, permitting only weak light from the streetlamps outside. The TV was on, but Chet was nowhere to be seen. He wasn't in bed next to her, or in the chair, though his cell phone and wallet were on the dresser. He hadn't left her.

Her head lagged, her eyelids heavy. The spinning effects of the nightmare lingered. She was severely terrified, but even more severe was her thirst. She felt like she might vomit. On the nightstand was a bottle of water. She snatched it, taking a greedy drink. Memories from the night before—or was it the day before?—flickered through her thoughts. Chet had been in and out of the room. He'd been on his cell phone a lot. She remembered something he said about Nogo Saucedo. What was it? Saucedo was south of the border. Chet was arranging reinforcements, utilizing connections, strengthening allies, even though Chet was still under an invisible contract to find Saucedo's lost money and drug shipment.

Putting the cap back on water bottle, Ayden glanced at the digital clock. It was one in the morning. She bent over the side of the bed and heaved, spitting some of the water onto the dirty carpet.

Remembering the running shower, Ayden lifted the sheets covering her. Her clothes had been removed. She was too exhausted to care. Her under garments looked and smelled terrible. Wrapping a sheet around herself, she crawled out of bed and padded toward the bathroom. Her head still felt unnaturally dizzy and she tripped, catching herself on the wall. An immediate sheen of perspiration seemed to pop up across her upper lip. Her stomach upturned again. There were no words to describe the stupefaction she felt. It was a dreadful sensation.

Steadying her eyesight, she regulated the frayed breaths in through her nose, out through her mouth. The fear of her nightmare motivated her, and she finished walking to the bathroom.

The door was ajar and, with a slight nudge, it swung inwards. Steam poured out into the hall. Chet smelling steam. Ayden stepped one toe onto the tile and peeked inside. The mirror was completely fogged up. As was the glass shower door. Behind the swirling mist, Ayden could see Chet's silhouette standing under the cascading water with his back to her. His black hair was flattened to his neck. His shoulders were curved forward a bit, chin lowered, and he leaned one hand against the tile. There was something defeated about his posture. A shiver rippled up her spine.

She wanted to feel the water on her skin, to be cleansed, but she left the bathroom until Chet was finished. If their circumstances had been different, if they'd been a married couple, she'd have joined him in the shower to wash away the plague of her nightmares, to feel his security. On her bed, she waited. He came out in a puff of steam, already dressed. Little droplets of water trilled down his brow bone and nose. His eyelashes formed star-like points, and he blinked against the moisture. She was immediately self-conscious. Ugly. Wretched. Hey eyes averted subserviently as she sat on the edge of the mattress, wrapped in a sheet that needed to be washed.

Emotion tugged Ayden's eyes back to Chet's when she noticed he hadn't moved. The flash of need in his expression reflected her own. He moved carefully to the dresser and opened a drawer, withdrawing a sack of women's clothing. They still had tags. He walked them into the bathroom and set them on the counter. When he returned to the main room, glancing at his cell phone, Ayden moved stiffly to the bathroom door. She desperately needed a shower.

Chet watched the back of her head disappear into the bathroom. He needed something else entirely.

9

Upon awakening, Ayden felt her stomach rumble with hunger. She was famished. Peeling her eyes open, the dim angles of the motel room came into focus. It was morning. She realized she was sprawled across the bed on her stomach. Her right arm was extended far out along the sheets, and a tattooed arm was stretched out on top of it. Slim fingers were interlocked with hers. Chet was kneeling on the ground at the side of the bed, asleep.

Swallowing hesitantly, Ayden looked at the time. Six in the morning. Her mind was much clearer now, despite the incessant throbbing. She lifted a hand to her head. Her hair was tangled, but at least it was clean. As if he sensed her rousing, Chet stirred. He sat up, alert, and then yawned. He was fully dressed, minus his shoes. Ayden wore one of the new outfits he'd purchased—probably when she was in a fit of withdrawal. It was a cozy shirt and leggings.

Chet slipped his fingers out of Ayden's and stood, stretching. Ayden thought she should say something to him, but no words came out. Bile threatened her throat instead. She went into the bathroom. The fatigue was plain as day in her sagging eyes. Her skin was wan-gray. A concaved belly suggested rapid weight loss. The inside of her elbow was dark blue. In repulsion, she turned away and went back out into the bedroom.

Chet was tugging his shoes on. His mouth was set in a granite line. A cranky wrinkle carved its way between his eyebrows. As Ayden stood near the foot of the bed watching him, she grasped for words to say.

Raising his face, Chet met Ayden's gaze with a look as sharp as a steal blade. She willed herself not to wince.

"I need a cell phone."

Chet didn't pause as he collected his own phone and wallet off the dresser, followed by his keys and the shotgun. Marching toward the door, he didn't so much as offer a word while ripping it open. Fresno's famous heat poured into the motel room. How long had it been since she'd basked in the sun? She wanted to sing and run outside, but her feet stayed rooted to the ground. Chet started his Mustang and then appeared back under the doorframe.

"Do you want to stay here or come pick something out yourself?" he asked quietly. "I'll get the rest of your belongings rounded up from the estate."

"I don't want to be here alone."

He nodded once. His eyes were sullen. She pictured him asleep, kneeling on the floor by the bed, his head resting on the mattress by her ribs, his arm across hers, their fingers interlaced.

"I said that last night, didn't I?" she asked.

He walked up to the doorway of room *12*, towering over her, shading her in his shadow. "You asked me never to leave you," he answered. "Ever."

It came out deadpan. As if Chet could either take it or leave it. Ayden reached up and touched the side of his face. He melted into her palm, his eyes closing. She wrapped her other arm around his neck, squeezing him as tightly as she could. His arms came up behind her back, pulling against her shoulder blades. He buried his face in her neck, allowing the sun to shine onto her face. It was more than a peaceful moment. It was a peace offering.

"You rescued me," she whispered.

Chet got into the driver's side of his Mustang after opening Ayden's door. The motel parking lot was empty enough, and traffic driving by was typical. Ayden settled herself into the car, concerned she might be recognized, unsure of who was looking for her, knowing Chet's vehicle wasn't inconspicuous. Neither was his driving. Chet cranked the stick shift into reverse and peeled out of the parking stall. Roughly jamming the gear into first, the car then shot out onto the street.

Without looking at the passing vehicles, Chet veered across all three lanes and took an immediate right. The tires squealed, and a few honks burped. Ayden didn't dare say anything. They were slowed by a red light, and she gazed over at him. His right hand gripped the steering wheel. The muscles of his forearm swelled against his tattoos. His left elbow was propped up against the window, and he had a finger against his lips.

The light turned green, and Ayden's head was glued into the headrest. He didn't ease on or off the breaks, causing her body to jolt forward and backward. They pulled into a large parking lot, and Ayden thought she was going to have whiplash. But then Chet parked, and opened his car door in one fluid motion.

"Stay here," he ordered.

Ayden watched him shut the door and pace studiously into the electronics store. Only ten minutes later, he appeared with a small plastic sack. He blended in with the environment, his clothing nonchalant, his attitude unperturbed. She wondered fleetingly if anyone ever guessed what he did for a living. She loved how Chet moved, every part of him. Gothic and debonair. She'd never been so attracted to a man.

He stopped near the hood of the car, stiffly, jerking his head to stare at something behind her. Ayden twisted to look out the back window of the Mustang but wasn't sure what he was seeing.

Chet moved fast. When he was reseated in his car, he tossed the sack at Ayden, and drove back down the road like they hadn't stopped at all. She realized his eyes were darting into the rearview mirror and found herself catching glimpses of cars that were behind them through her right side-view mirror. Nothing looked incriminating.

Except he said, "We're being followed."

"What?"

Ayden tried to shift onto her knees and peer behind them. Down the road, there were several nondescript cars. She looked specifically for black SUVs, like the one that she'd been stuffed into the night of her kidnapping. Which reminded her.

"Chet?"

He jammed the car into third, swerving through traffic. "Yeah."

"How long has it been since…since Craig's death?"

"You spent nineteen days with Rocco. Eleven more in the motel."

He said it just like that.

Ayden pricked her mind for the sparse memories she had of the last several weeks, but all she could remember were sensations of ecstasy and grief and loneliness. Was she clean from the drugs now? She didn't feel comfortable asking Chet about it. He'd taken care of her, of course. He must have nursed her, patted her scalp with a damp cloth, changed her sheets. Another debt she owed him, this eternally giving creature.

The Mustang pivoted again, and they were on the freeway. Ayden held on to the car door as they spun. Chet grunted.

"What's happening?" she asked, afraid of the answer.

Who exactly would be coming after them if Rocco, Armando, and everyone else at the warehouse were dead?

"It's not Saucedo's men," Chet muttered.

"How do you know?" She clutched the plastic bag in her lap, suddenly wishing she could call the police. "I don't see anything."

"Four cars back. Red Audi. Tinted windows."

His voice sounded like a recording, or a robot. Ayden stared at his profile a minute longer, the slant of his nose, his mouth.

"Do you know anyone who owns a red Audi?" Chet asked, eyes on the road.

They were approaching the tailgate of a pickup truck. Ayden screeched as she anticipated Chet ramming straight into the back of it, but at the last second he cranked the steering wheel right, and they darted around it. She placed a hand to her forehead, for once unsettled by the acceleration and speed. Her stomach felt upside down. When did she last eat?

"Ayden?" Chet demanded. "Red car? Audi? Who do you know—"

"N-no one," she stuttered. "No one. I mean…none of the girls at my salon drove a red car and Craig—" her voice caught in her windpipe— "Craig drove the Acura, you know. I don't have any other connections." She wanted to say friends. "Connections are liabilities, I'm informed."

Chet didn't respond. He adjusted his fingers on the leather stick shift. To her astonishment, he down-shifted, and the car chirped as the tires skidded. They decelerated until the red Audi was only two cars behind them, and one lane to the left. It was nearing, fast. Ayden felt like a sock had been stuffed down her throat. She sunk down until only her eyes peered out the window.

"What are you doing?" she gasped.

Chet continued to brake. The Audi pulled up alongside the Mustang, and Chet glanced out his window, directly at the pursuing car. Ayden felt herself chill with the iciness of Chet's eyes. She knew he wouldn't be able to see anything passed the tint of the

Audi's windows, but that didn't stop him. Whoever was in there could see Chet, and that's what Chet wanted. It was a threat. Chet didn't watch the freeway ahead of them, he just stared at the red car, a morbid, ominous expression on his face.

A second time, they were closing in on a vehicle ahead of them. Ayden called out Chet's name, curling up tighter in her seat. His eyes didn't stray from the Audi, but he jarred the Mustang into gear and gruffly rotated the steering wheel. The wheels protested as rubber burnt on the asphalt, and pewter exhaust sprayed into the California air. The next thing she knew, they were descending an exit, drifting the forty-five degree turn, and then racing onto a downtown street.

Chet must have been holding his breath. He let out a downward gust of air. Ayden sensed the imminent threat was removed and sat up. She glanced out the window. Familiar shops and bars and the theater blurred by. It was still early in the morning, and most Fresno residents were just heading to work. That would explain the congestion on the freeway. But where did the Audi come from?

"How did it know where we were?" Ayden thought aloud. "Or *who* we are? I mean, if it isn't Saucedo's men…Chet, who do *you* know? Is it someone else that might have—that you're associated with?"

His pallid expression told her he didn't know. He was asserting his calm and reposed demeanor. If he had enemies that weren't part of Saucedo's organization, what kind of enemies would they be? Was there a worse type of rival? If Chet was concerned, she was genuinely terrified. All the questions she had about him, the women in his life, how he escaped Rocco's men after being battered to a pulp, and what his plans were now, didn't matter.

Ayden felt like she couldn't trust anyone in the world.

10

One of them ought to turn on the radio. Ayden couldn't bring herself to do it. What if the station played Elvis Presley, or some sappy song about star-crossed lovers? She pulled out the contents of the sack Chet gave her in the motel. There were a couple of shirts, two other pairs of pants, and generic underwear. She contemplated asking him to stop by a church distribution center, but decided against it. Some other time. Beneath the clothes were a disposable toothbrush and a pair of white flip flops.

"It's a bit of a drive," Chet stated abruptly.

Ayden laid the clothing in her lap and looked over at him. Was there a more beautiful man? His milky complexion was a little more flushed than usual. She wanted badly to reach out and touch his arm. Even as her eyes dropped to the tattoos along his right forearm, he glanced over at her.

"How long of a drive?" Ayden asked.

"Several hours. Probably four."

She sighed, blowing a strand of hair from her face. "Where are we going?"

"The Sierra Mountains."

He was distant. There was still an awkward wall between them. Chet left her for Keeley. Ayden ran to Craig. Craig died. Ayden was captured. Tortued. Drugged. Chet and Ayden were reunited. They loved one another, obviously. How did they get passed the pain?

She ripped her gaze away and stared down at her elbow. She wished she had something to cover the markings there. Would they scar? Tracing a finger around the marred tissue, she thought of Chet's tattoos and pondered how hard it had been for him to quit using, considering he'd been surrounded by such negative influences for years.

Ayden was curious about Chet's relationship with his boss, Nogo Saucedo. They were closer than just employer/employee, which meant there was a deep bond between them. Several times, she'd heard Chet mention comments about his biological father. During some of his phone calls with Saucedo phone, Chet had said things like "I'm not him" and "that debt has been repaid". What exactly was going on?

It was strange to Ayden that she was so enthralled by him. Her ex-husband, Mitchell, had held an appeal when they'd first started dating. Craig was a good-looking guy, who was also a member of her faith. Yet, neither of those two men spawned the sort of longing, yearning, unstoppable, irrepressible, earth-shattering, love and care in Ayden that Chet did. There was this undeniable urge within her to take care of him. Whatever sadness tormented him, she wanted to remedy it. When the rueful regrets of his past washed over his face and clouded the gentle blue in his eyes, she wished she could transfer the burden from his shoulders to hers.

He also drove her crazy—literally, any time he was behind a wheel. His secrets pestered her. Danger followed them everywhere. Never before had a man made her feel so wild and out of control. Half of the problem was she enjoyed it. The night at Pismo Beach, when they first met and Chet took her for a ride on his motorcycle, was just the beginning. Every bit of his mysterious enigma thrilled Ayden. She loved his Mustang, and how he handled it with expertise. The vroom. His tattoos were even adorable to her now, because despite how harsh he could appear on the outside, he was soft and compassionate on the inside. The couple times she'd actually heard him laugh out loud made her heart soar.

Chet followed the road to the freeway entrance, running almost every light, red or green. Ayden ached inside, mentally and physically. With their lives at stake, she worried there would be no time to work things out between them. If they could at least have some quality alone time. An hour later, she was dozing against the window, dreaming of alone time.

***

Chet stole glimpses of Ayden while she slept, his temper taking a dive with each of her sleepy respires. In a sick way, he was jealous of her, of the drugs she'd been given. Deep inside, he felt his demons pining for it. It was like losing a limb depriving himself of them. Yet, he was strong enough now to turn them down. He had a replacement. *Her.*

It was necessary for them to go straight to the mountains, he told himself. Necessary to ask this specific person for help. Chet had killed dozens of Saucedo's men, and Saucedo had run out of reasons to keep Chet alive. His boss barely believed Chet that hadn't taken the money or drugs that were missing. Nogo even suspected Ayden of conspiring with another drug lord, or that she'd let slip information about when the deal would go down, how much money would be there, etc, and one of Chet's competitors swept it and lifted it. Nogo wanted the shipment returned, and Chet had promised to help find it in exchange for his life...and the lives of a few others.

The bad deal, the missing money, the deceased employees. It was typical drug heist business, but Chet was the one responsible for the exchange, therefore he's the one primarily accountable. Saucedo would not stop hunting them until Chet found his boss's lost money and drugs. Even then, Chet was worried he'd made his boss so mad that Saucedo would never let them live in peace. He hoped he had time to concoct a solution and prove to his boss he had nothing to do with the heist, before he or Ayden encountered any more life-threatening dilemmas. He also prayed for the help awaiting them in Lake Tahoe.

Chet could still remember sneaking up to the outside of the warehouse, listening to the bizarre clanking that was sounding around the walls. *Clunk. Clunk.* His gun was steady in his palms, in spite of his rapid heartrate. Tucked into the back of his pants was his trusty led pipe. He wore brass knuckles on his right hand. He wasn't used to facing dire situations sober-minded, and his bravery wavered. Wavered, but intensified with each step he took.

Thinking of Ayden with those men was all the incentive he needed. It boosted his courage like fire in his blood as he slinked from one wall to the next, in near pitch black, prepared to shoot his first target. The clatter came again. Chet had put his ear against the concrete wall and waited. *Clunk. Clunk.* He knew in a heartbeat that it was Ayden. She was leading him straight to her. Using the noise as guidance, he determined which area of the warehouse they were keeping her in.

The men guarding the outside of the warehouse were easy enough to dispense of. Inside the building, he followed the sounds of the clamor to a door. Two men were outside of it. He pulled the trigger, ending them both, and stormed the door. It was locked. Several men came jogging down the hall to his right, and Chet twirled to shoot them. He slammed into the door again, certain Ayden was being kept prisoner behind it.

Rocco and Armando let lose a hurricane of bullets after he broke through the door. Chet had to lie flat on his back, using his feet to propel himself back down the hallway as the walls exploded around him. He inhaled the blasting dust, clamped his eyes shut against the flecks of concrete stinging his face. When the men ran out of ammo, he took action. When he saw Ayden on the ground, it was like he'd blacked out the way he had the night he'd gone for Keeley.

Nogo Saucedo wanted vengeance for whomever was behind the drug heist. The druglord took Keeley, and that meant he could make Chet do whatever he wanted. Chet had arrived at the location sight several nights before rescuing Ayden. Men had been positioned there to murder Chet and retrieve all the money and drugs he'd supposedly stolen from Saucedo. Keeley was nowhere to be found. Chet hardly escaped with his life, but he ridded the town of every one of the pawns Saucedo sent, only after extracting valuable information about Keeley's whereabouts. After securing Keeley, Chet made a phone call to his boss. They came to an arrangment that both would honor until Chet located Nogo's lost shipment.

That's when Chet went back for Ayden.

He thought about going to Starla. Maybe she could help. But remaining in Fresno was jeopardous. Saucedo just wanted his money, and Chet could find a way to assist his boss. With Keeley and Ayden on the line, he didn't have a choice. He'd find the stolen shipment, but he needed time and preparation. The mountains would be his safest bet. He could ensure Ayden's protection, at least while he came up with a way to convince his boss he was not a traitor. Chet wanted out of the business, but he knew better than to double-cross Saucedo. Besides, Chet didn't care about money. Or drugs, anymore.

It didn't matter that Saucedo thought of Chet as a son—the man's business came first. Business and money. Chet was done having anything to do with it. He had to get Ayden as far away. The contact in Lake Tahoe was the one place Nogo Saucedo would never go.

The place Chet was taking Ayden to was far enough in the mountains to be an inconvenience, not to mention the owner of the cabin he hoped they could temporarily occupy knew who Nogo Saucedo was. The man knew all about the criminal organization. If that guy could get out, certainly Chet and Ayden could. They needed the help. If Ayden wanted to disappear, this man would help get her out of the state, get a new name, a new life. She'd be free.

Chet's gut twitched at the idea of sending Ayden away forever. He'd spent the past handful of years obsessing over her, and it only grew in force when she returned his interest. Then they touched…they kissed. The fact that she could so swiftly seek comfort from Craig hurt Chet more than his withdrawals. He felt more betrayed than he had when Brandylynn, his teenage love, abandoned him. He'd been left with an eviction notice on their rundown apartment, and a hefty debt to the local dealers that he'd had to repay.

While Chet drove, his mind drifted back to last night when Ayden'd asked him not to leave her, ever. It confused him, her desire to be free, her demanding he stay. She fell asleep grasping his arm, and he fell asleep beside the bed holding her hand. Her touch was reparative. Addicting. It filled him with the same ecstasy a needle would, but instead of darkness, he was overcome with light.

She'd been latent for days straight, succumbing to the shakes and chills of a severe withdrawal. He was tormented alongside her, holding her hand, brushing her hair out of her face, helping her sip on water and nibble on food. The only moments he left the bedside was to shower or run to the store for necessities, and only when she was deep asleep.

Chet thought he could demonstrate his selfless conduct by attending to all Ayden's needs, by loving her and asking for nothing in return. It was medicinal for him. It felt better giving than taking. He watched her sleep for hours, tracing her ear and giving her soft kisses on her shoulder. *Ayden* was his drug. He felt her love for him, and he shared his with her. They were going to survive because they had each other. How could he let her vanish from his life—for good?

Saucedo wasn't returning to California for another week or so. Having a few days to hide out with Ayden was just what Chet needed. Shifting in his seat, he gripped the steering wheel with determination and gassed the pedal. Things would be different in the mountains. There would be space. He'd also promised her he'd find her a church.

It made him grin. They were opposites, matched by destiny. He was sure of it. She had been robbed of everything, and yet wanted nothing but peace and comfort. Chet had everything, on the outside, yet was so void on the inside. Where he lacked, she excelled. When she was wary, he was fearless. When he was violent, she was calm and forgiving. They were duel edges of a sword. She helped him to see light in his dark world. He had experienced the goodness, and he longed to exist in it. He wanted to attend church and worship God, too.

Chet shook his head, blew out a stream of air, and sped out of the city limits. Three and a half hours later, Ayden was still deep asleep in the passenger's seat. They were approaching their destination. It had been awhile since Chet had driven so far into the never-ending forest. He appreciated the lush foliage and crisp pine scent, but he had a slight mountain-aversion. Only a few times in his life had he gone into the Sierras. His parents weren't big on camping, nor were they big on anything other than lounging back, glazed-eyed, possessed by the same drugs that had ruined their lives. And, ultimately, caused their deaths.

Chet would not think about his parents. He could not bear to think about his faults and incompetence in character, and where he'd inherited them.

His eyes kept sliding over to Ayden, her slim legs in the leggings, and her slight shoulders. The clothing he'd bought was simple and cheap. He would return to the estate and pack up more of her belongings in a few days—before Saucedo entered California—and also get her another cell phone. She wasn't wearing any makeup, and her hair was a haphazard jumble of waves from the previous night, but he couldn't have thought her more gorgeous.

Tearing his gaze away, Chet focused on the winding road. It wasn't much further now. The sun was blocked from the towering trees, and only patches of sunlight speckled the asphalt in tiny, dancing spheres. A few birds swooped down languidly, disappearing into the thick woodland. After a wide turn, the lake came into view. The magnificence was stunning. He kept winding further into the trees, toward the cabin. It was a miracle he even remembered how to get here, since he'd only been one other time. Was he thirteen? Fourteen? He'd been told the doors would always be welcome to him, and as he reflected back on that day, he wondered if it hadn't all been a foreshadowing.

In either case, Chet knew he needed an ally. With an ally it would be possible to drop off the face of the earth and help Ayden disappear. It was really his only hope. Chet promised Ayden he wouldn't kill anyone else. What would happen, heaven forbid, if Chet couldn't find Nogo's lost shipment? If he and Ayden stayed in town, they would be silenced. Dead. Or, worse, lifted and tortured. Up here, in the middle of nowhere, not even Nogo Saucedo would bother to try and find them.

Chet sighed, turning down an unmarked dirt road that was nearly disguised by the overgrowth of tree branches and gnarled roots. The Mustang creaked, snapping twigs as it drove over the brush. Stems scraped the exterior of the paint. His stomach had begun to tighten. He felt the common itch at the inside of his elbow that accompanied uncertainty, and withstood by clutching the steering wheel as if he might otherwise be swallowed up by the forest enclosing them. Soon, Ayden was going to meet one of the men Chet considered a friend, but feared more than any other man on the planet.

11

Ayden heard Chet calling her out of her peacefulness. For the first time she could remember, her slumber had gone without any nightmares. It was filled with quite the opposite. A green winery, a motorcycle, and a boy. Sitting up, she stretched the kink in her neck and took a look outside the windshield. The Mustang was stopped, and everywhere, all she could see were trees.

Ahead of them, there was a decent-sized cabin. A porch wrapped all the way around it, and two, handmade rocking chairs sat on the west side. Ayden's gaze traveled further west, through an opening in the thickness of pines and shrubbery, where she could see the glimmer of a blue lake. Tied to a small dock, was an old canoe.

Chet withdrew the keys from the ignition. He had a look of mild discomfort on his face, and she wondered why he had brought them here if it wasn't safe. Was he scared? She knew he had guns, at least one led pipe, and brass knuckles in the trunk. There were probably rocket launchers and grenades. Still, Chet's eyes darted around the peripheral of the cabin like he was searching for something to pop out of hiding.

"Come on," he stated under his breath, reaching to open his car door.

Ayden followed and was blasted with a cool breeze. While it felt refreshing, it also caused goose bumps to sprout up over her skin. Rubbing a hand up and down her arm, she followed Chet around the hood of the Mustang. She felt a sharp longing for the beach, replaced almost instantly by terror. She wouldn't be forbidden from visiting the California coast the rest of her life, would she? Would she have to move east in her "disappearance?"

Chet paused, staring at the front door to the cabin. Ayden had the impulse to grab his hand, to feel some kind of reinforcement or solace, but she didn't know what kind of impression they were supposed to make on this contact. At a splashing sound coming from the lake, they both twisted around. Emerging from the trees, they saw the figure of a man.

"Ayden," Chet stated. She moved only her eyes, meeting his gaze. He gestured out in front of him, and stated, "This is Nolan."

The man trudging out of the forest, fishing rod in one hand and beer can in the other, was a Hispanic male who looked peculiarly familiar. Thin scars cut across his face like white slivers Ayden could see even from fifty feet away. His hair hung down past his shoulders in unruly dreadlocks, giving him a grungy, Jamaican appeal. His neck was beefy against an even bulkier set of shoulders. Tattoos peeked over his collar. He was much shorter than Chet, but he didn't look less capable.

As Nolan tilted his chin up, he caught sight of Chet and Ayden standing immobile beside the Mustang. Nolan smiled, and his teeth boasted of silver fillings. Due to the scarring, his cheeks puckered almost to the point of grotesque, but there was something welcoming in his eyes. Endearing. He wasn't a threat.

Drawing closer, Nolan tossed the beer can toward a garbage can near the front porch. It bounced off the rim, joining a few other crushed cans littering the pine needles on the dirt. Ayden chanced a quick glance over at Chet. The taut look that inhabited his face diminished, the set of his shoulders were a tiny bit more relaxed. But he had rocked forward onto his toes, ready to pounce. He was guarded.

Intrigued, Ayden watched Nolan draw nearer. His shirt was flannel and plaid, worn and old. His jeans were the same. A mountain man, living the dream. This was the man who'd inspired Chet to use the name Nolan when they'd encountered one another in Las Vegas?

Nolan spoke first.

"I'd offer you a beer, but I understand you don't drink."

His voice was husky and quietly powerful, like Clint Eastwood in Dirty Harry. Up close, Ayden inspected the deep set of his near black eyes. He had the body and face of a man whose life was flourished with reckless adventure, but the effortlessness in his walk told her it had been a long time since he'd participated in anything remotely dangerous. He wasn't ready to pounce, the way Chet was. Nolan was muscular, and frightening, but had an easy smile and countenance.

"You told me not to," Chet replied softly.

Nolan looked once over the length of Chet. It pleased him, and his grin broadened. Then he took the remaining steps between them swiftly. He clamped a hand down on Chet's shoulder and gave it a fatherly shake. Chet finally let the ghost of a smile pull at his lips.

"Nolan, this is Ayden." Chet motioned to her, bashfully, and Ayden only then realized she had inched back.

"Nolan Saucedo," the man declared. "That's me."

Ayden nodded once, stuttered, and then extended a trembling hand. "It's nice to meet the man who actually owns that name."

Nolan's eyebrows quirked in amusement, and he smiled back at Chet. Chet gave a disgruntled sound and scratched the stubble on his chin.

"Well," Nolan beckoned toward the cabin, "why don't you come in and tell me what it is that brought you to my neck of the woods."

Nolan started for the cabin. Only when he reached the porch did Chet turn to Ayden. Something triggered her memory, a memory of being tortured. His boss entering the cold, pitiless room she'd been restrained in. Eyes the color of midnight. The South American accent. Nogo Saucedo. Nolan Saucedo.

Relatives?

"I'm not going in there unless you tell me who this man is and what we're doing here," Ayden heard herself whisper.

Chet cracked a grin that made her stomach flutter. His blue eyes were twinkling with mischief, just like the glorious, blue lake visible through the trees.

"I told you he could help you disappear," Chet said quiet enough that Nolan couldn't overhear.

From the front door, Nolan called over his shoulder, "Get in here, boy. It's been too long. Bring the babe with you."

Chet tilted his chin toward the door and offered Ayden his hand. She sighed, and then slipped her palm into his. He gave her an unexpected tug and she fell into his side, placing a hand on his ribcage. If he trusted Nolan, she could, too. Glancing up, she saw Chet's calm again, a nostalgia. This place made Chet happy. Maybe Nolan made him happy. Or was it the mountains? Ayden wanted all the answers.

Chet led her into the cabin. "We don't bring Nolan into our mess," he whispered. "Nolan paid the price to get out. He's here to help us, not be a part of it. He doesn't ask, we don't tell."

There was an open living room adjoined with the quaint kitchen. An old, stove fireplace heated the expanse with burning wood that smoked and smelled excellent. The furnishings were that of an outdoor enthusiast, with a few animal busts decorating the walls. It looked like any normal cabin, she supposed. She hadn't ever stayed in one. She'd never been a big fan of mountains in general. It was the beach that really captivated her. More than anything, she missed the waves and summer sun. Again, she shivered and wished for boots and a jacket.

Chet pulled Ayden to the couch and sat down beside her. Draping an arm casually around her shoulders, Chet waited while Nolan pulled a few drinks out of the fridge, and then returned to sit in the chair closest to the fire.

"Water?" he offered Ayden.

She took the bottle and thanked him.

Nolan handed the second bottle to Chet. "Nine years," he murmured.

Chet grinned again, perilously modest. "I'm sorry. Things have been…"

"I don't want to know," Nolan interjected with a dismissing wave of his hand. "What matters is, you are here now, and—" he let his eyes sweep over to Ayden—"you have her."

Chet *had* her?

Ayden gulped. They looked like a couple. Was that Chet's intention? Did that put her in more jeopardy? The unknown made her lean forward to rest her elbows on her knees. Chet's arm stayed on the back of the couch.

"Tell me," Nolan continued, popping the top to a new can of beer, "what brings you to my place?"

Chet swiped a hand across his face. When he slouched back into the cushions, making himself at home with their unfamiliar environment, his eyes fell onto the side of Ayden's face.

"Ayden and I have been friends for awhile now," Chet explained in a voice she hadn't heard him use before.

He sounded—what was it called?—humbled by this man.

Chet looked up to Nolan, revered him even, and Chet didn't revere anyone. This spiked Ayden's curiosity.

"It seems I couldn't stay away from her," Chet added hoarsely. He finally glanced back to Nolan. "I am in deep with Nogo. Fresno is my territory now. Roughly a month ago, a deal went bad. The money and drugs went missing, and I was set up. Nogo thinks I stole it, for Ayden and I, because I'd recently told Nogo I was done working for him. When Nogo found out about Ayden, everything went…haywire. Long story short, we're here because she wants to disappear. Right?"

Nolan and Chet both looked to Ayden. She felt their eyes burning holes through her. It was the first time she'd heard Chet talk about his boss so informally. He even referred to the man as Nogo instead of Saucedo.

"I—uh—sorry, I don't really know where to start," Ayden stammered. Blinking over at Chet briefly, she said, "I don't exactly want to be involved in…the business…but Chet and I—"

"You want to be together, run off into the sunset, and live happily ever after," Nolan finished for her.

Ayden's cheeks heated. Chet cleared his throat.

"It's not really that," Chet muttered. Ayden took a drink of her water, hesitant of what else she could do. "It is my fault she was brought into this mess. In reality, I've wanted to get out for a long time. I suspect you know that."

Nolan smirked dryly.

"The thing is," Chet expounded, "whether we run off into the sunset together or not, we both want to run off. We need your help."

Nolan steepled his fingers beneath his chin.

Ayden fidgeted nervously. Her eyes flitted to a staircase in the back of the room that led to a loft, probably bedrooms. Did Chet plan on keeping her here? For how long? Was there even cell service?

"You're the only one I could come to," Chet spoke reverently. His behavior left Ayden incredulous. "What else was I supposed to do? She is in danger. Nogo had her lifted for a few weeks. They drugged her. I got her out, but…Nogo has access to Keeley, and unless I finish the job for him, and return his money and drugs, I won't see her again."

"You got Ayden out?" Nolan asked, laughter glimmering in his eyes. "Away from Saucedo?"

Chet gave a lift of his shoulder.

"And you didn't get killed," Nolan mumbled. He clucked his tongue and added, "Boy, you've sure grown up. I always said it isn't the size of the man in the fight, it's the size of the fight in the man that counts."

"I wasn't sure if you'd even remember me, or…if we should even come…" Chet's voice dissolved into an uncomfortable silence.

After a moment, Nolan said, "Boy, I couldn't be happier to see you. As long as you didn't bring any baggage with you."

"I didn't bring it here," Chet replied wryly, "but I have to go back to Fresno to take care of it."

"You're going to face my brother?"

"Brother?"

Both men stared at Ayden. She felt a stinging sensation in the back of her throat. The room was closing in on her. It was becoming difficult to breathe.

"Nogo Saucedo is my brother," Nolan remarked. He sent a questioning glance toward Chet before returning his attention to her. "What else don't you know?"

"Everything," Chet answered for her, in a rush to be heard.

His expression was of pleading concern. He didn't want Nolan to say much more. Ayden watched the wordless exchange between the two of them. Wiping the back of her hand across her brow to remove some perspiration, she took another drink and tried to steady her pulse. Walking back outside in the brisk forest breeze sounded like a good idea. She was about to insist the men allow her a moment to do just that, when Nolan suddenly stood. Taking a long swig of his beer, he pointed a thick finger at Chet.

"Looks like you two have a lot to talk about."

Chet shifted his weight and retracted his arm that was hanging casually along the back of the couch. Bending toward Ayden, he rested one elbow on his knee, staring at the water bottle in his hands.

"Nolan, you and I have a lot to talk about before I go on saying things to Ayden she doesn't want to hear." Chet twisted the cap anxiously. "I don't see a need to…tell Ayden much of anything. There's no reason for her to know after she gets out and moves on with her life."

Nolan observed Ayden's reaction with a purse of his lips. She titled in and whispered in his ear.

"Chet."

When he turned his deep, blue eyes on her, she felt the scintillating connection between the two of them. His gaze was tender, gentle, and also a little tired. He looked exhausted and weary.

His throat hummed, "Hm?"

Nolan made a timely exit, disappearing up the stairs with noisy footsteps. Ayden took a deep breath in through her nose and then released it.

"What exactly are we doing here?"

12

Ayden felt more at ease sitting on the porch, even though she knew Nolan was upstairs in the cabin. She didn't know how sound-proof the walls were. Settling herself into one of the wooden rocking chairs, she wrapped her arms around her knees and tucked her heels beneath her. The distant lake was her focal point. It was a marvelous scene, one that could easily sway nomadic drifters, and people trying to escape the hustle of mobster life, into taking up residence in such a secluded place. Nolan chose this as his refuge. Ayden wanted the Cayman Islands.

The breeze was growing colder as the sun started its descent, causing her to shudder. She didn't have a jacket, or good hiking boots. Chet appeared just then, walking out the door carrying a Mexican serape. Ayden took it from his hands without making direct eye contact and draped it across her lap. Chet sat in the rocking chair beside her, immediately pushing himself back and forth. The wood porch protested with a low creak. The two of them stared out at the water, neither saying anything for close to ten minutes. Eventually, Chet brought his chair to a halt and planted his feet firmly. He leaned toward her, reached out, and then decided against it.

Slouching back into the chair, he said quietly, "Remember when you asked me about the place we were going to, and I told you the man who lived here should be the one to explain his story to you?"

Ayden nodded, still staring at the lake.

"Nolan should really be the one talking," Chet reiterated. "He could probably tell you any story better than I could. Even my own. He's Nogo's brother. You know that much. He used to be in the business, higher up than Nogo. There was a big family fall out, but in the end Nolan's wife wanted out. The only thing more important to Nolan than money, was his wife. Nolan basically killed anyone that got in his way, and then they disappeared. It was so legendary no one bothered to look for him. He's the most savage, brutal man I've ever met."

And this was their hope for survival?

Reading Ayden's next thoughts, Chen continued, "He's also

the kindest."

Ayden felt her throat grow tight. She'd often felt that way about Chet.

"Nolan is different than I remember," he continued. "He could pass as a lumberjack."

Chet's handsome chuckle dragged Ayden's attention over to his face. He met her gaze with his own, holding it steadily.

"You think he'll help me disappear because he feels sorry for you?" she asked.

"I think he'll help us both disappear because he's the only man who has ever cared about me," Chet answered. And then said, "I think."

"Where are your parents, Chet?"

His eyes snapped up to hers. He closed his mouth, opened it.

"Dead," he finally replied.

"How?" Ayden questioned, trying to sound empathetic. "When?"

Chet fidgeted. He did not want to talk about it, so he used his mechanical voice. "Because of the world they lived in." He looked at his hands, watching a memory play out on his palms. "I was ten. I've endured a great many catastrophes in my life, the majority caused by them."

He spoke rapidly, but she translated the contempt in his tone. Gazing out into the trees, he masked the discomfort in his face.

"Is that what happened—the day that picture was taken?" she questioned. "The one I found at the estate right before we, um…the picture…You said 'this was the day my life changed forever'. What happened that day?"

"They were killed," Chet responded. An ugly glaze crossed over his eyes. He was no longer seeing the forest but something gruesome. "Nogo slaughtered them, and I was sold into the business."

A hard, mass of disgust choked her, and she lifted a hand to her mouth. "Sold?"

"Nolan, he purchased me. As an employee."

She felt rage next. "Nolan purchased you? Why are we here

with him, Chet? How awful—"

"It saved my life," Chet replied curtly.

Ayden blanched, so confused by the organization Chet worked in. "What happened when Nolan left?"

"I was sent to work for Nogo. The brothers lived together on a large ranch near the border. They sent me back and forth into California, as north as Fresno. Nolan was kind to me, and he saved my life, but he was gone less than a year later. I've worked for Nogo ever since."

It made sense. That's why both of the Saucedo brothers treated Chet like a son. The situation was perverted, and despicable, but it was starting to click.

Ayden said the only thing she could think of. "I'm so… sorry."

Chet kept his face away from her a few seconds and replied, "Never ask me about them again."

"Okay," she said, but only to comfort him. Of course she wanted to know more about Chet's past, his family, why he ended up the man he did, and why he sought out Nolan today. She would have to take it on good faith that Chet would bring it up on his own terms later. "So, what about Nolan?" she pried gently.

"Nolan is a man of integrity," Chet responded a bit more easily. "If I do anything right in this life, it should be owed to him."

"I thought you said Nogo raised you like a son?"

"Nolan was the favorite," Chet interjected with a hint of humor. "The one who feeds you ice cream for dinner."

"Nolan fed you ice cream for dinner?"

"It was a metaphor," he answered, finally smiling a little. "I think Nogo knew I was partial to his brother, that's why Nogo tried to sway my loyalties. It was part of the rivalry between them—besides money. Nolan…he's got a soul. He cares about humanity. A little. I've never seen a man love a woman more. Everything to Nogo is about money. He trained me to believe that, wired my brain to respond to numbers and possessions. Taught me to kill."

Ayden huddled beneath the wool serape, watching Chet's eyelashes flutter up and down. He was gazing out over the lake, retrospectively. It was serene and quiet up here in the mountains. She felt like they were so far from society they could shout and not be heard for miles. Above, the sky was clear except for a jet stream crossing from one cluster of trees to the other, like it'd been drawn there with chalk. The air was crisp with the scent of pine and wilderness.

They finally had a moment, just the two of them, without anything chaotic to cause a disruption. Ayden decided to try and ask Chet a few more questions.

"What will you do? When we disappear?"

He stared, unmoving. Then, he began rocking his chair again. Extending one leg out ahead of him, he used the toe of his other foot to lazily swing the chair.

What she really wanted to know was if he'd go back to his old habits. If Chet had truly changed, not for her but for himself, he wouldn't return to drugs and misdeeds. She needed to know if he honestly wanted a better life, if he was interested in God, and if he would stick to it even though she wasn't there. There was a bit of Chet's childhood stuck inside of him—the boy she met at the grocery store—who just wanted acceptance and love. Would he seek it elsewhere, if she refused?

Chet said something too low for her to hear.

Ayden asked him, "What did you say?"

He angled his chin at her just enough to make eye contact. "I could go away someplace. Like this."

"Is Nolan always up here alone?"

"Yes. He doesn't seem to mind." Chet paused. "He once said 'Success is relative. And it brings a lot of relatives.' He prefers to keep to himself. Now that Lina is gone."

"That's what you want?" she couldn't help questioning. "To live alone in a remote cabin?"

"It would be better than going back to Nogo, or anywhere in Fresno. Too many memories."

She agreed it would. "So…"

She was dying to inquire about Keeley, the other woman in Chet's life. They met in rehab? Was that conversation off-limits? Maybe if Ayden got him talking about his rehabilitation, information would spill out on its own.

"What was it like to be in rehab?" she asked.

Chet gave a vague wave of his hand, but his eyes seemed to

smile. "Which time?"

"How many were there?"

"Three."

"For the same drug?"

He gave a short laugh and Ayden grinned. It was a contagious sound.

"Nah," Chet stated. "For lots of drugs. Each time it got worse. You know, it always starts with cigarettes, then the gateway drugs, then the hardcore stuff."

"You should be a D.A.R.E. instructor," she teased.

The sideways glance in his eyes made her heart scuttle.

Ayden was happy he was opening up to her. They were finally discussing things about his past he'd kept hidden. She always felt like he knew way too much about her. He'd spent years spying on her, even if he did so from a distance. This was good. It was going to help her trust him more.

"But you never drank?" she asked, remembering the dunes over spring break.

He hadn't touched alcohol in the time she'd known him. Chet was saying, "I'd never say never."

Ayden recalled another person who seemed to know about Chet's habits *and* his transformation.

"Starla told me she saw a change in you," Ayden mumbled.

She braced herself for a furious retaliation, but Chet's face gave nothing away.

"I've known Starla as long as I've known Nolan," he said, slowly, and with an underlying message. There was something he was trying to tell her.

Gradually, Ayden's stomach did an unpleasant roll.

"Is she…Nogo's daughter?" she asked timidly.

"Close," Chet answered.

A gust of wind burst into the side of the house just then, and Ayden trembled. She felt like going back in the house and cuddling up next to the fire, but she didn't want Chet to stop talking, and she didn't want Nolan interrupting.

This time Ayden asked, "Is she Nolan's daughter?"

Chet's lips crimped up into an unconsciously, sexy smile. He stopped rocking his chair and looked straight at Ayden.

"By blood, yes. They're estranged."

Ayden could imagine why. She thought Starla was a nasty, trashy woman, and almost said so out loud.

Instead, she inquired, "What happened between them?"

Chet stretched his arms out in front of him, linking his fingers and popping his knuckles. "She got involved with a screwed-up junkie, got pregnant at sixteen, lost custody of the kid, began hustling for Vlad at seventeen," he explained. "Vlad is head over... the women." As if that said enough. "Vlad liked Starla, but he liked her profits more. Starla was so doped up and brainwashed that Nolan couldn't persuade her to stay clean, nor could he keep her away from Vlad. Vlad is our go-between with our Vegas contact, Elias. Do you remember Elias?"

Ayden did. The Venetian.

"Elias is head over the women in Vegas," Chet commented.

Ayden hated that she felt sorry for Starla, so she tried to reignite the feelings of jealousy and rage. She knew just by looking at Starla that the woman was ethnic. She tried to remember if there were any similarities between the woman and Nolan, but all Ayden could see in her mind was a silk robe. Chet had gone to this woman. During their ten days apart, while Ayden was trapped at the estate. Chet said he had gone up north, and something went wrong, and he relapsed. They'd been intimate, Chet and Starla, even though he didn't say it—Ayden could feel it. It didn't take much for Chet to charm a woman, but Ayden knew it didn't take anything to persuade Starla. Just the idea of Chet and Starla in the same room made Ayden want to gag.

"So, Nolan left Starla—"

"And everyone," Chet finished. But there was no bitterness in his tone. "He felt like the deceived one when the family, including Starla, turned against him. Lina was all he needed in life."

"I see," Ayden murmured.

Her eyes strayed down to his arm and the sleeve of tattoos. *Lina.*

She'd pressed on his wounds enough for one day, but she would come back to that.

The way Chet was speaking now, and the way he so obviously had a high regard for Nolan, Ayden deduced Chet envied the older man.

It was officially dusk, and Ayden was now too cold to remain outdoors. Though the sunset was beautiful, it fell quickly behind the trees. The lake glowed yellow, and the breeze picked up. As she thought this, Chet stood and stepped in front of her.

"Let's get you warmed up," he said, and he held out his hand.

Ayden wondered if they should have a new verbal agreement, for their relationship. She didn't know if they were all going to be sleeping in the same room, under the same roof. No one had mentioned sleeping arrangements. Ayden didn't want a one-on-one sleepover with Chet, but there was no way she was sleeping in the cabin alone with Nolan. She let Chet take her hand and lead her back inside.

Nolan was in the kitchen, frying some kind of gamy meet. It didn't smell like chicken or steak, but it made Ayden's stomach rumble with hunger. Spices wafted throughout the room in delicious mixtures. Chet dropped her hand when they stood by the wood embers glowing inside the old, stove fireplace, and he paced into the kitchen. She sat down on the rug, watching him. He asked Nolan what kind of mess he was making for dinner, and Nolan barked out a laugh. Clapping Chet on the back, Nolan handed him a knife and told him to set to work cutting potatoes. Ayden grinned into the serape around her shoulders, watching them.

"Hope you're not a vegetarian, babe," Nolan hollered over his shoulder.

Ayden sat cross-legged and had to strain her neck up high to see them over the couch. The pan was sizzling loudly, spewing grease.

"I'll eat whatever you've got," she yelled back.

And she did.

The meal was basic. Meat and potatoes. Nolan told them it was deer, and went on about how proud he was of his hunting skills. Chet made some offhand comment about Nolan being unable to quit shooting things that made the two of them rupture with laughter. It made Ayden feel like she was sitting at a family dinner table, watching them interact. She hadn't seen Chet so content in a long time. Even when they were at the estate together. He carried around troubles, his eyes always looked bruised, he harbored secrets. But here, that all dissolved away. His guard was down. He was genuinely happier.

There was a tiny, very outdated television in storage, and Nolan dragged it downstairs to set it up beside the couch, where Ayden insisted she sleep. Chet offered her the largest bed up in the loft, but she didn't want to leave the warmth of the fire. Anyway, Nolan would be up there, behind a flimsy door down the hall. She wanted to be a little bit further away from strangers, just in case. With Chet sleeping just beyond the staircase, not enclosed in a bedroom, he'd be a barrier between her and the retired villain. Nolan would have to walk past Chet sleeping in the loft to get to the staircase, and she had a feeling he wouldn't get far without Chet waking.

Nolan gave Ayden some ludicrously huge socks to warm her legs, and she pulled them up over her leggings to her knees. They looked silly with the rest of her outfit, but she was grateful. She thanked him for his hospitality, but he just gave her a gaping smile of fillings and said, "My pleasure, babe," then winked at Chet.

Her cheeks would flame a little every time she heard Nolan call her that. He didn't say it in a derogatory fashion. He said it like a kind, old grandpa, and it made her feel adored. Chet only smiled to himself at Nolan's new nickname for her. She couldn't be certain, but she thought it made Chet blush, too.

Withdrawing to the couch in the living room, Ayden made a list of the things she still knew she needed to talk about with Chet. Starla was Nolan's daughter, which meant the four of them lived together, until Nolan left. Chet and Starla likely grew up together, which gave their history some meaning. That made Ayden feel out of place. She knew these kinds of organizations were like enormous family trees. Everyone was connected somehow, except for her. But she was also feeling extremely welcome, by both Chet and Nolan. They were two very charismatic and charitable men.

Nolan grabbed a final beer from the fridge and then bid them a goodnight. It wasn't that late, but the mountain sky was black as night. Nolan joked about not owning a clock. He said, "It's either light or dark. That's all that matters."

Ayden was worn out and drowsy. Slouching on the couch, she stared at the orange coals in the fire and let the blaze hypnotize her. Chet was changing in the bathroom, and when he stepped out Ayden had to cover her mouth with a hand. He was wearing a flannel button up and brown long johns. He ruffled his hair. The pants were a little too short, coming to an end at his ankles, and the shirt was five sizes too big. At least it covered his crotch, where the long johns had a built in breach.

Chet folded his black clothing, tucking them away. He then straightened his shoulders, pasted an expression of confidence on his face, and strolled over to the couch.

"That's a grade above pink floral," Ayden quipped as he stood beside the couch.

Chet placed his hands on his hips and glanced at the TV. "Thank you."

She glanced at the TV, too, and wondered if this was Chet's way of asking if he could stay up with her for a while. Pointing at the screen, she asked if he wanted to watch something.

"There's only and old VCR," he responded, hooking the television up to a nearby outlet. "I can't promise Nolan has a wide variety of movies to select from, but I bet he's got at least one that isn't a gory, horror film."

Ayden was yawning as she said, "You pick. I'll probably be out in a couple of minutes anyway."

Chet walked to a cabinet along the wall, staring at a collection of videos. He picked one up, dusted it off, then put it back with a whistle. His second decision resulted in a nod, so he closed the cabinet and returned to the TV. Ayden glimpsed the cover of the movie as he put the video in the VCR. *Shawshank Redemption*. It was a classic.

"I like this one," Chet stated.

Ayden didn't protest.

The TV flickered to life, the screen fuzzy and aged so that the color came through distorted. Chet took his place on the couch, sitting by Ayden's heels that were tucked to her side. He didn't attempt to get close. He simply crossed one foot over the other knee, hiking up the long johns a few inches to accommodate his long legs. His feet were bare, and regardless of the hideous plaid shirt,

Ayden thought he looked ravishing. And ordinary.

The movie started, and Ayden squirmed. The fireplace was burning low, emitting a quixotic essence. The room was bathed in skipping shadows. It was kind of ironic. The setting was ideal for romance, a cabin far up in the Sierra Mountains, situated beside the luxurious Lake Tahoe. But Ayden's head was already drifting. Her eyes closed of their own accord. She leaned her head on the armrest, folding her hands beneath her chin. It was so nice, so nice to be here instead of a cheap motel, or chained up and drugged, or even in a plush bed with Craig. She fell instantly asleep.

She woke up with a jolt to something loud happening in the movie. Chet's eyes were trained on the television, but when she glanced over at him she noticed her feet were in his lap. She was lengthened along the entire couch, and he'd moved to the furthest end. Her blanket was pulled tight up around her shoulders, exposing most of her legs. The thick socks were bunched up around her ankles. One of his hands rested on her calf. He might not have realized she awoke, so she stayed deceptively immobile. Though sleep teased her with lulling breaths, she peeled her eyes open just a minute longer.

The fire had been stoked, and the dim light reflected in Chet's blue eyes. He was a beautiful man, inside and out. She couldn't wait to have him beside her in church again, to watch him sit and listen in wonder, to see the guilt and shame lifted from his shoulders. Hopefully, he would have a chance to speak with a bishop soon. What she wouldn't give to be a fly on the wall in that discussion.

Silently, she said a prayer of gratitude, giving thanks for her many blessings, and for the two men in her life who were going to help her. She prayed for their wellbeing, too, and for anyone who might be hurt by Saucedo's men. In conclusion, she asked for guidance and support. Then, she smiled at the man rubbing her leg.

Chet deserved a happy ending, she thought dreamily.

13

Ayden was dreaming.

In her dream, wood was crackling, and the heat was exuded on her face. She smiled, moaning, tunneling deeper into her blanket. Something soft brushed her cheek, like a feather, but left her skin feeling cool. It was a pleasing contrast to the warm cinders. She wanted more.

A car growled to life, and she startled awake.

Nearly flopping off the couch, Ayden shook off the morning stupor. She stood. She was in the cabin. Daylight was beaming through the windows. Outside birds were chirping. The stove was still hot, but had not been stocked with wood in a few hours. It was warm enough. She didn't need to wrap the blanket around herself, but she kept the socks pulled up to her knees. The engine of a car rumbled again, and then the sound grew distant.

Ayden ran to the window and peered out front. The Mustang was gone.

Turmoil erupted inside of her. She flung the cabin door open to leap outside. The air was still brisk, but the sensation of sunshine on her skin was pure bliss. She closed her eyes, tilting her face up to let the sun tickle her face. Forest aromas encircled her. The lake was twinkling in the distance. Gazing around the vicinity, she gathered Chet had left, and Nolan was nowhere to be seen. Chet was good at leaving. Surely he wasn't planning on abandoning her up here in the mountains with Nolan. Was he?

The Hispanic male came waltzing out of the trees a few seconds later, hoisting a fishing line above his head. Strung all over it, were dozens of fish.

"Breakfast?" Nolan shouted.

He gave Ayden a friendly smile that was distorted by his scarred face. Today, his dreaded hair was pulled back into a ponytail. He donned a different plaid shirt and jeans, roughed up cowboy boots, and had a blunt tucked behind his ear. Ayden was glad to see him, to have company, but she had her reservations about being alone with any kind of man—this far from civilization.

When Nolan approached the deck, he swung the fish over his shoulder and jerked a thumb at the road.

"Chet will come back for you," he said assuredly. "Don't worry 'bout that, babe."

Ayden crossed her arms, transferring her weight.

Why couldn't Chet have told her that himself? Where did he go? Why?

This last question came out of her lips, and it sounded like a complaint.

"I would too, if I were him."

She quickly cleared her throat. "I mean, where is he going and why?"

Nolan trotted up the steps and into the cabin. Ayden followed but stayed in the living room as he took the fish to the sink and proceeded to gut them. The sight of blood made her feel queasy. Not the odor of fish guts. It reminded her of Chet being hurt, and her imprisonment by Armando and Rocco.

"Oh, you know Chet," Nolan was saying. "He can't ever stay here or there. He's got a gypsy's soul."

That wasn't exactly reaffirming.

"You didn't see him this morning?" Ayden hoped she didn't sound needy or clingy. Chet wasn't her boyfriend, and she had no right to claim his whereabouts. Still, she wanted to know where Chet went without her. If he was going back into town, she wanted to go, too. There were things she could pick up, like more suitable clothes. She *had* to get to a church distribution center.

Nolan tugged the spine of one fish out and tossed it into the garbage. "He left before I got back from fishing." He waved a decapitated head at her, simultaneously propelling a fishtail into the trash. "Boy won't go far. Not without you."

Ayden wanted to dispute that. She wanted to mention Keeley, and the fact that Chet had already left her for that girl. Chet had left Ayden numerous times. Maybe Nolan knew something about Keeley. It felt evil to pry, and Ayden knew Chet would feel horribly violated if she asked Nolan anything about his personal life behind his back, so she didn't do it immediately. The thought stayed in her head though.

What was she going to do up here with Nolan all day? Clearly, Chet trusted Nolan enough to let them stay way up here in the mountains without a chaperone. Chet'd been so crazy, envious of Craig it made Ayden feel a bit more comfortable with the stranger who owned the cabin. She'd be better off trying to get to know Nolan. It could be to her advantage.

"Nolan," she began, "what do you do up here? I mean, for fun?"

"Fish. Hunt." Nolan was pulling dishes and pans out, preparing to sauté the fish. The way he handled the creatures, their bones and innards, the blood, she had the fleeting idea that he missed his old lifestyle. "The lake is my sanctuary. There's a pathway that leads all the way around it. I like to walk it. Every day. Never gets old. The water is always shifting, the trees bend, the sky is never quite the same shade of blue. And winter—" he whistled —"you should see it for yourself."

Ayden sat back on the couch, leaning her arms over the back of it while she spoke to him. "I've never fished or hunted. A stroll around the lake sounds wonderful. Do you ever go into the city?"

"Meh," he replied. "Now and then. There are some dumpy food marts I stop at. Mostly I get what I need up here." He pulled the refrigerator door open and withdrew a beer. "Except for these."

Ayden smiled.

Beer and fish for breakfast.

After they ate, Nolan ventured off into the woods with a rifle and a serape wrapped on his back. Ayden didn't pester him about his daily regimen. She used the toothbrush Chet bought for her and brushed her teeth, took off the socks Nolan lent her, and stuffed her feet into the flip flops. They were so unconventional in this environment, and made her crave the beach even more. Next, she grabbed a spare blanket, and then headed outside.

The sun was cresting above the tops of the trees, breaking through the foliage in pillars of light. It was splendid. The scents of pine and lake water mixed with various plant life deserved a candle at the bath and body store. She followed Nolan's directions down to the lake and spotted the tiny dirt trail. In some places it traced parallel to the shoreline, and in others it led her into a grove of trees. Her feet were noisy on the path, snapping twigs, crunching pine cones, and scuffing pebbles. If it was warmer, she might have thought to dip her toes into the lake. Later, she hoped to take the canoe out for a trip across the water's surface.

A mile into her walk, Ayden stopped for a break. The lake was enormous. Draping the blanket over one shoulder, she traipsed down to the water's edge. She picked up a pinecone and chucked it out into the lake, watching it bob on the surface. Little ripples flowed outwards in giant circles until they collided into the beach. *Ripple effect.* That's what her life had been. She grew up as a strict Christian in her religious culture, sheltered by her parents, and pressured by them to marry young. Ignoring the miniscule rebellious stint at Pismo over spring break, she diligently heeded their requests. She married Mitchell, in a temple, for time and all eternity.

Ayden's marriage had been the single worst years of her life. Mitchell abused her in every way imaginable. In some ways, unimaginable. His hands were heavy and quick to strike, but his words inflicted more pain than anything. She still suffered mental injuries from Mitchell's damaging remarks. Every time she looked in the mirror, she heard his voice. When she got dressed, when she walked down the street, when she went to bed.

On top of that, Mitchell was an adulterer. Not only did he force himself on his wife frequently, but he philandered with women all over Fresno—probably other cities, too. Ayden had often glanced at girls at the super market, musing whether or not they had been with her husband. It always made her feel unclean. Sometimes, she resented her parents. There was nothing wrong with religion, but they'd sheltered her so much from the world she didn't know how a bad man who was a good liar, from a good man who was a bad liar. She didn't know how to combat certain situations, like abuse, because she'd never been educated on it. No one taught her about the dark side of the world.

The only positive thing Ayden could take from her marriage was the opportunity that had taken her to Las Vegas, where she encountered Chet for the first time in years. If she hadn't ran into him, he might not have saved her from Mitchell the night her husband was going to kill her. The notion made her quiver. Chet had come to her defense, and the ensuing weeks had been a riot of emotion. Ayden got divorced and started a new life. Her new job provided her with income and friends. She met Craig. She grew attached to Chet in ways she never dreamed.

The first time Chet disappeared, he was gone six months. What else was she to do but move on? Her heart hadn't fully recovered, and she missed Chet every single day, but she did not want to wallow in pity like she had over Mitchell. Nothing was quite as crippling as being the divorced woman—feeling utterly worthless. Nothing she did could please Mitchell. She was never enough for her ex-husband. When Chet left, it brought back feelings of inadequacy. Ayden began dating Craig in Chet's absence. Craig, the wholesome gentleman who was now in his grave. That was the effect she had on him. The consequences of *her* actions led to the murder of an innocent man. Chet was right. Craig's blood was on her hands.

Maybe God's way of punishing Ayden for Craig's death was allowing her to be kidnapped by Saucedo's men, tortured, and drugged. It certainly taught her an invaluable lesson. She would not get involved with anyone.

Ayden smiled sardonically at the lake. Connections are liabilities. How she hated it when Chet was always right.

She resumed her hike, ambling around the lake to take another rest on a hill where she could see the rooftop of the cabin. It was such a spectacle she wished she had a camera to snap a picture of it. She thought of the picture of Chet she'd found at the estate, the one that was taken the day his family was destroyed. He'd been such a young and haunted boy. It hurt her the way his eyes had been tear-drop shaped, his shoulders slumped and browbeaten. No wonder Chet hated pictures and never had any displayed in either of his homes. They displayed the depths of his pain.

She'd probably never see any photo of his parents, or any more of him as a baby. He was so handsome, his parents must have been fine-looking people. They were killed by Saucedo, Chet said. She wondered if it happened in front of Chet.

The whole thing was such a tragedy. Chet had no hope of escaping his perfidious life. Being raised by parents who were addicted to drugs, tangled in the world of distributing them, and then dying at the hands of the men they worked for, selling their son into the business. If Chet wanted to live, he had to become one of them. That's why he had a weak spot for Nolan *and* Nogo Saucedo. Nolan was obviously a caring man, but despite Nogo's murderous conduct, Chet saw the man as a father figure as well. Chet felt indebted to his boss.

The complications ran deep, and Ayden worried she'd never see a resolution. She prayed for Chet, for Nolan, for the lost lives and their loved ones. Comfort and peace wound their way toward her on the breeze, and she grinned at the infinite compassion God was capable of. Continuing around the lake, she forced her mind to roam elsewhere, and instead breathed in the fragrant air, appreciating the way the sun dazzled off the trickling water.

***

It was nighttime, the stars dotting the black sky overruled by a full moon. Ayden sat on the porch. She was bundled up in blankets, the thick, men's socks adorning her feet, cradling a cup of cocoa. Nolan had offered her coffee, but Ayden explained she'd never drank it. It smelled delicious, however. Nolan seemed relieved she turned down the coffee. He popped open a can of beer and told her he had an abundant stash of hot chocolate. She made herself a mug and snuck outside to perch herself on a rocking chair.

Chet was not back.

The Mustang had such a distinct sound, she was sure she'd hear the grumbling engine long before the headlights appeared. It unnerved her to think he could have been caught in town. His life might be in danger. If he ran into any of Saucedo's men, would they have shot him? Would they give him time to finish the deal Saucedo forced upon him? Chet was so brave and dauntless, but he was human. And breakable. She could hear the crunch of his bones over and over, the day those masked men entered Craig's bedroom and kidnapped them. It was a nightmare she relived time and time again. It caused her more misery even than Craig's death, which weighed her down with guilt. Her feelings for Chet were so much stronger.

Nolan hadn't cooked as fancy of a meal for dinner tonight, and Ayden settled for a can of soup. It was bland on her taste buds, but only because she was stressed. She wanted Chet back at the cabin, to see his face unharmed, and hear him laugh. The cocoa warmed her belly, but even the flavor lacked sweetness. She sipped from the mug because it was in her hands, but all the while her head was clogged with frustration.

She was paranoid.

The sounds of the forest grew eerie in the dark. Every snap of a twig or crack of a branch made her jump. She squinted into the black surrounding the porch. It was amazing. The lake was completely invisible in the dark. Only sometimes would she catch a glimpse of it shining under the moon.

The clock read 11:00pm when Ayden dumped her mug in the sink. Disgruntled, she stood by the fire, extending her fingers toward the warmth for a few minutes, before returning to the porch. Chet had a cell phone, but she didn't. She didn't bother asking Nolan if he had any kind of phone service. It was obvious he didn't. He enjoyed being disconnected from the world. He'd gone to bed an hour earlier, hinting to her for the fourth time that Chet would return when Chet would return. As if that was supposed to soothe her. She had resorted to chewing her nails and waiting impatiently.

The wooden, rocking chair creaked as she swayed, staring into the night full of buzzing insects. Trees rustled in the wind, sending earthy drifts over Ayden's skin. At this hour, she felt swallowed up by the mountains. The cabin was a tiny speck in miles of lush backwoods, off the grid, safe from intruders but also too far from help. She hoped they wouldn't have need for any law enforcement. There wasn't another source for transportation that she could see. Nolan got around, which meant he either had a vehicle or a small motorcycle stored somewhere, but he didn't offer it to Ayden and was not planning on leaving her at the cabin alone.

She was too frazzled to find sleep. The last time she checked the clock it was one-thirty. The rocking chair was now still with her curled up in a ball on top of it. It was like music to her ears when she heard the distant sound of a car and tires turning over gravel. She clung to the blankets, squinting into the dark. The first sight of headlights made her sigh. A V8 engine purred over the driveway. However, when the car emerged from the trees, the headlights shone so bright at the cabin she was momentarily blinded. Lifting a hand to shield her eyes, Ayden wondered what she would do if it was someone else. A person sent to kill them? But then the headlights shut off and the engine killed. Ayden recognized the sleek body and red paint.

Chet got out of the driver's side door, leaning across the car to grab a duffel bag from the passenger's side. He was dressed in all black, and his hair was perfectly tousled. The moon caught his bare arms and shone his sleeve of tattoos in glimpses. When he shut the car door and glanced up at Ayden, she saw no signs of distress in his eyes. His journey into town had gone unflawed. It made her almost light-headed with relief.

"You're up?" Chet asked, tucking his keys into his pockets and heading toward her.

"Can't sleep," Ayden responded wearily.

It wasn't even a lie.

There was a single bulb illuminating the porch, and Chet met Ayden underneath it. They stood staring at one another in silence for a second, before she inquired about the bag.

"Some essentials," Chet proffered.

"To get by?" Ayden asked.

Her voice sounded flirtatious. Subconsciously, she figured if he hadn't met trouble in Fresno, he might have met enjoyment. It brought jealousy to her cheeks.

Chet nodded. "I went to the estate, but it took some time to make sure the place was clear. Saucedo might have it bugged. I've got some cash. Clothes. Shoes." He pointed a slender finger at her socked feet. "And I got you this."

He set the bag down on the porch, unzipped it, and withdrew a cell phone.

"Thank goodness," she murmured.

"Won't do much good around here," he mentioned under his breath. He hoisted the bag back up over his shoulder and straightened. "But there's a hill not far from here where you can get service. You just have to hike to the top."

"Got it."

He took a step closer. She caught the scent of his minty breath.

Why couldn't you love only me? Ayden plead internally.

"Come inside, toots. You've got to be freezing."

Chet gave her a small smile and lifted a hand. She thought he was going to touch her face, take her chin in his two fingers. In anticipation, she leaned a fraction toward him. Instead, he reached for the door.

14

It was day two at the cabin.

Chet was outside, chopping wood. Ayden was crouched by the window, gaping at him. He'd removed his shirt, and his chest was moist with perspiration. The hair around his temples was flattened to his skin. She could faintly see his tattoo below his ribs. The one that read, "Mi ami?" The sleeve of ink on his arm stood out in contrast to his bare abdomen. A name was drawn in those designs. Lina. Ayden assumed it was the same Lina whom Nolan had been married to. Hopefully today Chet would finally tell her what it meant.

Every couple of swings with the ax Chet would take a break, wiping the back of his hand across his forehead and licking his lips. A glint of silver reflected the afternoon sun. Ayden'd grown accustomed to Chet's looks, including the piercing, but she knew there would come a time when she'd had to discuss the boundaries her religion put on those things. It didn't make Chet a bad person to have tattoos or piercings, and she was so used to them she liked him that way, but her church set standards for the sake of obedience and sacrifice. It was good for the soul. It would be good for *his* soul.

It shocked her out of her wits when a voice spoke up behind her.

"Get on out there after him, babe."

Ayden whirled around to see Nolan. She hadn't heard him come in. He hauled some logs over to the stash he had stacked by the stove and headed up the stairs.

"A man's efforts should be rewarded," he called, and then she heard his bedroom door shut.

Her cheeks burned with embarrassment.

When Ayden glanced out the window again, Chet was coming toward the house. His arms were full of sliced wood, his muscles flexing beneath the strain. She ran to the front door to open it for him, and he grunted out a thank you. As he walked by her, she breathed in the scent of his body, the familiar aroma mixed with pine and dirt. Chet dropped the wood in the same place Nolan had, then stood and craned his back. Ayden's feet were moving of their own free will. She was at Chet's back before she knew what she was doing. Her hands were raised, her fingertips prodding the slabs of muscle running vertical on either side of his spine. He had his hands pressed into his lower back, by his waistband, but they lowered as she began kneading his muscles.

That half-groan, half-moan vibrated through Chet's body and into Ayden's palms. She rubbed as low as she could, then slid her hands up to his shoulders using the skills she'd acquired in cosmetology school to dig into knots and massage out tight zones. His skin was damp and the oils from her hands made it easy to work through his tense muscle with ease. His head rolled to one side, so she dug her knuckles into the back of his neck, circling her hand around and around. Then she made the mistake of splaying her fingers up into his hair. Chet froze.

"Sorry, I…" Ayden stammered.

She took a step back.

"Don't apologize," he replied. "Unless you've done something you regret."

He gave her a small smile over his shoulder. She returned it.

"I'm sorry I have to go into the bathroom now," he stated, and then took two huge strides to vanish into the bathroom.

A couple minutes later, the shower turned on. The hum of spraying water made her think of the motel room, their first night there when he broke down the bathroom door in search for her. He'd looked at her so tenderly under the bathroom counter. And whenever she looked into his eyes after that, she saw it there. He cared about her. She cared about him.

But what were they going to do when he was in love with someone else?

***

Ayden was standing at the water's edge. The windy, mountain air steamed her breath. Evening always brought a chill. Chet was slouched against a tree trunk in the shadows, but he turned as he sensed Nolan approaching. It was a gift. Everyone in the organization—anyone who was intelligent—knew when another human was approaching simply by sense.

"She's cold," Nolan declared.

Chet smelled tobacco on his friend's breath. He gave Nolan a look out of the corner of his eye.

"She's always cold."

"And you don't see that as a gift from the Almighty?" Nolan laughed. "She's practically begging you to take her to bed."

Chet rolled his eyes. Nolan took a drag of his cigarette and let out a puff of smoky tar. It wasn't the ideal time to bring up Ayden's religion.

"Where did you meet her?" Nolan asked.

"Not where you think," Chet answered quietly.

"I assumed that already," Nolan jeered. "She's not your type."

Chet turned a scornful eye on him. "Thanks for the reminder."

"You know, I never expected anything to happen with you and—"

"Don't say it," Chet interjected. "Don't."

Nolan nodded in acquiescence. It was dusk, and Chet knew his face wasn't very discernible in the dimly lit trees, but he spun away from Nolan to keep his emotions hidden just in case.

"She was never right for you," Nolan carried on, as if he were speaking to the wind and not Chet. "I respect you for—wanting to do the right thing. You were always a bigger man than your father. I hope you know that. It is best that you didn't end up with her."

It had been so long since Chet had seen Nolan. He couldn't remember if Nolan was a sensitive guy or not. The conversation was making Chet's skin feel too tight. He didn't want to dig up old memories, let alone discuss them. No one ever discussed Chet's father, especially not Chet. Nolan knew that Chet had once been involved with his daughter, but Nolan also knew it had never been extremely romantic. Starla and Chet's codependency spawned from mutual careers and addictions. Chet hadn't explained their history to Ayden thoroughly, though he could tell Ayden was beginning to suspect the worst. It wouldn't be long until Ayden put all the clues together.

Nolan knew the kind of life his daughter lived. Chet was raised in the business. Nolan knew what sort of activities took place in those kinds of "relationships." When Chet pulled up to the cabin two days ago, and Nolan first took a look at him, Chet thought for sure his old friend would withdraw and turn he and Ayden away. Chet was ashamed of his past. He didn't know how to face the man he looked up to—the man who had the guts to get out of the family business. Instead of turning Chet and Ayden away, Nolan did the opposite of withdraw. Nolan looked so genuinely happy to see Chet. It was like…Nolan could see Chet had made the changes to better himself, and Nolan was proud.

"All is right in the world," Nolan commented to himself. "This. You. Her. It's all right."

Chet didn't realize Nolan had retreated to the cabin. He was standing in the trees by himself, watching Ayden. She was dressed in the clothes he'd brought her from the estate. Snug jeans that hugged her curves, and a long-sleeved thermal shirt. It was cool enough at night that he'd brought her a jacket and some boots. She'd left the jacket in the cabin, and instead had the blanket wrapped around her shoulders. He'd been observing her for over twenty minutes and wondered what she was so entranced by. The lake? The stars? The way one reflected the other?

That was one thing the mountains had. The sky.

Chet felt much closer to heaven up here. If he believed in heaven.

What he didn't feel close to was Ayden. They'd hardly spoken all day. There was a wedge between them. Chet knew what it was, but he also knew it wasn't going anywhere. He wanted to be able to talk to Ayden without lying to her, but there were stories he wasn't ready to tell her. He had a feeling if she knew the last remaining details about his life, the ones he'd struggled so diligently to keep hidden, that she would never want to see him again. It terrified him.

He tried to think of something to say to her. Tipping his head against the scratchy tree, he moved his foot and a twig snapped.

Ayden's head whipped around. Her face was shrouded by

moonlight, but Chet could tell her hazel eyes were massive with fright. Swiftly, he stepped out from the trees so she could see it was only him. He knew what it was like to fear the dark, to fear sound and movement.

"Just me," Chet said. His voice was constricted. "I thought I'd go for a walk. It's a nice night."

By then, Chet was by Ayden's side. She didn't look him straight in the eye, but she offered a polite smile. He had his hands shoved deep in his pockets, but when she turned to head toward the cabin, his arm shot out to stop her. She paused with his palm on her shoulder, glancing up at him. If he didn't say something now, he was going to throw her against the tree and kiss her.

"I'm going to have to go back into town," Chet ground out. "Probably tomorrow."

Ayden nodded hesitantly. "You'll be gone all day again?"

"Yes. But this time I thought you might want to come with me."

"I would've gone with you yesterday," she responded.

Chet looked up at the stars. "I know. But…there were some things I had to take care of…"

"Yeah, yeah," she sighed. "I got it. You have your life with me, and you have your life with them. Don't want to get them mixed up, now would you?"

He returned her gaze. "Ayden."

"Chet?"

She took a few more steps toward the cabin, but he stopped her again. The words popped out of her mouth.

"Did you go see Starla?"

"Actually, yes. But it's not what you think."

"Don't call me Ashley."

It made Chet grin, and then they both felt the gravitational pull of the world reallocate. She was putty in his hands when he smiled like that.

"I do have dignity," Chet chided playfully. "I would never two-time my girlfriend."

Ayden rolled her eyes. "You went to see Starla."

"We happened to cross paths. I didn't go to see *her*, specifically."

"What about Keeley?"

Chet felt his cheerfulness die a sudden death. He wouldn't lie to Ayden, but he wouldn't tell her about Keeley.

"She is currently residing with some of Nogo's associates," he answered rigidly. "I can visit her, but it's hazardous. I'm looking for a way to get her out. Possibly out of the state."

"What was she in rehab for?" Ayden questioned.

"Hm?"

She held Chet's gaze firmly. "You said you met her while you were in rehab. What was Keeley in there for? More drugs?"

He flinched. She saw it.

"Um…kind of." His teeth were working over his bottom lip, giving her fleeting glimpses of his piercing. Speaking of Keeley made him more anxious than a dozen armed mobsters. "It was more…emotional…trauma and healing."

Ayden didn't exactly believe him, but she didn't question him further. She grew irritable at once and stomped back to the cabin. Chet waited in the yard until she'd gone inside, and then cursed aloud. He knew he was pushing her away, but anything else would push Keeley away. He never wanted to have to choose between them, but his situation was growing trickier by the day. If he didn't find some way to resolve it, he feared he would lose them both. Time was running short. So much occupied his mind. He still had a job to do.

15

The next morning dawned in a creepy silence. Only the sun streaming in through the windows gave light to the dim cabin. It couldn't be long past daybreak. Ayden stretched a foot out the bottom of the blankets and propped herself up on an elbow. She'd slept on the couch again, which was surprisingly comfortable. The fire was a delight. She gazed up the stairs, where Chet was sleeping in the loft. Down the hall was Nolan's room. The man was typically an early riser. He'd go out and fish when the lake was undisturbed, before anyone else rose. Today, however, nobody was stirring. Nolan's galoshes were sitting muddy at the front door next to his fishing pole. Chet's Mustang was parked out front in the misty, mountain air.

Climbing off the couch, Ayden padded to the kitchen for a drink of water. The clock read eight in the morning. She'd just go back to bed.

The wooden beams creaked above her, and she glanced toward the staircase, expecting to see Nolan coming down in his head-to-toe plaid ensemble. Instead, Chet appeared. His hair was flattened on one side, his eyes not quite all the way open. He wore the same huge, flannel shirt and brown long johns, which were adorably rumpled. He yawned, lifting the over-sized shirt to scratch his navel. In a wild moment, Ayden pictured watching him come down the stairs for the rest of her life.

Giving a vague wave of his hand, Chet strode into the bathroom and shut the door. Ayden moved back to the couch, kindling the fire. It didn't burn as hotly as her insides. She knew what she felt was love. A raging, passionate, Shakespeare-worthy love. It was also the most bewildering emotion. She knew it was pure, like Christ's love, but there was also attraction involved. Working through her emotions would be easier with the help of a kind and understanding bishop.

When Chet reentered the room, he stared at the clock.

"I thought Nolan would be up by now," he muttered to himself.

Ayden wrapped a blanket around her shoulders. "Maybe he decided to get a few more Z's. I'm headed that way now. Goodnight." And she plopped down on the couch.

She could hear Chet ascending the stairs. He stopped at the landing to tell her he was going to inform Nolan that they would be in town all day. Chet liked to have a backup plan. If he and Ayden ran into trouble in Fresno, Nolan was to be their source of deliverance. She settled into a slumberous preparation, listening to Chet knock lightly on Nolan's door. There was no response. Chet called Nolan's name quietly. After a moment, a door squeaked open. The planks in the ceiling groaned as Chet moved about upstairs. His footsteps stopped.

Ayden opened her eyes. In the same instance, a strangled cry rang throughout the house. She sprang off the cushions, ditching the blankets on her flight to the stairs. At the loft, she slid into the wall with an agonizing thud. Nolan's door was open at the end of the hall. No light was on inside. She sprinted to the doorway, wheeling into the bedroom where she located Chet kneeling on the ground. Nolan's head was in his lap, eyes half-open, body unmoving. The sound was coming from Chet.

"What happened?" Ayden demanded, dropping to her knees beside Chet.

She reached out and touched Nolan's forehead, terrified that he would be cold and dead. To her dismay, his body was feverish. She checked for a pulse in his neck. The thick skin was leathery under her fingertips. There was a faint heartbeat.

"He's alive," she gasped.

Chet was rocking back and forth. His eyes were wide, blank, aghast. He remained in this state for several minutes, the time it took Ayden to run downstairs for her cell phone, just in case she managed to get service.

"Don't," Chet stated upon her return. "Don't call the police."

"But—he needs a hospital, or…"

Chet hoisted Nolan into his arms and laid him on his bed. Nolan's mouth slackened, deepening the creases of his scars. Ayden shoved her phone in the hem of her pants and helped Chet situate Nolan's body.

"What are we going to do?" Ayden questioned, near panic. "He needs medical attention. He could be dying."

"He *is* dying," Chet answered. He pulled away from the bed and glared down at the body emotionlessly. "He overdosed."

"*What?*"

"He overdosed," Chet said again, just like that.

"How do you know? I mean, is it that bad? Should we do something? We have to do something!"

Chet started backing into the doorframe. The paleness of his face was worrisome.

"Chet?"

He didn't respond.

"Chet!"

He licked his lips. "What's the date?"

Ayden gawked. "Wh-why?"

"What's the date, Ayden?"

She grabbed her cell phone again, reading it to him.

"It's the anniversary of Lina's death," Chet murmured. "I should've known. I should've…I should've been in here."

"Lina's death?" Ayden repeated. Fear gripped her. She wanted very much for everything to make sense. "Nolan overdosed because today is the anniversary of his wife's death?"

"Suicide."

Chet's face remained carved of stone. His voice was cold.

Lina committed suicide?

Why, after all these years, would Nolan overdose *now*?

"Please," Ayden begged, "we have to help him."

"He doesn't want help," Chet said calmly. "This is what he wanted. Let them be together again."

"Chet, how can you say that?" she spat. "We can't let Nolan die. Maybe he didn't want to overdose. Maybe he just accidentally took too much of—whatever he took."

"Prescription pills."

"How do you know that?"

Chet raised a finger and pointed at a bedside table. Ayden strode to it and yanked open the top drawer. Six pill bottles rattled forward against the wood. She slammed it shut.

"Okay," she breathed. "Okay. Doesn't he need his stomach pumped? I saw it done once, in the movie Almost Famous—"

"Life is not a movie," Chet barked suddenly. His eyes

stayed on Nolan's dormant body, but he directed the insult at Ayden. "Give it up."

She quieted her mouth, but her heart was hammering against her ribcage. Arguing was pointless. She decided that the box had been opened. It was time to pry.

"What happened to Lina?" she questioned firmly.

To her surprise, Chet did not hesitate to respond.

"She couldn't handle life outside the business. Once Nolan relocated their existence up here, he cut off contact with everyone. Including Starla. It tore Lina up inside. She was divided from her family, her child, her money, her friends. The seclusion was a lot to take. Plus, she had vices of her own. One day, she just lost it. She overdosed."

Ayden took a deep breath. So, the love of Nolan's life, the whole reason he wanted to get out of the organization and live a wholesome life, ended up committing suicide. That left Nolan more alone than ever. Lina was obviously important to Chet as well.

"Chet," she said softly, "why did you have her name tattooed on your arm?"

This time, he did hesitate, but it wasn't with malice. His eyes glazed over as they lifted to the window. A brighter ray of sun came in. Morning was kissing the mountain range. The pillar of light danced off specks of dust in the room. Nolan's breathing was audible in their silence. It was a minor comfort. He was still alive.

"Lina was more of a mother to me than my own," Chet replied. "She took me in and loved me like her son. She showed me what true love was. Her relationship with Nolan was a fantasy, something you only see in the movies *you* speak of. Their love was strong, unbreakable. I felt it living under her roof as a boy. Once, when I was sixteen, she wrote me a letter. It—" his voice cracked with emotion –"it told me how proud she was of me, and that she knew I had it in me to become a bigger influence on those around me than any of Saucedo's men. I thought she meant by gaining rank in the business, but I see now…I see now she meant otherwise."

"Chet?"

"Mm?"

"We need to go into town today. It's Sunday."

He finally glanced her way. "And leave Nolan here?"

She raised her palms outward. "We need to get to a church building. I know people who can help Nolan. We can bring them here, and they can give him a priesthood blessing—"

"No one is coming here," Chet shot back. His bladed hand swiped through the air. "No one. This is Nolan's sanctuary. He would kill me for bringing anyone up here uninvited."

She had a feeling that was a literal warning. Still, she countered, "You brought me here."

He paused only briefly. "I was lucky. Nolan trusts me, and he trusts my feelings for you. No one else steps foot up here."

"Fine," Ayden assented. "Then we must go to the church and ask them to pray for Nolan. I can talk to the bishop. He can say a special prayer. You and I can fast for Nolan."

Chet was looking quite skeptical. "What is fast? Like, Lent?"

"Kind of." She almost smiled at his knowledge of the traditional Catholic holiday. "We will give up food and water, and we will pray. Together. If you won't let me take Nolan to a hospital, that's our best bet."

Chet closed his eyes and pondered her request. After a minute, he stroked his brow bone with a thumb.

"Alright, Ayden. I will find you a church building. But I have business to attend to. I can drop you off. You'll have about an hour or two. Will that be long enough?"

"Yes," she almost cried. "I wish you'd come with me."

"I would, any other time. Today, I have to meet with some of the men I think stole Saucedo's shipment from the heist. They know I've gone 'rogue' and if I do a good job convincing them I'm against Saucedo, they'll tell me the truth about the drugs, and whether or not they have the money. I can pick you up afterward. Keep your cell phone handy."

"I will. And Chet?"

He was halfway out the door, his wrinkly flannel shirt partly over his head. "Yeah?"

"Remember your promise."

They were seated in the Mustang, cruising down the road that bent and curved through the mountains. It was a long drive into Fresno. Ayden didn't feel as aggravated as she had that morning. Instead, she felt totally drained. Her head thumped, and her stomach felt queasy. She had zero appetite. A few bites of bread and half an egg were all she managed to consume. They were driving into town, leaving Nolan upstairs on his bed. It was ludicrous. She prayed and prayed for the man's life to be spared, even as Chet's words thrummed in her skull.

Let them be together again.

Ayden didn't know if she was affronted by Chet's reaction to Nolan's overdose, or if it had kept her panic at bay. Perhaps Chet had seen dozens of overdoses, suicidal or not. He could be apathetic to Nolan's heartache, but she doubted it, not with the way Chet spoke of Lina. There was compassion in his voice when he stated, "Let them be together again." Like he knew Nolan was going to a better place. It made Ayden second guess the words of her prayer.

Lord, let thy will be done, she revised.

Chet glanced at Ayden discreetly, but said nothing. Once she got cell service, she looked up the address of a church. There would most likely be a worship beginning a half hour after they arrived, if this building followed standard church schedules. Chet explained they could pick up anything Ayden desired at a grocery store on their way out of town. She was having a hard time paying attention. Every red car that drove by made her stomach flutter unpleasantly.

"Is something wrong?" Chet eventually asked.

"You know," she said lowly, "you have far more connections than I do. I'd say that red Audi following us on the freeway was probably your liability, not mine." Chet gazed at her with a brotherly annoyance. Before he could reply, she added, "Are you going to tell me who you're going to meet?"

"A few other people that have it out for Saucedo."

"Any women?" she asked.

"Yes."

They remained silent the next hour, staring out the windshield.

Eventually, the silence was so smothering that Ayden turned on the stereo. It didn't bother her that the Elvis CD was playing. The King's rich, melodic voice sang through the speakers, Kentucky Rain. Despite the tension in the car, things were fine until they got closer to city. Pine trees diminished to fields, which morphed into orange groves, that disbanded into palm trees and neighborhoods. They passed through the countryside of Clovis, the smell of barnyards, cattle, and citrus transitioned into smog when the muscle car entered the borders of Fresno.

Chet became rigid. He developed a nervous habit of checking the rearview mirror. It made Ayden scan the cars behind them on the freeway using the right side mirror. Every time a car passed them, she would sneak a glimpse of the driver through her window. When it was a red car, her heart did a little joggle. If there was an SUV in any lane, near or far, her head swirled, and she felt nauseas. Flashes of the concrete cell that held her captive tortured her mind. Everyone was a criminal at this point.

They had just pulled up to a stoplight when Chet's cell phone started ringing. He had to lift his hips up to pull it out of his front pocket. The caller ID read Saucedo. Ayden felt a sudden dread. She knew Chet's boss was out of the country. If Saucedo was calling the second she and Chet arrived in Fresno, there was obviously a spy who had recognized Chet's Mustang. She also breifly wondered what Nogo would think if he heard his brother Nolan was on his deathbed.

Family blood wasn't guaranteed to be influential. Nogo Saucedo might view Chet as a son, but this was all getting messy. Messy meant mistakes, and any mistakes cost Saucedo's money. He would kill Chet if Chet didn't find his boss's missing shipment.

Chet let the phone ring only twice before shutting off the radio and answering the call.

"You got my message," he murmured.

Ayden knew by Chet's tone that he was carrying the burden of Nolan's condition.

Saucedo responded. Ayden strained her ears to hear what the man was saying. His accent was too thick, and he spoke much too fast. She was pretty sure it wasn't all English. Chet listened tranquilly. When he replied, his tone was even and composed.

"I agree." Then a few seconds later, "I told you. I'll help you, and we'll make a trade. If I can help you get what you want, you can give me…what's mine." He paused, turning his head in the slightest degree toward Ayden, as if he meant to look at her, but changed his mind at the last second. "I'll get your money, Saucedo. My loyalties have been to you. Not your minions. From one man to the other, I give you my word I'll keep my end of the bargain."

There was a jumbled reply.

Chet cleared his throat silently. "Whatever it takes."

Ayden was subconsciously nibbling her finger.

"Then it will be over," Chet asked through a statement. "You and I go our separate ways."

He changed lanes, swerving into a parking lot of an old tattoo parlor.

"Good. I'll be there."

Chet snapped his cell shut and parked the Mustang in the back. The building was small and perfectly square. The exterior was dilapidated, the stucco rusty and discolored. Bars lined the windows. A neon sign in the front flickered. Chet leaned across the car and opened the glove box. Ayden recognized the gun as he withdrew it.

"Stay here," Chet ordered. "Be my lookout."

It was a lame command. He just didn't want her inside with him.

"Aren't you going to take me to the church?" she asked.

"This won't take long. Then I'll take you to the church." He bent forward and reached below his seat, showing Ayden the handle of a second gun. "Just in case," he stated.

"Am I at liberty to ask who *you* are planning on shooting?"

"At the moment, no one." Chet's eyes held hers from across the car. "I'm planning on persuading."

"Whatever it takes?" Ayden repeated his words from the phone call with Saucedo.

"Exactly."

She rubbed her arm, glancing up and down the sidewalks. They weren't in a family-friendly part of town.

"I thought—you promised me you wouldn't kill anyone."

"Oh, I won't," he nearly smiled. "Trust me. They're much harder to persuade that way."

"Are you recruiting people?"

He smacked a loaded magazine into the bottom in response and reached for his car door. "I need a team."

"I see," she muttered.

He got out of the Mustang and tucked the firearm in the back of his pants. Ayden was a sucker for his bad boy image. Was it to much to ask for less of the bad deeds accompanying the image?

He bowed at the waist, one hand on the hood of the car, the other on the door. His expression grew solemn. The glint of mysterious playfulness dissipated.

"This could all be over soon," he said. "I'll be quick in here. You'll be to church on time."

Ayden swallowed and nodded once. Her hands were clammy. She tried to wipe them off on her jeans and look casual, but Chet read her apprehension. Too bad she didn't have a skirt. The members in the ward would assume she was an investigator. The bishop would think much different once she explained who she was, and what she wanted.

Chet gave a quick grin. "Chin up, toots."

Then he shut the door and walked into the parlor.

He'd said it the way he used to, probably to try and make her smile. But Ayden felt odd and cold inside. Being around Chet stirred many emotions within her. She always knew he was meant to come into her life. He'd taught her so many valuable lessons and brought her joy—sometimes pain—but mostly joy. It felt right, being with him. She had to admit, she felt safe when she was with him. At least, being his friend. Their kiss had been magical, yes, but foolish. She didn't want a physical relationship with a man who loved other women simultaneously.

Ayden's idea of "quick" was a couple minutes. After ten, she grew concerned. She had twenty minutes to get to the church building on time. Chet said it wouldn't be long, and she now had to go to the bathroom. She didn't know how furious Chet would be if she got out of the car to walk down the street to the fast food restaurant on the corner. He'd asked her to be the lookout, but she couldn't hold it. Hopping out of the Mustang, she decided it would be safer to remain closer. There had to be a restroom inside the tattoo parlor. Gulping down her nervousness, she exited the Mustang and paced through the front door.

It chimed as it shut behind her. She did a rapid, visual scan of the parlor, where some weathered chairs surrounded a glass table. It had stacks of magazines on it, the top one exhibiting a raunchy woman with a leg high in the air. There was a crude expletive printed across the top. A receptionist sat at the desk to her right. The girl couldn't have been older than nineteen. Her face was decorated with various piercings, and she had a strip of bright green in her asymmetrical hair. Ayden's cosmetology skills rose to her mind, and she began to miss her career. *She* would've textured the receptionist's hair a bit more. The girl smiled at Ayden.

Ayden peered toward the back of the room. There were two chairs, separated by curtains. A man was reclined in one, while the male artist doodled on his bicep with a tattoo gun. In the furthest left corner, there was an unmarked door. She'd forgotten about Chet in general, and was prancing from foot to foot. Sidling up to the reception desk, she asked the girl if there was a bathroom available.

"Of course," the girl replied, pointing to the door with no label. An aroma of stale tobacco wafted off her punk rock shirt. "Just go through there and take your first right. There's laundry going, so excuse the racket."

Ayden grinned back. "Thank you."

She hustled to the back of the shop, only briefly glimpsing the tattoo the man in the chair was receiving. It was a mermaid with raven hair.

At the door, Ayden heard voices. Her fingers closed around the handle and she turned, pushing it inwards, just as Chet was pulling it toward himself. It was like he knew she was coming. Sensed her approaching. His eyes were a scalding blue, but he pasted a neutral expression on his face.

"Bathroom…" Ayden stuttered.

The room was hazy and smelled strongly of marijuana. Ayden stood stagnant a few seconds before daring to glance away from Chet. Opposite her, a male sat in an open office. Junk was scattered over the desk, with piles of papers and cigarette butts. There was a computer, telephone, and trash can full to the brim with empty, glass bottles. To the side of the office was a bathroom door.

"It's over there," Chet pointed a finger.

"Thanks," Ayden mumbled.

She avoided direct contact with the grimy, porcelain toilet as best she could. Beyond the thin walls, she could hear Chet speaking with the other man. They sounded like long time buddies. Finished, she washed her hands extra carefully, and then slipped out of the bathroom. She tried not to gaze into the office, but a quick peek revealed a tall bong sitting on the desk. It was emitting plumes of smoke. She couldn't hold back the abhorrence from her face as she stared from one man to the other.

"Ayden, this is Pasquale," Chet announced.

Pasquale had a sideways grin on his face, and his eyelids were shuttered at two different heights. Ayden stood in the office doorway as both men surveyed her. They seemed to be calculating, drawing the same conclusion. It was taking longer than she wanted. The air was too potent, and she needed to get outside so she could breathe. Tucking a strand of hair behind her hair, she faced Chet with what she hoped was her most condemning frown.

"I'll wait in the car."

It was meant to remind him she was going to be late for church.

Pasquale stated, "She's perfect."

Ayden transferred her glare to him, even as Chet replied, "I know."

"She's perfect for the job," Pasquale reiterated.

"That, too."

"What job?" Ayden demanded.

"Let's get going, toots," Chet remarked. "I'll explain on the way."

He didn't wait for a response as he angled his chin toward Pasquale. The two clamped hands and leaned in to thump one another on the back. Chet lingered, asking under his breath, "I can count on you?"

Pasquale drew back and peered out the office from side to

side as if someone were eavesdropping. Then he said clandestinely, "I'll tell you everything I know. There's a new guy around. They call him Louie. Big Italian guy from back East. He's been sweeping the streets south of Shaw."

Chet murmured in agreement and backed out of the room. Ayden followed.

"You'll be hearing from me," Chet said in farewell.

Pasquale jerked his nose up once. "Looking forward to it."

Ayden and Chet passed the tattoo chairs and paced toward the exit. As they walked by the receptionist, Chet's eyes grazed over to the girl with green in her hair.

"Bye," he said.

The girl smiled and wiggled her fingers at him as he loped out the front door. It tipped Ayden over the edge. Her frustration morphed into jealousy, then disappointment, then anxiety. When they were sitting in the Mustang, Chet returned his gun to the glove box. He was whistling. He didn't say anything as he started the clanky, muscle car and drove onto the main road. Out of the corner of her eye, she saw him slouch back in his seat. He turned down First street, in the direction of the church building.

"You'll pick me up in an hour or two?" Ayden questioned.

"Louie's the one who lifted Nogo's cash," Chet replied. "I know it."

She shook her head in disgust, gazing out the window. Her clothes would reek when she entered the sterile, reverent building.

"…and is now a major contender in the city. I've heard of him." With lips turned down in a foreboding manner, Chet added, "We'll dispose of him, then it will all be over for me."

He sighed wistfully as if he were speaking of retirement on an African safari rather than plotting the murder of a rival druglord.

16

Ayden was weeping when she entered the chapel. Sitting in the very back row, in the very last chair, away from any other members, Ayden clutched a hymn book in her hands and cried. It shamed her after she'd sworn to be strong.

Most of the speakers went unheard. Her thoughts were disjointed. The cabin. Nolan. Keeley. Lina. Chet. False expectations. Differing paradigms of reality. Right. Wrong. Good. Better. Best. She prayed, feeling worthless. What would God think of her?

By the closing prayer, Ayden sucked in a breath and hushed her tears. She wiped her face dry, not caring that her clothing was unsuitable for church. The odor of cannabis had hopefully abated. Welcoming the familiar comfort of such a congregation, she walked up to the pulpit. Identifying the bishop, she strode up to him and extended a hand.

"Bishop, my name is Ayden."

He smiled in the way a man would greet a convert, barely glancing at her apparel. "It's nice to meet you, Sister."

"I have an enormous favor to ask," she continued. "Can you spare five minutes of your time, please?"

"Of course, of course," the bishop replied. "Brother," he called to a passing man, "I'm going to speak with this fine sister a moment."

The bishop led Ayden into his office, where they sat opposite one another, a giant desk separating them, biblical doctrine on shelves on either side. A picture of Christ hung on the wall. It threatened Ayden's eyes with more tears. The peace she felt just being…home.

"Bishop," she croaked.

The ecclesiastical leader handed her a tissue.

"Look, I literally cannot explain to you in five minutes what I'm doing here, or why, but I need your forgiveness and blessing."

The bishop looked genuinely concerned. "Sister, the Lord shows mercy on those who seek repentance. Showing up here today proves your willingness to be made clean."

"It's not just me," she sighed. "Oh, gosh. Where do I even

start?" She gave a small, embarrassed laugh. "I'm a good person, right? I don't commit huge sins, or partake in anything sinful. By rule, I'm a temple worthy individual. This isn't…I don't dress like this on the Sabbath. I haven't been home…I don't have a home. I'm not homeless, I'm just…No—I'm not here for that. This isn't even my ward. I—I don't know where my records are or who—"

Ayden started crying again.

The bishop's concern grew deeper. For the first time since their introduction, his eyes flicked over her appearance. Did she imagine him sniffing the air?

"I need you to pray for me and another man I know," Ayden whimpered. "His name is Nolan, and he is greatly suffering. I know he needs our help. He needs God to watch over him in this time. Could you please, bishop, pray for my friend, Nolan?"

"I can do that," the man answered softly, extending a box of tissues.

She sobbed into the tissue in her hands. Everything was sinking in. Her tangled reality. If she said it out loud, which she was considering doing, it would sound like the 90's mafia classic, Scarface.

"Bishop?" Ayden asked. "What would you do if you were in a bad situation, but you knew you had the power to do good? What would you do?"

"Like war?" he questioned.

"Maybe. If you were surrounded by evil, evil people doing evil things, and you wanted to help. Perhaps make a difference in just one person's life. Is it wrong to associate with those people?"

"We are cautioned to stand in holy places," the bishop replied.

"I understand that. How does our influence then extend into unholy places?"

"Are you in a situation you need help getting out of?" the bishop asked.

She laughed again. "You have no idea." He opened his mouth, but she continued, "I don't know if I'll see you again, because I don't know where I'll be in a month. A week. A day. But I knew I needed to come see you and confess. I needed to ask for your blessing and your forgiveness. I hope you can believe me when I say I'm trying to do what is right. The people around me might be making poor choices, but I'm remaining as righteous as I can. I'm—stuck—in this 'place'. It's a matter of safety. Soon, though, I'll be able to move and start over. When that happens, I hope the Lord truly forgives all my trespasses, and I can return to regular worship."

The bishop frowned, thumbing through his scriptures.

"Bishop," Ayden said, "if after all of this, I bring even one soul into the gospel, the Lord will forgive me. Won't He?"

The man quoted a scripture about faith and forgiveness that provided great solace for Ayden. Still, the wise man warned Ayden not to get involved with anything illegal or dangerous. She wanted desperately to tell him about Nogo Saucedo, and the men after she and Chet, but she held back. That would have to wait until her records were transferred to a permanent ward. Her confession would be hours long, more than she had today.

"Thank you for your time today," Ayden sniveled. She wiped the soaked tissue beneath her eyes. "I'm so sorry. I wish my life was different. I'm doing the best I can."

"Let us pray together," the bishop suggested.

They bowed their heads, and the ordained man spoke to God in a direct, pastoral manner. His words were powerful and strong, and they invited peace into Ayden's heart. Her tears subsided. She knew God was watching over her, and that He would continue to guide her along this crooked path.

***

She was sitting under a cherry blossom tree when the Mustang roared into the parking lot. Several members glanced suspiciously at it. Or the driver.

It was Sunday, and the service at her church building had been pleasant. Most of the members she'd gone to sacrament meeting with were heading to the third hour block. All the women would be gathering in Relief Society. Ayden wouldn't even know how to talk to those women. How many of them had been through what she'd been through? Their worst day was flubbing a chicken pot pie they needed to take visiting teaching.

Ayden rapidly got into the Mustang. Chet had his cell phone magnetized to the dash with a nifty gadget. The screen was lit up and she could see Nolan's face on the other end. In a tiny square in the bottom, right corner, there was an image of Chet's face seated in his car. Ayden leaned over into view of the camera. Nolan was laying on his bed. He grinned at the sight of Ayden and waved.

"How you doin', babe?" Nolan asked hoarsely.

Ayden smiled back. "Better, seeing you conscious."

Nolan was a sight for sore eyes, but he was awake and speaking.

"I prayed for you," she added.

"Prayed?" Nolan questioned.

Chet adjusted his seatbelt and glanced out the window at the church building. A couple of deacons strode by his chugging Mustang, admiring it. Chet gassed the throttle, much to their pleasure. Ayden smirked at him, talking to Nolan.

"When did you come to?"

"Right before Chet called," Nolan answered. "It was the strangest thing. I was having the best dream. There were..." He paused, finishing in a masculine voice, "...white, fluffy clouds."

Chet cleared his throat. "Time to run, old timer. You've got everything you need until we make it back?"

Nolan waved him off. "Don't you worry about me. And don't call again. I can't figure this technology out."

"I'm glad you're okay!" Ayden called as Chet disconnected the call.

He took his cell off his dash and stuffed it into the pocket in his pants. Stomping on the clutch, he wrenched the stick shift into reverse. There were more cars in the parking lot now, and a fresh wave of church-goers arriving to attend another sacrament meeting. Chet swerved around them, exiting the religious premise.

"Where are we going?" Ayden said.

"To see Starla."

Ayden's peace was eviscerated by the car door as it shut. "I do not want to be in the same room as that woman."

Stand ye in holy places.

Chet drove on. Ayden recognized the streets. They were almost to the nightclub.

"Listen, I've got a plan," Chet commented. "Pasquale and two of his men are in on it. I have a job for *you*, too. One you will excel at. I need your help." His tone dove serious. "Do this for me, please. And I'll give you anything you want. I'll pay you for your time, more than you could imagine. When it's over, I'll help you vanish. Just like you asked."

He sounded sincere, but Ayden didn't want to have anything to do with his business transactions, didn't want to be paid for it. She didn't want to add to her list of confessions. But she wanted to vanish. If it were *that* dangerous, Chet wouldn't ask her to do it. That's what she kept telling herself while the car eased into the parking lot of the nightclub. When he parked and asked her to follow him, she felt sick to her stomach. A weird sensation. One she wouldn't label jealousy. She could not believe she was walking back into this establishment, especially after she'd just left church, where she'd felt good and whole again.

Forced upon this crossroads, Ayden murmured a prayer. If she helped Chet with this job, and they both survived, she could bring Chet to church. It was like war. One must do what others could presume as evil in order to reach a resolution of righteousness. If she refused, if she walked away from Chet now, he could be killed. *She* could be killed. Saucedo knew her face. She knew too much. Chet might never taste the goodness of the gospel. If she were diligent, she wouldn't be committing any sins, but neither did she feel right being swathed in the sins of others. She kept justifying herself by saying all of these afflictions would be consecrated for her good. And, if she was lucky, for Chet's good, also. He may be redeemed.

Deep down, that's what motivated her most. Ayden, despite her religious instincts to avoid iniquity, wanted to save Chet.

Hank was behind the bar inside the nightclub, like last time. He sipped a glass of scotch. The music was low, but the lights were pulsing on stage. No one was up there dancing, but as Chet and Ayden strolled toward the curtain in the back, Starla came strutting out. The woman appeared just as Ayden remembered. Slutty. Wearing a short, silk robe that left nothing to the imagination. Ayden averted her gaze, but Chet looked Starla right in the face. They exchanged sociable greetings.

"Just got the call," the stripper said. Her gaze skated to Ayden. "She's ready?"

"Ready for what?" Ayden asked.

Chet leaned an elbow on the wall and let his eyes travel the length of Ayden's body. His gaze enveloped her in observation, like he wanted to devour her. He hadn't looked at Starla that way.

"Saucedo will be back in California in a few days," Chet told Starla. "I just spoke with him about our plans. He's on board. Pasquale is in, too."

"Pasquale?" Starla questioned, amusedly sardonic. "The independent contractor? Saucedo won't be thrilled. And you're up to the challenge?" Starla directed that question at Ayden.

Ayden still didn't know what she was getting herself into. What she wanted more than anything was for it all to be over, and to be able to disappear, like Chet said. To go back to a normal, semi-boring life. She also wanted to rescue Chet, to show him what kind of world it would be with a clean soul. Her heart beat for him, and she feared it would stop beating altogether if he were hurt or killed.

"Tell me what I have to do," Ayden grumbled.

Chet pushed off the wall and put his lips right in her ear. His hand pressed into the small of her back as he spoke quietly, "Practice."

17

"I will not wear that!" Ayden protested.

Starla sighed impatiently. If *her* boss gave the orders, Starla would comply. Ayden was insubordinate at its finest. Chet was near the bar, talking with Hank. The other girls were behind the curtain in Starla's dressing room, sorting through some of the dancers' performance apparel. Ayden was still in shock. She hadn't totally committed to the job, but she hadn't said no either. If Chet hadn't beseeched her with those incandescent, blue eyes, she would have immediately declined.

Starla held up another pair of tassels and a sparkly band she called a skirt. Ayden scoffed.

"Well, I don't suppose you brought your own wardrobe?" the woman asked tetchily.

"I didn't know this was part of the plan," Ayden rebuked. Her cheeks were hot. She wouldn't fill out any of the fabric tops the way the other females would. Tassels were Starla's alternative. "I've never worn anything remotely so…scandalous."

Starla gave a rapid eye-roll-eyebrow-raise that meant, *Clearly.*

Ayden didn't want to start a fight with Nolan's daughter, but this was out of her element. Out of most women's ordinary. Ayden was a born and raised Christian girl, with morals and ethics and modesty. Her idea of sexy was wearing her hair down. She was *not*...two inches of dark regrowth, fake red hair, fake eyelashes, fake breasts, fake everything, a pound of department store make-up, and a sleazy smile in need of dental work. It was troublesome enough to be forced to dance—for an audience—but to wear an outfit *that* disgraceful? She saw her reputable honor skittering away. Hours in a bishop's office confessing turning into days. Worse, she was going to be instructed by Starla. The girl who Chet had been involved with.

"Just take your pants off," Starla commanded. "We'll start with that, okay? You can keep your shirt on."

"Sounds like you've said that a dozen times."

Ayden tried to match the woman's catty vibe. Snark didn't come natural to her.

Starla sneered. "Don't flatter yourself, honey. I've had plenty of women."

The dancer handed Ayden a pair of nude tights, ordering her to put them on over her generic underwear.

"This is horrible," Ayden complained.

"It's not so bad," Starla replied with a laugh. "Especially when you get paid."

Ayden did not want payment for her performance. She wanted to help Chet, and then get out of town. She removed her shoes, socks, and pants, and stood facing Starla. The woman examined Ayden's bare legs, circling to get a better look at her backside. Ayden gritted her teeth. Starla made a sound of accord.

"Impressive."

Ayden pushed her sleeves up to her elbows and took a deep breath. "Okay, let's get this over with."

They walked out into the club. Starla led the way to the stage, dropping her robe at the stairs. She was wearing strappy heels, which made her taller than Ayden, but Ayden was slimmer. The lights were so bright, Ayden couldn't see further than the two chairs closest to the stage. She blinked and tripped. Starla escorted Ayden to the pole, giving her hair a dramatic toss, and then shouted to Hank to cue the music. A computerized tone blared through the speakers, the beat dripping like honey.

"We'll start with the basics," Starla coached. She had to speak loudly to be heard over the music. "Can you move your hips?"

Ayden's eyes darted to where she thought the bar was. "Does Hank have to watch?"

Starla smirked. "You're not the first girl he's seen up here, and you certainly won't be the last. Pay him no attention." She was conceited. Despite her aging looks, and hard-partying complexion, she was confident in her routine. "Do you want a drink to give you a little boost of courage?"

"No."

"Fine. Here." Starla dug her fingers into Ayden's scalp and gave Ayden's loose hair a ruffle. "Excellent. Now, start by taking the pole in one hand like this."

Ayden pursed her lips in irritation, but did as she was told.

"Slowly, up on your toes. Revolve around once or twice."

Starla demonstrated, then stood back so Ayden could have her turn.

"This is ridiculous," Ayden whined.

The veteran dancer placed a palm to her forehead. "Listen." A sorrow Ayden wasn't sure a junky stripper could display rose into the woman's face. "If you do this, you'll probably save his life."

Ayden felt spotlighted on the stage. The song was obnoxiously repetitive.

Save his life?

It was all she could dream of doing.

"Chet has a chance to…" Starla trailed off before locking eyes with Ayden. Arrogance gave way to a chafed ego. It was her turn to be jealous of Ayden. "He has a chance to start over. You're giving him that chance. *You* are the only one who can. He needs you."

Ayden closed her eyes to shut out the room and tried to subdue her angst. "Whatever," she murmured. "I'll try."

"Thank you," Starla said, placing a hand on the pole once more. "I mean it."

It was five in the afternoon by the time Starla concluded her first tutorial. Ayden was exhausted. Her fingers were shaking and cramped. Her arms felt like dead weights. In a strange way, it reminded Ayden of her high school days competing on the dance team. At least, when she focused on the skills in that manner, it made the situation easier to swallow. She'd always been a talented dancer. Her flexibility was almost non-existent at her current age, and her endurance lacked, but finding the rhythm came effortlessly.

As Ayden dragged her body up the pole, palms stinging and calves throbbing with fatigue, Starla clapped from the sidelines.

"Cut!" the woman yelled.

Hank killed the music, but Ayden's ears continued ringing. She was panting heavily and sweating. This was the best work out of her life. If her job in Chet's scheme was going to work, she had to be convincing. She would not wear tassels, but she had to keep the audience's attention for a few minutes. It was crucial to Chet's plan.

"Get some water," Starla ordered with a congratulatory nod.

Ayden didn't return the nod.

"Come see me tomorrow, alright?" the dancer added. "Although, I don't know if you need it. You're a natural. Don't you think, Chet?"

The strobe lights shut off, and the stage darkened. Ayden froze by the pole, staring out into the chairs. Chet sat in one, reclined, with his legs sprawled out in front of him. One of his hands was fisted at his temple, a finger touching his brow. Starla was descending the stairs, but Ayden couldn't get her feet to move. How long had he been there? Watching?

He had no expression on his face. His eyes were glued to Ayden's.

Starla grabbed her robe and slipped her arms into the sleeves, tying it loosely around her waist. Her heels clicked as she sauntered to the bar, where Hank poured her a vodka, and then she was gone behind the curtain. Ayden was humiliated. She'd been legitimately attempting to dance, to be believable. If Chet witnessed this inappropriate conduct, did he think less of her?

Ayden did not want to be compared to Starla—to be in the same category as such a wanton...harlot! She considered turning down the job a second time. Without saying anything to Chet, she jumped off the stage, avoiding the stairs and a potential trip-and-fall in the heels, and flew into the back room. Starla was nowhere to be seen. Ayden snatched her pants off the floor, jammed her legs into them, and haphazardly put on her shoes. She stood behind the curtain for several minutes, debating whether or not she should go out the rear door and run down the street to the nearest church for confession—her church or not.

Hank turned the music back on, but it was a classic rock radio station, playing at a decent volume. Ayden listened to the words of a popular Bon Jovi song.

'We're half way there. Oh, livin' on a prayer.'

Ayden stepped out into the club. Chet was in the same exact position, facing the stage. Inch by inch, his head turned until his eyes locked on hers. He sensed her there. From across the room. A tension in his posture was palpable. He stared at her so hard, she thought his gaze would sever a vital organ. She had to summon more bravery than it took to grab the pole to meet him at his seat. With each step she took, she felt her feet grow more leaden. Chet's lips didn't move. He didn't blink. She couldn't even tell if he was breathing. His eyes glimmered darkly as she approached. He sat motionless, his tattoos an odd color under the iridescent lights.

Once at his side, Ayden expected Chet to stand. He remained sitting, though he'd bent one knee and flattened that foot. She shuffled her hair over one shoulder and grabbed her elbow, glancing up at Hank. The bartender was busying himself scrubbing dishes.

"I've changed my mind," Chet stated.

It made Ayden jump. She looked down at him, puzzled by his frown. He stood, almost knocking her over.

"We need to get out of here," he declared curtly. "I'll take you back to the cabin."

Ayden treaded carefully behind him while they strode toward the door. Chet didn't bother saying farewell to Hank. He pulled open the door, following Ayden into the evening air. The sun was setting, casting orange rays into the polluted sky. It would be dark by the time they reached the mountains, and very late when they reached Nolan's cabin. The Mustang was parked in a nearby stall, but she noticed a few others had filled in. The club's hours of operation were day and night, but the trending hour was night. She could see why Chet wanted to leave.

After they got into the car, he began driving them toward the freeway. Ayden was rubbing her legs. She coughed.

"I won't make you do it," Chet murmured.

"Hm?"

"I won't let you do it."

Ayden's eyebrows knit together. "If I'm that bad at it—"

"Ayden!" he nearly yelled. His palm thudded into the steering wheel, and it caused the car to jerk. They stopped at a red light, partially merged over two lanes.

"What's wrong?" she asked.

Chet ran a hand across the top of his hair.

"New plan," he grunted to himself. "You're staying at the cabin. I'll figure something else out. I can—I'll just—I still have those plane tickets. Tomorrow, first thing, I'm dropping you off at the airport."

"You only have a few more days," Ayden stated. "A few days until Saucedo returns to California. Can you finish the job by then? Without me?"

"I'll get by."

"Chet, what happened? It will be okay. I'll get better. Tomorrow, Starla said she'd show me a few more moves."

"You won't be going to see Starla tomorrow," he responded crisply.

"But Chet—"

"Ayden," the light turned green, and he punched the gas, "do not fight with me on this. I cannot let you go in front of those men alone and…and…dance like that."

She was starting to understand what he was saying. He didn't think she was bad. He thought she was good.

"You said Pasquale would be there to keep an eye on me," Ayden mumbled. "You said it would be safe."

"That's because I thought you'd merely be a distracting entertainment. When those men get a glimpse of you up there, they won't be able to take their eyes off you. They'll want to hire you. And by hire I mean they'll lift you and force you into work against your will. What if one of Louie's men gets to you before I do? It's too dangerous. No. No, I won't let you. If Louie's men take you away, it will be worse than if you'd worked for Saucedo."

They were speeding up the freeway. Cars blurred by. Chet was clicking his tongue ring against his teeth, and Ayden was munching on her fingernail.

"Do you think," she began, but hesitated. "Do you think I could distract them long enough for you to find out if Louie has Saucedo's shipment?"

"Distract?" Chet guffawed. "More like mesmerize."

Ayden thought she should blush, but she was shocked that she didn't. She pressed her hands in between her knees and gazed out the window at the setting sun. They both knew if she didn't pull this off, there was a chance Nogo would not get his revenge on

Louie. That meant the lost money and drugs would not be returned, and Chet would take the fall. Chet seemed desperate to get out, and for deeper reasons than just evading a life of crime. There was something else.

"Chet," Ayden spoke gently, "I want to help you."

He glanced at her, fleetingly, returning his eyes to the road. All of the stress of the impending confrontation with Louie, not to mention Nolan's close call with death, weighed heavily on Chet. He was strained, and such strain took a lot of strength to conceal. She saw the forlorn drifter in his eyes, the man who would skip town often.

"I...appreciate your concern, but...I couldn't live with myself if you were trapped, and I could have done something to help you get out. We'll pull this off. Then, you can buy your freedom."

Chet wasn't persuaded. "It's more complicated than just you and I," he breathed out.

His voice held restraint and, she gathered, remorse.

"Because of Keeley?" Ayden asked.

He nodded only once.

"Can we get her out, too?"

His voice was unemotional. "That is part of the deal."

"Good," Ayden stated, her contentment forced. "See? We'll all get to start over."

But the longer they drove, the darker it got, and the colder she felt.

***

Pasquale told Chet about a man who'd been living in Columbia for several years but was in California.

"Benecio," Pasquale said to Chet.

Benecio was another independent, like Pasquale. He was a sociopath and couldn't be trusted to do anything except show up where there would be money. Chet decided to meet with him. Pasquale sent Chet alone, giving him the address of a trailer park on the outskirts of Fresno County. Ayden implored Chet to take her with him, but he insisted she work more with Starla.

Chet drove his Mustang to the trailer park. A gated entrance with barbed-wire along the top forced him to coast to a stop. There was a keypad. It was broken. Two men stood on the outside of the gate. They were packing. Striding toward Chet's car, one of them waved a signal in the air with his hand. Chet rolled his window down. One man pointed a gun into the car. Chet lifted his palms, empty. The other man was pacing around the outside of Chet's car.

"Open the trunk," the man holding the gun at Chet's ear ordered.

Chet did as he was told.

Both men searched Chet's trunk. Finding nothing, they shut the trunk and waved Chet forward with their weapons. Chet eased on the gas, his car rolling up to the gate. It creaked open. He drove slowly inside, where three more men sat in chairs out front of the first trailer. They each had a loaded weapon in their lap. Chet continued on to the address Pasquale gave him. The ground was dusty, clouding Chet's rearview mirror when he glanced behind him. He turned down a narrow street. A picnic table littered with garbage sat abandoned. Metal trash cans lined the road. The engine of a broken down Buick sat next to the open hood of its car. One of the tires was missing, and it was propped up on a jack.

The street came to a Y. Chet took a slight left. A rundown trailer with several guys, and two girls, standing outside of it came into view. One of them was flinging a switchblade around. Another one had a long, heavy semi-automatic firearm. He was bald, with tattoos on his scalp and face. Wearing a white tank and jeans, the man lowered his weapon, pointing the tip at the nose of Chet's Mustang. Chet hit the brakes and jammed the parking break down. The two girls, early twenties, craned their necks to watch him climb out of his car.

"Benecio?" Chet asked.

No one moved. The other men said nothing. One of the girls was more impressed with Chet's car than with him. The bald man with the long gun spit in the dirt.

"He's expecting me," Chet stated.

The sun was high overhead, the air stale. One of the girls said something to the guy toying with his switchblade.

"Esta aqui," Chet said a final time.

The door to the trailer opened, and a man stepped down. He was a handsome guy, with one big diamond earing. His hair was cropped short, and he had a smear of facial hair including a groomed mustache. He smiled in Chet's direction.

"Mi familia," the man said.

All the people outside of the trailer seemed to relax. The man aiming the semi-automatic at Chet turned around. He stalked past the others and vanished inside the trailer, leaving the door open. The girls returned to chatting with each other, taking out their cell phones. Heat from Chet's Mustang wafted out against his legs. The handsome man with the earring ordered the girls to "get busy" in Spanish. Chet wasn't sure if it was an invitation to move or not, and the wrong move would get him shot. His gaze slid over to the guy with the switchblade and then back to the handsome man coming forward.

"Benecio," the man said, taking Chet's hand and shaking it.

"Chet."

"Tu eres Lina's chico?" Benecio inquired.

Chet's mind raced. "Lina Saucedo."

"Si. Lina es mi familia."

It made Chet grin. Small world. Many connections.

18

They didn't have anything on the agenda for the day. Ayden knew they'd be sitting around. Chet would be chopping would outside. Nolan would be gone fishing. The extrovert inside of her summoned the courage to force Chet into taking her into town, but not just into town—to a church building during the mutual hour for the young, single, adult women's and men's activity. Ayden made plenty of excuses about how Chet loved to drive his Mustang at full speed through the mountains, the tires chirping as they clung to the winding roads. It didn't take much convincing. She mentioned needing to stop at a mutual activity for her church, speaking about her spirit needing replenishing, and only as they approached the church building did she profess it to be a young, single, adult activity.

"There will be a bunch of YSA's here," Ayden said as Chet slowed the Mustang into the church parking lot.

One of his eyebrows dipped when he glanced at the plethora of cars.

"YSA's?" he questioned.

Ayden smiled at knowing something he didn't.

"Our age people," she replied.

Chet pulled sideways across three parking stalls in a back row, glaring out the windshield at the college-priced, V6 abominations. Several young, single adults stood in a group on the sidewalk chatting. They glanced in Chet's direction. His car engine rumbled loudly.

"You can kill the engine," Ayden murmured, unbuckling her seatbelt. "But that's about it."

Grinning, she got out of the car. The sun was lowering. It was warm out, as usual. She wore her cowboy boots and a flannel shirt open over a plain T. Behind her, Chet turned off the car and exited. Ayden strode across the parking lot, waving at the group of people on the sidewalk. The eldest of them, a late-thirties businessman, stepped toward her.

"Good evening, Sister," he greeted warmly. "I'm Bishop

Bommgardner."

"Ayden," she smiled politely.

Two of the people in the group were girls, early twenties with nice hairdressers. They glanced beyond Ayden's shoulder and froze. The other three people were males, one of which spoke animatedly about his favorite sports team. He wore a graphic T that fit his hunky figure. Bishop Bommgardner followed the gaze of the two girls, his lips forming the word *who* without actually speaking. Ayden didn't have to look. She gestured with a thumb, assuming her mystical companion had approached from behind her left shoulder by the fish-faced expressions on the females.

"This is Chet," Ayden announced.

The sports fanatic and his guy friends looked up. One of them quickly appraised Chet's appearance, the black ensemble, tattoos, and vintage classic with fierce competition. The other two nodded in a welcoming fashion. Bishop Bommgardner took Chet's hand straight from Chet's side and shook it.

"Nice to meet you, Brother."

Chet's eyes slid over the bishop's white collar, to the gawking girls, to the three guys. His countenance was reserved. Ayden almost told him he'd need a gun. Just for kicks.

Sports Fanatic made a bold move, stepping toward Chet. "Are you new in the ward?"

The guy's tone was friendly enough, but Chet didn't appreciate anyone stepping toward him. Chet squinted.

"We're just visiting," Ayden answered, her eyes exchanging a fleeting blink with Chet's. "But Chet wanted to meet some of the YSA's in case he's ever in the area again. Isn't that right?"

Chet stood stiffly, a cynical frown forming on his lips.

"That's awesome," a second guy responded, moving up to Sports Fanatic's elbow. "I'm Philip."

"No hablo ingles," Chet stated.

Philip's face lit up. "Oh, enserio? Que padre! Hablo espannol. Donde serviste?"

Chet slowly looked over at Ayden.

"We're heading to a service project," the bishop was saying. "Chandler, can Philip, Ayden, and her friend Chet ride with you? I can fit Connor, Maria, and Francesca in my Explorer."

"Sure," Chandler, Sports Fanatic, replied. "I'll shove all my textbooks in my trunk. This semester has been crazy."

He gave Chet a nod. Chet was still dubiously regarding Philip. The third male, Connor, held an expression of being threatened. He kept staring back and forth between Maria and Chet. Eventually he followed the bishop to a ten-year-old Ford Explorer parked at the curb. The two girls, who Ayden watched highly consider jumping into the back of Philip's car instead, begrudgingly got into the back seat of the Explorer. Ayden thwarted a grin and stepped after Chandler, who led the way a few cars over to his Mitsubishi. Philip told Ayden their service project was doing yard work for some elderly people. Chet remained a few paces behind. Chandler opened the back door of his Eclipse and withdrew several heavy school books. Popping his trunk, he tossed them onto a pile of dirty laundry.

"My Bachelors is gonna kill me," Chandler said, once more directing the conversation at Chet.

Philip opened the passenger's side door. "Chet, you can ride shotgun."

Ayden almost burst out laughing. She slid into the back seat opposite Philip, while Chandler took his seat in the driver's side.

"Chet loves riding shotgun," she remarked gleefully.

Chet stood by the front tire looking like he'd rather ride all around Fresno in a pink caterpillar from the Disneyland ride Alice in Wonderland than be seen sitting in Chandler's Mitsubishi.

"Come on, toots!" Ayden called, buckling herself in. "We don't have all night."

Chet reluctantly took his seat in the passenger's side. He shut the car door, his hands awkwardly rigid in his lap. He probably hadn't been chauffeured by another guy, let alone a young single adult, since he was a kid. Chandler started his car, revving the engine a few times. Ayden died watching Chet's profile. She turned her attention to Philip.

"I don't speak Spanish," she said. "Did you serve a mission somewhere Spanish speaking?"

"Yeah," Philip said. "Argentina."

"That's cool. What about you, Chandler?"

He put his stick shift into reverse and followed Bishop Bommgardner out of the parking lot. "I served in Italy. I've been back a year and a half now. Work and school are so intense. I'm fulltime at college, hoping to get into a graduate program back East. My parents won't pay for my student loans once I get in, though. You know? I'm going to have to get a second job. Probably even a third, if I wanna pay for my tuition."

Chet grabbed the dash with his right hand while Chandler veered onto the road, the car's hubcap nicking the curb. Ayden snorted at Chet's muffled curse. His forearm flexed beneath his tatoos. Chandler had the grace to look embarrassed, quickly accelerating to show off. The bishop's Explorer cruised on ahead of them. Philip's interest in Ayden grew.

"Where are you visiting from?" he asked.

Ayden watched Chet's jaw while she thought of a good way to tell the truth and change the subject. "I've been staying up North. I haven't been to a Singles Ward in a long time, but I wanted to get out and be with people closer to my age tonight. Service projects are fun."

"Yard work sucks," Chandler murmured.

He slammed on his brakes at a red light. Chet flattened a hand against the window. They all jerked forward.

"Brand new pads," Chandler stated, glancing at Ayden through the rearview mirror. "They're sensitive."

Chet's neck twisted just enough for him to make eye contact with Ayden.

"Brand new pads," she reiterated with a touch of educational sarcasm. "They're sensitive."

They arrived in a rundown community where many trees needed pruning, leaves needed raking, grass needed mowing, and flowerbeds needed weeding. The bishop parked in front of a tan, stucco house. Chandler swerved up behind the Explorer. Chet was out of the car before it was in neutral. Ayden headed to the driveway where Philip met Maria and Francesca. They hadn't recovered from their fascination with Chet. The bishop began delegating orders, pointing to the three houses that needed yard work. Francesca offered to mow the lawn, but when she took her place behind the lawn mower resting in the front yard, she didn't even know how to get it started.

"Can someone help me?" she called, her eyes honing in on Chet.

Ayden smiled wryly while her chest simultaneously burned possessively. Chet sighed, crossing the lawn to assist Francesca. Connor looked temporarily relieved.

"I'll start in the rose bed," Philip said, beckoning to Ayden. "Wanna help me?"

"Sure," Ayden nodded.

Chandler and Connor swiftly began pruning trees. Chandler's skills with yard work proved to be more efficient than those with his stick shift. After helping Francesca start the lawn mower and instructing her on how to use it without inflicting serious injury or death upon herself, Chet was sucked into raking leaves with Maria and the bishop. Ayden observed him fondly while plucking weeds from the rose garden. Maria desperately wanted Chet's attention and tried in every way a girl knew how to get him to compliment her. Unbeknownst to Chet, Connor was simmering with envy. Ayden silently dared Connor to attack Chet with a chainsaw. She was half tempted to turn it on Maria if the girl didn't calm down. As they worked, Bishop Bommgardner began his ecclesiastical duties by fishing for information about Chet's background. It was obvious Chet wasn't a member of the church.

"A couple of young adults from the ward are heading up to Utah for the next General Conference," Bishop Bommgardner told Chet. "Ever been?"

Chet stroked the grass with his rake. "To Utah?"

"To General Conference," the bishop inquired.

"I heard they have the best ski resorts," Maria commented.

Chet gave her a winning smile, which she accepted despite ignorantly assuming his smile was for her knowledge about Utah's climate and not the direction it took the conversation.

"You like to ski?" Chet asked Maria.

"I've been snowboarding. Twice."

She pulled her pile of leaves closer to Chet's. The bishop

dropped his religious debriefing momentarily.

Philip interrupted Ayden's thoughts. "How did you two meet?"

She glanced over at where he was kneeling a few feet from her. "Chet and I met at the beach when I was a senior in high school."

"Wow," Philip nodded. "High school sweethearts. That's adorable."

"Ha!" Ayden laughed, using a dirt-smeared hand to tuck a piece of hair behind her ear. "Not even close."

Philip paused, also getting a kick out of Maria's behavior toward Chet. "You guys aren't dating?"

He said it as casually as a single, returned missionary could.

Ayden grinned, pulling out a wilted dandelion. "We're something, that's for sure."

Philip accepted that. By the time they were finishing up on the third house, Chet made his way over to Ayden. She stuffed a bag full of leaves into a trash can. Chet held the lid open for her.

"Converted yet?" she grunted.

Chet shut the lid to the garbage can, his eyes scanning the houses on the opposite side of the street.

"What?" Ayden asked.

"I used to buy tamales from an old woman that lived over there," he answered.

He saw an image from his past, leaning up against the garbage can. Ayden stepped close to his side so their shoulders were touching. She examined the house Chet stared at.

"How did you know the old woman?" she questioned.

"I knew her son," Chet replied.

It said enough.

"Speaking of tamales," Bishop Bommgardner interjected, approaching from beside them, "we're going out for Mexican food after this. You two interested?"

Ayden gave Chet the opportunity to decline. He'd thus far been a champ about their impromptu service project. He'd mowed, raked, and weeded three yards and was now thoroughly covered in bits of grass and dirt. If he was ready to go back to the cabin, she'd go with him. To her astonishment, however, Chet gave the bishop a polite smile.

"I'm starving," he said.

Bishop Bommgardner lifted a closed fist. Chet bumped it with his own, then winked at Ayden while the bishop hollered to the others.

"Chips and salsa are on me!"

They cleaned up the tools and set them back near the first house where they'd be picked up by a neighbor later. Connor was trying to salvage lost time with Maria. Francesca asked Chet if he liked spicy food as she moved over to the Explorer. Ayden knew it was Francesca's sneaky way of hoping Chet would engage in conversation and join her in the bishop's car instead of Chandler's Eclipse, but Chet was not to be manipulated.

"It's my favorite," Chet answered, and he got into the back of Chandler's car before he could be offered shotgun.

Ayden scooted into the middle seat in the back to sit next to Chet. It didn't go unnoticed by Philip who took the front, passenger's side. Chandler slumped into the driver's seat and started his car.

"I'm gonna smell like grass for a week," he stated.

He drove to the Mexican restaurant Bishop Bommgardner told them to meet at. Philip put up a good effort at finding compatible topics for discussion with Chet but was mostly unsuccessful.

"How do you feel about the Lakers this season?" Philip questioned.

Chet was more reclined and at ease in the back seat than he'd been in the front, even though the Eclipse didn't have much space. His long legs were bent, and his knees parted on either side of Philip's seat. His left hand, the one closest to Ayden's leg, picked at an invisible piece of lint on his black pants.

"I'm not a good judge of sports," Chet responded honestly.

To which Ayden exclaimed, "Chet's athletic. He can play volleyball really well."

Chet shot her a teasing scowl.

"That's rad," Chandler said, pulling into the parking lot of a cantina.

He parked next to the Explorer. Maria and Francesca exited the Ford, giggling down at Chet.

"We get into some pretty heated tournaments in the YSA," Philip added. "You should come sometime."

"Yeah, you should," Ayden agreed, nudging Chet's ribs.

Chet nudged her back.

She wondered if he'd ever hung out with friends his own age. Thinking back on their first time meeting at the beach, she wondered what Chet's buddies Gavin, Reese, and Gage had thought about Chet. What had it been like to be one of Chet's "friends" back then? Or even now?

All four got out of the car. Ayden exited on the same side as Chet, pleased that he waited for her and shut the car door behind her. Connor was glad the others had decided Chet and Ayden were a thing, but he couldn't get Maria to give him the time of day. They entered the restaurant and Bishop Bommgardner told the hostess they needed a table for eight.

"Philip says you're gonna join us for volleyball?" the bishop asked Chet as the hostess led the way to a long table in the back of the restaurant.

Ayden smiled watching Chet scramble for words.

"He's got a wicked…" she began. Chet skewered her with another jesting glower while she finished, "Serve."

They sat four to each side of the table, Chet on one end in case he needed to make a dash for the exit. Ayden sat on his right, her arm brushing his sleeve of tattoos. It was a cute cantina. Their table was in the very back next to an open floor that was brightly tiled. A setup for a live band sat in the corner with a sign that mentioned music and dancing on the weekends. The waitress appeared, taking their drink order. She left a basket of chips and a bowl of salsa on the table with a promise to promptly return. Chet opened his menu, holding it just high enough that it boxed he and Ayden into privacy.

"Is this my initiation or what?" he whispered out of the side of his mouth.

Ayden bent her forehead against his temple. "I believe that's a chimichanga with beans and rice."

His eyes slid down her face, the blue twinkling mischievously. Ayden pretended to read the menu that offered them some short-lived seclusion. He smelled like gasoline, which she loved. Ayden savored the moment of closeness and committed to memory the vision of Chet doing yard work—extra yard work considering Maria spent most of her time messing up piles of leaves so Chet would help her.

"I'm concerned," Chet continued under his breath. "Are they going to force feed me jalapenos and make me recite the bible?"

"They haven't yet," she shrugged, turning her face to his. Their noses touched. "But if they do, I'll make sure they're mozzarella stuffed jalapeno poppers."

The waitress returned. Chet lowered his menu. Ayden grinned.

Maria's cheeks turned bright red. She took a sip of her water and finally batted her eyelashes at Connor.

"So, do you have Professor Conrad this semester?" she asked him.

The waitress stepped up to Chet's side, lifting her pad of paper and a pencil.

"Tacos al pastor," he said with a perfect, Spanish accent. "Con guacamole."

"And for you?" the waitress asked Ayden.

"Tamales," she replied. "Chicken."

Conversation flowed smoothly throughout dinner. The young adults breezed through all pop culture matters and school subjects. Ayden commented where appropriate, but Chet stayed mostly silent. He would cordially nod or answer when a question was directed at him, but he remained reticent and observant. Ayden liked how amiable he was in spite of being completely out of his element. He was so talented at being in control of himself, at being Chet. These people had no idea who he was, or what he was capable of. How amazing he was…

"Want a bite?" Ayden asked Chet during the course of their meal.

Chet stuck his fork into Ayden's plate of tamales.

"How does it compare to the ones you used to buy?"

He swallowed. "Not as good." He then lifted his eyes suddenly.

Ayden looked around. "What is it?"

Chet's eyes misted over. "This song."

She listened, tuning out the restaurant goers around her. A reggaetón track played through the speakers. Chet's mouth opened into a nostalgic smile. Ayden watched him relive a particular memory. She loved watching Chet. His emotions were always neatly concealed, but at times he opened up chambers of himself and gave her glimpses of his life. This was one of those glimpses. She felt like holding a menu up again so she could stare shamelessly at his beautiful face.

"It's a catchy song," Ayden said.

Philip overheard. "It's a great beat. Do you dance?"

"Oh," Ayden stammered. "I…"

"She loves to dance," Chet answered for her.

Payback.

Philip smiled and asked Chet while motioning toward Ayden, "May I?"

Chet kicked back in his chair. "Be my guest."

Before she knew it, Philip pushed out of his chair and walked over to Ayden, lifting his hand. Ayden felt obligated to take it. She gave Chet a scolding smile and let Philip lead her onto the tiled dance floor.

"It's not an Elvis song," Ayden hollered over her shoulder. "You traitor."

Chet kept his eyes on her. She turned her attention to Philip who had to be at least a year younger than she.

"I learned some bachata on my mission," Philip said, putting one hand on Ayden's waist. He took one of her hands in his.

He began a few steps to the rhythm of the music. Ayden did her best to follow. It was easier than she thought. Rhythm and dance came naturally to her. She chanced a glance over at Chet, slightly terrified that he might be ready to steamroll Philip the way he'd wanted to steamroll Craig the time he saw Craig and Ayden outside of Ayden's salon. Confusion crept over Chet's features. He was still reliving a memory. Reliving the song.

"I'm not very good," Philip laughed, ushering Ayden around the vacated dance floor.

She ripped her gaze away from Chet's eyes, longing to fall into them. Chet stared directly into her, but she knew he was seeing something else. He had that haunted look on his face that she'd seen in the photograph of him as a kid that she'd discovered at the estate. It made her ache to hold him.

Philip sensed her feelings for Chet. He had a gentleman's manners.

He asked, "Do you want a try, Chet?"

"Hm?" Chet gazed up at Philip. "No. I can't bachata."

Philip was a decent dancer. He spun Ayden around. "It's not that most men can't dance. It's that they won't."

"Exactly," Chet affirmed.

The song ended. Philip released Ayden. She took her seat again, sipping from her water. The room felt warm. Even warmer was the breath Chet exhaled on her neck as he tilted into her and gently kissed her cheek.

19

Ayden had her misgivings about returning to Las Vegas. It wasn't her ideal destination vacation. She had bad memories about the last time she'd been in Vegas, but she also had some good ones. The last time she'd been in a casino, she was standing at the Craps table in the Venetian. Chet had come up behind her. It was her first time seeing him since Pismo Beach, and she hadn't even known it was him. He'd rescued her from Mitchell. He'd driven her across the state back home to California. This time she was arriving to Vegas on Chet's arm. And it was out of necessity, for Chet had to get permission from Benecio's superior if he was going to gain their assistance.

They would attend an event at an extremely high-end club. The list was exclusive. It even had a dress code. Chet didn't reserve a room for more than one night, but he'd checked into a suite at the Bellagio where he and Ayden could get dressed. There were clothes waiting for them in the closet. She didn't ask questions.

They stepped out of the Bellagio onto The Strip. It was early afternoon. The sun was out, and the temperatures were nice. Warm, but not hot. There weren't many people out, but a few devoted partiers with yard drinks around their necks stumbled by, laughing. One of them was joking about a new tattoo he just got on his bicep. They had some time to kill. Chet glanced down the street.

"As many times as I've been here," he said, "I've never been here other than for work."

Ayden smiled up at him. "This is only my second time to Vegas. I'm not sure whether my experiences were for business or pleasure."

Chet took her hand. His fingers spread naturally in between hers. It was so comfortable, so reassuring.

"Should we make it a pleasure?" he asked her, pulling her down the sidewalk.

"It already is."

They walked by a family of five. Chet smiled at them.

A beautiful, loud melodic song began to their right. They paused in front of the Bellagio fountains. Water started shooting up into the sky. Several other people gathered by, too. A well-trained classical vocalist serenaded the pedestrians. Chet and Ayden admired the streams of water, the synchronization with the music. It was a fifteen-minute-long display. When it ended, Chet started down the sidewalk again. Hand in hand, they made their way passed a few hotels and shops.

"The M&M factory," Chet said, pointing across the street.

"Shall we?"

He nodded. "We shall."

They crossed an intersection, and Chet opened the front door. Ayden passed by the larger-than-life sized M&Ms and stepped underneath the big, pretend bag of M&Ms dumping over the threshold. Chet entered behind her. There were candy kiosks and chocolate bars the size of laptops everywhere. An entire wall dedicated to tubes of every color and flavor of M&Ms ran the length of the store. There were stuffed animals, hats and beanies, t-shirts, baby's onesies.

"I have an idea," Ayden stated.

Chet was trying on a yellow M&M beanie that had two strings of yarn dangling down over each ear.

"I'll pick out a bag of flavored M&M's for you, and you pick one out for me."

He took off the beanie. "I like it. Then you have to eat them, no matter what."

"And guess the flavor correctly."

"Bingo."

They took off in different directions. Ayden walked toward a red tube. She peered over her shoulder at Chet as she grabbed any empty sack to fill.

"No cheating!" she hissed at his scheming grin.

He turned away.

She filled her bag with orange and red M&Ms from the Chili Nut flavored tube. After purchasing them, she waited for Chet near a wall of green M&M pillows. He arrived a minute later holding a bag that was twice the size of hers. It was filled with brown, white, and yellow candies. They exchanged bags and left the store. Ayden opened hers first, popping a trio of M&Ms into her mouth.

"Hm," she murmured. "Good. I'm not sure. Try yours."

Chet already was.

"Not my favorite flavor," he replied, eating a few more.

"Is mine butterscotch?" she questioned.

"Close."

They walked through an intersection, returning in the direction of the Bellagio.

"Is mine paprika?" Chet asked.

"HA!" Ayden barked a laugh. "Good guess. I have no idea what mine is. Cinnamon something? Tell me."

"You're not good at this game," Chet laughed. "Yours is Pecan Pie."

"Dang it."

"I'm not eating a single one more of these. What's mine?"

"Are they that bad?" she asked, stealing one of Chet's M&Ms. She ate it. "Chili Nut," she revealed. "Yeah, I don't want any more of those either."

Chet gave the bag to a homeless guy standing at the corner of the street. Ayden shared the rest of hers with Chet, but she noticed how he picked out the white M&Ms. She smiled.

"Here," she made him carry the bag. "I shouldn't have any more."

Once more at their hotel, they made their way up to their hotel suite. They had a chunk of the day to pass before it was time to get ready for the evening. Ayden plopped herself down on the bed and crossed her ankles. She'd been content with their M&M adventure, but Chet was trying to find other activities to do to pass their time.

"Seriously," he said from the window. "There is so much to do here. We could see a show? I'm sure there's one starting in an hour or two."

Ayden didn't know how comfortable she was with Vegas shows. "That's okay."

He took a seat on the bed next to her, also crossing his ankles. "Are you sure?"

"Positive."

"If you say so," he sighed. Then glanced over at the telephone sitting on the nightstand at the head of the bed. "I've got an idea."

He reached for it, stretching the cord out as he pulled it onto the bed between them. From within the top drawer of the nightstand he withdrew a menu.

"Let's see what they have from Room Service," he added.

Ayden grabbed the menu and flipped through it.

"Just about everything," she declared.

"Even Chili Nut M&Ms?"

"Well, they don't wanna go out of business," she remarked. "But they have lobster. Steak. Fries. Ice cream sundaes."

Chet leaned over to peek at the menu. "Banana splits?"

She breathed in his scent. His breath smelled like mint.

"Banana splits, even," she confirmed. "I'm leaning toward lobster." Her eyes darted to the closet where her gown was hanging. "I have to make sure I fit into that tonight."

Chet took the receiver off the phone and pushed some buttons. "Room Service," he said. He whispered to Ayden, "I wouldn't mind if you didn't."

"I wouldn't go nude, if that's what you're eluding to. I'd go buy M&M pjs from that candy factory and rock those with a fluffy beanie before going naked."

Chet's mouth slanted into a smile. "I'll take two lobster dinners." He mouthed to her, "Please do."

***

Ayden wanted to spend every night for the rest of her life wearing M&M pjs with Chet, laughing at how silly the other looked wearing fluffy beanies. This was the closest to a legit couple they'd ever felt. Chet had ordered two lobster dinners from Room Service, two slices of chocolate cake for dessert, and two mini bottles of sparkling cider to drink. Ayden didn't finish her dinner, and only took a bite of her cake, because regardless of how funny Chet thought she was being, she was dead serious about fitting into her gown. He didn't feel the same pressure she did about making sure they impressed the right people tonight. This was the most she'd ever seen him act his age.

"You know, I saw this movie once where this girl drags her boyfriend to a Celine Dion concert," Ayden said as Chet cleared their Room Service. "Maybe after our event tonight I'll make you take me."

Chet licked his fingers and set their plates outside their hotel door. "Celine Dion is my jam. But I don't think we'll have time tonight. We'll probably be gone until morning."

"Really?" She underestimated the length of these kinds of things. "I hope I can stay awake."

He gave her a look. "Do you want to nap? I can wander downstairs or…"

"No," Ayden replied. "I think I'm just nervous about the whole night."

"It'll be fine," he said in that way of his.

She didn't believe him any more than she believed Celine Dion was his jam. To prove it, she sang, "'There were nights when the wind was so cold.'"

Chet gazed over at her, one of his eyebrows arching. She laughed, wanting that expression painted on a canvas that she could hang in her front room…if she had a front room. It was strange not having much. Yet, she never felt like she needed more. All she want-ed was Chet. Their friendship was growing through all of this. She felt like their afflictions drew them closer together. Hopefully, their trust grew so much that Chet would listen to things she wanted to tell him about God. And she wanted him to tell her more about himself.

His phone dinged with an incoming text message. He checked it, typing a response.

"Should we go over tonight again?" Ayden asked him.

Chet put his phone on the top of the dresser. "You'll be fine!" he stated with mild chastisement, bending to pat her head. "I've had fun today."

She saw that he meant it. "Too bad we're not staying longer.

148

There's a ride on the top of the Stratosphere that looks exciting."

"Next time we're here," he said, "I'll take you on it."

"If there's a next time," Ayden countered.

"You're not scared of heights?"

She shrugged. "Not really. If I'm locked in, rollercoasters or rides don't scare me. I wouldn't skydive, or anything like that."

"No?" Chet grinned. "Lover of the X Games wouldn't go skydiving?"

"I'd watch other people skydive on TV."

He moved to the bathroom. "I'm gonna take a quick shower. Then I'm afraid it is showtime. I'll be fast. You'll have plenty of time to glam up and primp."

She rolled her eyes. When was the last time she glammed up and primped? She barely had any makeup. Chet never treated her like she needed it, but for a formal event she would want to look presentable. Glamorous. It terrified her to admit how badly she wanted Chet to find her attractive. She hadn't yet unzipped the bag around her evening gown, but she knew it was expensive. The designer label on the bag was a brand she'd never before dreamed of wearing, or hoping of affording. While Chet was in the shower, she picked up his phone. The screen lit up with a passcode requirement. She set it back down.

20

Chet's suit was perfectly tailored. Ayden's gown was immaculately fitted. Inside the large, grand bathroom, Ayden slipped into the floor-length, silk dress. It was royal purple with a high neckline and long sleeves. The back had a teardrop opening in between her shoulder blades. She'd never worn anything so opulent, not even on her wedding day. Her heels were simple, silver t-straps. They fit like Cinderella's.

"How should I wear my hair?" she called through the door.

"However," Chet replied from out in the suite.

Ayden twisted her thick, wavy brown hair up into a classic French twist. It was easy, and she wanted easy. Besides, the dress was decadent enough. Even though the evening had nothing to do with how Ayden looked, she didn't abandon her sense of fashion entirely. She could appreciate the fine apparel and chose a hairstyle that would complement the entire ensemble. Fixing the straps of her heels onto her ankles, she smoothed the front of the dress down, amazed at the perfect fit.

The last time she'd put on a gown, besides her wedding dress, must have been high school. She'd gone to most of the school dances. Getting dressed up and girly was fun. Ayden and her girlfriends always went in big groups. They'd go out on a day activity first, then split up from the boys to get ready, and meet up for dinner. She'd never had a nice lobster dinner for prom. The Bellagio Room Service was better than most restaurants.

Thinking of hotels and prom, Ayden remembered a few of her friends leaving a dance early to go have a party at a hotel room their parents didn't know about. Ayden's date had asked if she wanted to go with them, but she'd declined. Her parents would be horrified. Whose older brother paid for a hotel room for a bunch of high school kids, anyway? It seemed irresponsible to her.

Ayden took a final glance at herself in the mirror, and opened the bathroom door. This wasn't prom.

She stepped out into the suite to find Chet adjusting his cuff links. His black suit was a custom, European fit. The plain white button-up he wore under it was stiff with precision ironing. His dark hair was styled differently, more conservatively. Black dress shoes that were neatly polished completed his outfit. Ayden floated onto Cloud Nine. She had never seen a more handsome man. He smiled as she stepped closer, tugging on the lapels of his suit coat.

"My," Chet sighed.

Ayden gave him a languid twirl. "Someone has good taste."

He whistled. "That color purple."

"That suit!" Ayden returned approvingly. "You look absolutely dapper."

"Enough to blend into the High Rollers?"

"Are you kidding? They're going to fall to their knees at your feet."

He offered her his elbow. She took it.

Together, they made their way downstairs and outside to the valet parking. A stretch limo awaited them. Chet opened the door for Ayden. Inside was a bucket of ice and an unopened bottle of champagne. Champagne flutes hung upside down all along one of the walls. A flat screen TV hung on the other. The windows were heavily tinted. Chet said nothing to the driver, who took off down The Strip toward the nightclub where Chet would be meeting his contact. A high-stakes poker tournament was going to take place this evening. It was not like the streets of Fresno. These were big time money changers. Chet had full confidence, but Ayden was nervous. She was just a country girl.

A man wearing an earpiece, holding a clipboard, stood by a curtained entrance to the exclusive club. There were a few people standing in front of Chet and Ayden. One of them Ayden was pretty sure she recognized as a movie star. Her heart shuddered in her chest. Chet escorted Ayden after the movie star, and told the man holding the clipboard their names. He stepped aside and let Chet and Ayden pass by. Chet pulled back the curtain, and Ayden stepped through first.

Her first thought was: peacock feathers.

Everything was neon blue, vibrant purple, hot pink, and sparkly. Her eyes settled on the four poker tables that were set up. Men and women gambled as cocktail waitresses in formal gowns pranced around the room. Vegas music played in the background. Cigar smoke wafted toward the glitzy ceiling. Funds were traded electronically, but Chet collected his chips from a dealer's booth and moved to an open seat at one of the tables. Ayden stayed close to his side, her eyes scrutinizing everyone in the room. None of the men looked like Saucedo's boys. These were not rough, hood thugs. They were classy men with money to burn.

Ayden rested an arm on Chet's shoulder as he sat at the table and accepted the cards the dealer dealt him. He had several stacks of chips in front of him which he organized based on color. The dealer laid two cards flat on the table for all to see. Chet glanced discreetly at his own hand.

"What's this game called?" Ayden whispered.

"Texas hold 'em," he answered, tossing a bunch of chips forward.

Everyone at the table went in a circle, placing bets. The dealer laid a third card flat. Two deuces and a queen of spades.

Chet lifted the corner of his cards. He gave Ayden an inquiring glance, but she smiled and leaned into his ear.

"Don't ask me."

He flicked some more chips forward. "It's only money."

Two other players folded. The dealer laid a fourth card flat. Ayden let Chet do his thing. Her eyes wandered over the room and its lavishness. She felt so much more comfortable here than at the nightclub in Fresno with Starla. It wasn't as dirty. Men kept their eyes on their cards instead of her body. Women were being respected, and several were gambling with more guts than the men. A gray-haired woman a few seats over from Chet puffed on a cigarette stick. Her pearl necklace shimmered. She had more chips in front of her than any other the other players at their table. She also won the hand.

"High risk, high reward," Chet sighed, sitting back.

He relaxed a little bit through the next game. The tournament continued. Gamblers thinned as crowded spectators thickened. Ayden pegged the movie star. She'd seen him in a few action flicks as a favorite supporting actor. A waitress came by with drinks for the table. Chet declined. Everyone else requested a Jack 'n Coke.

The dealer set up a new hand. Chet slid one of his arms around Ayden's backside, pulling on her hip. His fingers brushed the silk fabric of her waist. She nuzzled closer to him, happy to be claimed as his date for the evening. There wasn't a better looking man in the room—or on the planet.

"I see our guy," he said to her quietly.

The dealer laid another card flat on the table. Bets were placed around the table.

"Where?" Ayden asked, glancing around the room.

Chet nodded to his right, his eyes on the adjacent table. "Shaved head. King of the Jungle."

Ayden spotted the man with tribal tattoos along his arms and neck. He had a shaved head, a textured scarf, a bright orange dress shirt with the sleeves rolled up to his elbows, and snakeskin boots. She thought he could give Elton John a run for his money.

"That's who Benecio answers to," Chet remarked. "If we get *his* approval, we've got Benecio and his guys on our side."

Ayden exhaled a downward breath. "So, what do we do?"

Chet threw a handful of chips onto the cards in front of him. Grandma Moneybags scoffed and did the same, raising Chet five-thousand dollars.

The dealer motioned for Chet and the other players to reveal their cards. Chet's hand won.

"We work our way to the top."

Several hours later, only six gamblers remained. The dealers shut down three of the tables, condensing the players to one center table. Chet sat in a chair on the very end of the table. Ayden stood at his left, the other players all sat to his right. Benecio's superior was at the table. He had two, African American goddesses flanking him. Sipping a drink, he gave the other poker players a cocky smile.

"What's his name again?" Ayden asked Chet.

"The Amethyst Tiger," he answered, accepting the cards the dealer slid across the table to him.

Ayden did her best not to gape at the cockatoo a few seats over. "You're kidding me."

Chet gave her a grin. "Why do you think your dress is that color?"

"Amethyst Tiger," she muttered with a tiny shake of her head. "It's like a James Bond movie."

The players placed some bets. It was now crowded in the club. The music continued to play loudly. Private couches were gathering popularity. Ayden recognized a few more famous people including professional athletes. She was way out of her element.

"I have the nicest car and the prettiest woman," Chet commentated. "Does that make me 007?"

Ayden smirked over his head, watching The Amethyst Tiger. "I'm not answering that."

"Why?" Chet asked, taking a stack of ten-thousand dollars' worth of chips and sliding it out in front of him. "Afraid I might impress you with all my groovy, way-ahead-of-the-century, gadgets?"

"Focus," she scolded.

The dealer laid all the cards flat. Everyone folded, even Chet. The Amethyst Tiger took the pot. His hand was a measly two pair.

"Why didn't you keep going?" Ayden asked.

"He's a big bluffer," Chet answered clandestinely.

She didn't see how that was super relevant. Chet could easily take him with a better hand.

"Some people are big players," he added. "Others are big bluffers. They play off the other players' hands."

Ayden figured Chet would play his cards right, both figuratively and literally. They went through two more rounds before only three players were left with chips. The Amethyst Tiger, Chet, and a French woman in her seventies. Chet was dealt a winning hand. He had an ace of hearts and a jack of clubs. The dealer laid out a three of clubs, a jack of diamonds, a seven of spades, and an ace of spades. Bets topped a hundred thousand dollars. Ayden couldn't fathom the amount of zeroes in that number. She watched people give away chips as if they were just plastic and not representations of boats and cars and mortgage payments.

Chet bet The Amethyst Tiger out of everything on the table. They were both all in. As the dealer instructed them to show their hands, Chet received the winning applause. The French woman congratulated him and departed with only a mild rebuff for losing what Ayden considered a sizable inheritance. The Amethyst Tiger waited patiently as the dealer cleared the table and other spectators diminished. He approached Chet with an eccentric shake of his hand, his lady friends in tow.

"Okay, how do I know you?" The Amethyst Tiger asked Chet.

Ayden tried to slink to the side, but Chet took her hand firmly in his.

"Benecio," Chet said, standing.

He left his chips on the table unsupervised. Ayden's eyes kept flicking toward them, almost certain it was near half a million dollars. Neither Chet nor The Amethyst Tiger seemed concerned about the winnings. They stood eye to eye. The King of the Jungle definitely described the man Benecio worked under. He was a giant man. Chet was a slender, black jaguar in comparison. Ayden proudly stood at Chet's side. As his woman.

"Benecio," The Amethyst Tiger repeated. "You have my respect."

Chet's lips turned up at the corners. It was what he'd come for.

The Amethyst Tiger left to join the other partiers in the club. Chet asked a passing waitress for a water. Ayden felt a huge pressure release from her chest. Her elegant gown didn't feel as tight or hot anymore. The song switched to an upbeat, Latin pop hit. People abandoned their private couches to dance on the floor as tables and chairs were cleared. Lights dimmed, colored spotlights shone throughout the room. A bubble machine produced translucent bubbles. Some underage girls that must have snuck in climbed onto a podium.

"That's that," Chet stated.

He straightened fully and buttoned his suit coat, still holding Ayden's hand in his. She squeezed his palm.

"Where to?" she asked.

He ran a hand through his gelled hair, giving it a Chet-inspired tousle. "The dance floor."

Ayden followed him through the crowd, holding fast to his hand. Bubbles popped against her cheeks.

"The dance floor?" she gasped, briefly glancing backward. "Hey, your chips."

"Leave them," he replied casually. At the dance floor, he spun her to face him and pointed to the club patrons. "Drinks on me."

He'd won a small fortune.

"Drinks?" Ayden smiled. "And multiple round-trip airfares to Europe? Maybe a Scottish castle, or two?"

Chet raised his chin and grinned. A neon light strobed across his cheekbones, flashing in his eyes. An NBA player was hustling a few girls next to them. The movie star she'd first seen at the entrance of the club was spraying a bottle of champagne. Ayden ducked to miss getting wet. Chet laughed.

"Come on," he teased, taking both her hands in his, interlocking their fingers. "Bailando."

"I thought you didn't dance," she said dryly.

A group of people jumping up and down in the bubbles bumped into her. She fell against Chet's chest for a second, pulling back as he started lightly moving to the tempo.

"I said I don't Bachata," he retorted, speaking loudly to be heard above the music.

His movements were subtle and effortless, a slight Latino sway to his step-step-step. Ayden mimicked his body. The song ended and faded into another equally upbeat tune. Most of the younger crowd knew the lyrics and sang along. Ayden couldn't move too much given her long gown, but Chet wasn't trying to swing dance. Their dance moves were unembellished. They enjoyed just being close together, their worries far away.

She couldn't get over how he looked dressed in such refinery. He wasn't as browbeaten as he'd been at the cabin. It was nice to see him in a good mood. They needed some positivity to rejuvenate. By dawn, they'd be driving back to Fresno to undertake their formidable plan. Ayden had no idea what time it was, but she was surprisingly awake. She also was surprised that she wanted to stay with Chet on the dance floor just a while longer, dancing to the music together, savoring the taste of what freedom would be like when they could belong together.

"That was easier than I thought it would be," Ayden said as she and Chet left the club and made their way outside.

It was the middle of the night. Their limousine was parked in the valet. Chet opened the back door for Ayden once more. She hiked her dress up a little and climbed in, letting her hair down from the twist on her scalp. She shook out the waves as Chet scooted in next to her. The driver took them back to the Bellagio where Chet's Mustang was parked in the large, parking structure on the backside of The Strip. Once inside their suite, Ayden changed into her daily clothes, replacing her heels with her cowboy boots. Chet left his suit laid out on the bed's duvet, donning his black shirt and pants. She hoped it wouldn't be long before he joined her for Sunday worship and could wear a suit to church.

"Can you at least keep the cuff links?" she asked.

He glanced down at his suit and considered it. "Are you gonna ask to draw me wearing them, and only them?"

Ayden swatted at him.

"Let's go," he beckoned. "We have one more place to go before we leave town."

"Oh, yeah?"

"I have to pick up my car," he said, opening the hotel room door.

Ayden walked out into the hall. "Your car? It's in the parking garage."

"Not the Mustang," he said, dangling a silver key ring with a fuzzy, flamingo keychain on it.

Her eyes widened. "Where did you get that?"

His eyes narrowed. "More importantly, what does it drive?"

He tossed the keys over to her. She caught them.

"You won a car during the tournament?" she asked.

"I think I won the French lady's firstborn son, too."

Ayden giggled.

They took the Mustang out onto The Strip. Chet drove past the skyscrapers toward Fremont Street. As they drew closer, Ayden recognized the happenings of a drag race. Suped up cars with glowing lights lined the curbs, barricading perpendicular roads. People were everywhere. Music thumped from multiple stereos. The owners of the cars stood near popped hoods or trunks, checking out all the upgrades to their vehicles. Chet's Mustang, though plain by their standard, gained its own attention as he pulled it off to the side of the road and parked.

Ayden got out of the car and walked behind Chet as he approached an Asian-made car with yellow detailing. A girl with pink pigtails sat on the hood. She was holding an inflatable flamingo. Chet took out his keyring and looked at the fuzzy keychain. A flamingo. The girl blew a huge bubble with gum and popped it.

Chet eased his way between bodies to the owner of the car. "Kane?"

A guy standing in the center of his buddies looked up. He saw the keychain in Chet's hand.

"Race is in five minutes," Kane stated.

The girl sitting on the hood chuckled.

Chet's gaze swept across them. The bass from Kane's stereo pounded in Ayden's ears. She wondered how any of them weren't deaf.

"I'm just here for collection," Chet said, throwing the keys toward Kane.

Kane caught them, jingled the keychain, and threw it back at Chet.

"You won the keys," he stated. "You have to race for the car."

A blowhorn sounded across the street. Standing in the middle of the road was a woman holding a flare. A guy next to her was collecting pink slips.

Kane looked Chet up and down. "Race is in one minute."

And he and his entourage vanished into the crowd. Chet watched the girl with pigtails climb into Kane's car and drive it over to the starting line. Two other cars pulled up along side of it. Chet grumbled to himself.

"I'm too old for this."

"Don't tell me you've never raced the streets of Las Vegas?" Ayden probed.

Chet gave her a chastising smile. "It's against the law. You want me to race against these kids for a car I've already won? I could buy all thirteen of these cars with my winnings."

"The winnings you left at the nightclub?"

He quirked an eyebrow at her with an expression that read, "I can't believe I'm going to do this."

"If you want me to race for…" Chet held up the keychain. "For whatever this drives, I'll do it. It's probably not even worth it. I'll do it. But you're riding passenger."

Ayden felt a little thrill. Chet tucked the key into his pocket and they returned to his Mustang. Chet got into the driver's seat and started the engine. Ayden climbed in, and he drove it up to the starting line. Kane was discussing Chet's participation with the guy in charge of the pink slips. Chet rolled his windows down.

"Look at these dudes," Chet murmured.

Ayden did. She buckled her seatbelt and made sure it was tight.

The other drivers got into their cars and revved their engines. Another woman holding a second flare joined the first, and they took their positions in front of the cars. Chet's headlights shone down the street along with the other race cars'. Even though Chet's Mustang was a nice, vintage classic, the bystanders showcased their skepticism that it belonged in the same race as the other cars. Several people even pointed and laughed. Kane was in the vehicle directly to Chet's left. Chet glanced over at him. Kane put on a pair of sunglasses, regardless of the late hour, and stared forward again.

"Oh, boy," Ayden sighed.

"You sure about this, toots?" Chet asked.

"He didn't say you had to win the race," she said back. "He just said you had to race for the car."

"Good point," he replied, although she'd never have guessed if he was concerned about losing. "I hope it's a bubblegum pink Fiat. I'll give it to you as a birthday present."

"Don't pretend like you don't want to show these guys what your muscle car is made of," she joked.

"I could just run them over and get this over with a whole lot faster. I'm kidding."

Ayden flipped down her visor and closed it again. The women in the street raised their flares. The racers revved their engines.

Chet's Mustang growled deeply. His right hand eased onto the stick shift. Ayden tensed. When the flares lowered, each car shot forward. Kane's was first off the line. Chet held second position, his powerful V8 thrusting him to the front of the other two racers. He shifted into second, then into third. Kane's car pulled one car length ahead of Chet. The yellow detailing blurred as their speed increased. Chet shifted.

"This is just a quarter mile stretch, right?" Ayden shouted.

She flattened one hand against the roof of Chet's Mustang.

Kane's car spat out fire. Chet swerved slightly. The flames licked the Mustang's grill. In the side view mirror, Ayden saw the other two racers falling behind. Four and a half seconds, and Kane crossed the finish line. Five point six, and Chet zoomed past it. There were more people gathered around the finish line as Chet coasted to a stop, just behind Kane's bumper. Chet got out of the car, unfazed by the people either mocking or admiring him. He approached Kane, who actually graced Chet with a smile.

Chet was about to offer the same argument Ayden had about not needing to win the race to collect the car he'd already won, when Kane turned and waved to the side of the road. Ayden swiveled to follow Kane's gaze. Chet took a step further into the street. A crowd parted to reveal a shiny car with a pink flamingo dangling from the rearview mirror.

"I just wanted to prove to these guys," Kane said behind Chet's shoulder, "that classic muscle never goes out of style."

Chet pulled out the key he'd won from his pocket.

"What is that?" Ayden asked, her eyes glued to the car.

"A Yenko Chevelle," both he and Kane answered at the same time.

It was gorgeous. The silver paint was multi-dimensional. Chet paced over to it, sliding a finger along the body. Ayden crossed the street and peered inside. The seats were white leather with faint, pink stitching. Chet handed her the keyring.

"Happy birthday," he grinned.

Ayden took the key, smiling at the ridiculous, fuzzy, flamingo. Chet returned to his Mustang as Ayden slipped into the driver's seat of the Chevelle. Rolling down her window, she adjusted the seat and the mirrors. Chet reversed and turned his car toward another street. People split so he could inch between them. Ayden stuck the silver key into the ignition and turned on the Chevelle. It roared to life. She felt like she was about to drive a rocket ship. Putting the car into gear, she started after Chet. The Mustang's taillights glowed as he left the street racers behind, Ayden cruising behind him until they pulled up to a stoplight. Ayden drove up to the side of Chet.

"It's a six hour drive," Chet called out his window at her.

"Let's make it four," Ayden hollered back.

The light turned green, and Ayden took the lead. She drove toward the freeway entrance, and once they were on the onramp, Chet shot past her. She stomped on the gas and shifted, grasping the steering wheel with both hands. A hint of sunlight teased the horizon as they made their way onto the freeway, driving south on the I15. She knew Chet could leave her in the dust, but he gave her a fighting chance. The Chevelle had torque like she couldn't believe. The vroom siphoned through her blood like a drug. She was neck and neck with Chet's Mustang, her pulse racing faster than any modified automobile.

21

The next day was overkill on Ayden's routine. Winning Benecio's help meant Chet doubled his forces the night of the meeting at Starla's nightclub. The men would be positioned all over the nightclub, inside and out. Ayden had to keep Louie and his men distracted long enough for Chet and Saucedo to take action.

It sounded like a video game to Ayden. Every time she and Chet went over the designs, she giggled out of nervousness. Her sole task in the operation was to dance on stage and captivate the attention of Louie and his associates. A deal was going down, or so Louie thought. Pasquale aligned a fake transaction. As the men took their places around the vicinity, Chet and his boss would seize Louie. So much could go wrong in such a short amount of time.

"If anything goes askew, anything at all," Chet sternly told her, "you run like mad. You hear me? Run and don't look back."

It was seven-o-clock at night. They were gathered in the nightclub in downtown Fresno. Ayden and Starla were on stage, concluding the choreography for Ayden's routine. Hank was behind the bar, pouring glasses of gin and setting up for a busy evening. Seated on the stools were a few men Ayden had met only hours earlier. Carter, Sebastian, and Benecio. They were all smoking or chewing. Dozens more were outside and behind the curtains. Chet's team consisted of the unruliest men she'd ever seen.

Anytime Ayden mentioned her worries that one of them would turn against Chet, he replied calmly, "This is my town, toots."

Chet's town. So much so, that only Nogo Saucedo could control who went after Chet. Even then, Chet stated, some of Saucedo's associates wouldn't dare confront Chet. This gave Chet a small advantage, but it wouldn't save his life if they didn't recover his boss's shipmet.

Ayden finished her dance, reluctantly. The men, surprisingly, weren't paying her attention. She was wearing her leggings and a plain t-shirt. It would be different than her uniform the evening of, but she absolutely put her foot down on rehearsing in what Starla picked out. A few steps away, lounging in the chairs in front of an empty podium, Chet spoke earnestly with Pasquale. Starla had draped her robe around her shoulders and walked over to them, sitting on the armchair of Chet's seat. Ayden's face warmed instantly, though she forced her thoughts elsewhere. The night's activities were over, and Ayden didn't have anything else to do before tomorrow. All she wanted was to buy a big, fat, pizza, and sleep.

Just as Ayden descended the stairs, the spotlight came on and shone straight at her. Ayden stood on the last step, shielding her eyes with one hand. Everyone in the room began circulating toward the stage. Starla was at the bar by Hank. The music dimmed, and Chet's voice carried over the speakers.

"Alright guys, let's do a quick rundown."

Ayden felt like she was in a circus. This was orchestrated like a show. A movie. They were all actors, and Chet was the director. She could act. She could do this.

"Hop back up on stage, Ayden, so that the men know exactly how much time they have to get in position. Hank, cue the music."

That was it. Chet marched toward Pasquale, and they exited the back of the nightclub. Benecio remained near the front entrance, arms crossed and a surly glare on his face. Meanwhile, Sebastian and Carter maintained their positions at the bar. The dozens of men scattered around the inside stood behind curtains, in corners, in doorways. They were all armed. Starla approached the front of the stage, motioning for Ayden to hurry over to the pole. She then sat front and center.

Ayden gulped. Every eye was on her.

She wasn't naked, but she might as well have been. Tomorrow night, it would be a full house. Louie's men were coming for the deal, but the nightclub would also open for business. There would probably be a hundred male spectators examining her every move. In a strange way, she wanted Chet back in the building. It would make her more comfortable. He was the only person she remotely trusted. And it was pretty remote.

Starla clapped her hands. "Let's go!"

When Ayden's hands found the pole, Hank punched the stereo. The music blasted through the quiet club. Immediately, the men started to move. They were following their orders, pretending to interact with one another or socialize with Louie's invisible contacts. The only person watching Ayden was Starla. It gave her a little relief. She blew out a long breath, tightened her grip, and struck her pose. The song was long, close to seven minutes, but she remembered the sequence of steps Starla had instructed her. About the four-minute mark, Chet and Pasquale reentered through the back hall.

Ayden tripped when Chet's eyes met hers. His face was calm and inexpressive. He glanced away after only a moment, as he and Pasquale joined Benecio. Ayden climbed halfway up the pole, and then spun down and around. Out of the corner of her eye, she saw Sebastian and Carter coming closer. They joined Starla on the front row, grinning up at Ayden. A few seconds later, Chet, Pasquale, and Benecio were seated there as well.

Seven minutes.

Seven minutes and Louie would be taken.

Ayden knew there was only about thirty-seconds left in the song. It seemed the rehearsal was over. She was not going to be put on display like a monkey. Planting her feet firm, she released the pole and tucked her hands into her hips. She made the cut signal, slicing across her throat. Pasquale reached over to smack Chet on the back. Ayden didn't hear what they were saying. The music was still too loud, but she watched Starla lean in to join the conversation. The woman placed a hand on Chet's knee.

The music ended. Hank clicked the radio back on, turning the volume down. Chet was speaking rapidly with his recruits, discussing the anticipated night tomorrow. He didn't particularly acknowledge Starla's advance, but he wasn't rejecting it either. It made Ayden's chest burn. She tried not to stare. This was not her place, with these people.

"Hey!" Benecio shouted.

He was looking up at Ayden, fondling his wallet. She wrapped her arms around her stomach.

"How about one more go, just for us boys?" Benecio asked, and he tossed a handful of fifty dollar bills onto the stage.

The men hooted and roared with laughter. Except Chet. He grinned, but it lacked any mirth. His eyes moved over his team, calculating. Beat them all up now or later?

Ayden shook her head vigorously, shooting a pleading stare

to Starla.

"Come on, pretty girl," Starla hollered. "Give us a private showing!"

"Yeah," the men chanted in a chorus all around her. They were pulling out their own stacks of cash, throwing bundles of singles at Ayden's toes.

Chet's eyes roamed over the small multitude. He glimpsed back at Hank subtly, who had turned on another electronic beat. His head shook. Hank lowered the volume, and the men booed. Ayden was smothered in shame and humiliation. She took her heels off, one by one, left them on the stage, and fled into the dressing room.

The music continued to hammer the walls around her as she covered her face and sunk down along the wall. She had ripped the curtain closed behind her, aware that the men were laughing, but she didn't care. Her eyes grew swollen with the bristling of tears, and she scolded herself by not holding them back. It wasn't worth crying over. Tears were not an advantage in a life or death situation. Instead, she tugged on the boots Chet brought her from the estate—imitation cowboy boots that suited the cabin life—and caged her emotions.

Abandoning the make up and hair tools Starla had spread out on the station, Ayden took one final glance in the mirror and stormed out into the club. The men were smoking a substance other than cigarettes. It was not tobacco residue wafting heavily toward the ceiling. Ayden didn't bother even looking in their direction. She strode purposefully passed Hank and reached for the front door. Her cell phone was in her pocket. She'd call a cab or… or just roam around the city. It's not like she had money. She had hardly anything. A bit of cash to get by. Her only source of funds was—right behind her.

"Ayden!" Chet called.

He reached out and took hold of her hand. She rotated around with the objective of punching him in the face, but chickened out. It wasn't Chet's fault all men were pigs. His eyes were lustrous, a hypnotizing blue. They stood in the doorway of the nightclub, within eyesight of the chortling team of men and Starla. Ayden could feel her cheeks aflame. She jerked her hand away from Chet's and pushed through the front door.

"Wait," Chet stated, tugging Ayden back inside.

The door closed, but she refused to face him directly.

"I'm glad you didn't oblige them," Chet said coolly.

"You thought I might?" Ayden hissed.

She hated this bar and everything about it. After tomorrow, she never wanted to see any of these people ever again.

Chet let out a downward breath. He glanced around taking in the group of people he ruled.

"Just watching you do what is right makes me feel like an entirely different human being."

Was he joking? Was this some sort of a test?

"I'm leaving," Ayden grunted. "I'll be at the cabin, waiting for tomorrow. You can count on me, but I swear, after midnight tomorrow, I am gone."

Chet's gemstone eyes swiveled down to hers. He wanted to placate her distress. "Ayden, I never would've allowed it. Besides, if it were me, I would have thrown a lot bigger bills."

Ayden gasped and slapped him. It was weak, but effective.

Chet was stunned, but she didn't stand around to watch. His sarcasm stung her fragile self-esteem. She ran out the door into the evening air, grateful to be breathing in California pollution instead of toxic, drug fumes. She glanced right and left, choosing left, and sprinted down to the crosswalk.

Starla had her hand on his knee, and he didn't brush it aside. The thought fueled Ayden's rage. Dusk had fallen, and traffic was diminishing. It wasn't a nice part of town, but Ayden hoped that by holding her cell phone in her hands she could ward off prowlers. If she kept her chin up, and appeared defiant, she was less likely to be targeted. She was kind of hungry, therefore she decided to stop by a fast food mart to pick up something to eat, and then she'd worry about hitching a ride to the cabin. Four-plus hours in a cab? Four-plus hours with a bearded truck driver?

The rumble of the Mustang engine startled her. She peered over her shoulder as Chet pulled out of the parking lot and drove leisurely to the curb where she stood.

"Get in the car," he said.

Ayden disregarded him.

166

"I'm sorry. It was a rude thing to say."

Chet was leaning out the window. He drove at an irregular angle, causing traffic to veer around him. Several drivers honked, and one shouted. Chet didn't care. He stared up at Ayden as one might stare at a disobedient child.

"It was a joke, Ayden. A poor one. I take it back. I won't let them do it again. I'd never let anyone touch you."

"No?" she snapped, keeping her eyes on the lights as they changed from green, to yellow, to red. "No. You would have just *bought* me for a higher price. Is that how you swoon all your women?"

Chet grumbled something under his breath and got out of the car. He left the door open, causing even more infringement upon incoming vehicles, and paced over to her on the sidewalk. Ayden was so perturbed she wondered if she was emitting steam. She was trapped until tomorrow night. It hurt. The more she thought about it, the more she admitted how it hurt her to see Chet in his natural environment. How the men listened to his every word. How the female employees whispered his name behind curtains. She wanted the sweet, gentle man who kissed her and swore to be everything she wanted. This—this powerful druglord and mastermind—was not what she wanted.

She chanced a glimpse up at Chet's face. He was observing her, more gravely than before.

"You've disappointed me," Ayden murmured.

Chet's eyebrows lowered, and he looked away. "I know. I made a mistake. I told you I wanted to make a different plan. You and I know there isn't time. I don't have options. But Ayden, I'm doing this all for you too, you know."

"I doubt that," she rebuked.

A tiny bit of Chet's temper emerged. "You forget that we should be dead right now. Saucedo has the means to kill us, and he would have if it weren't for two reasons. One: he thinks I can get Louie to cough up stolen money and drugs. Two: he is somewhat concerned about my wellbeing. That's a miniscule somewhat. There is no such thing as 'getting out', Ayden. Nolan can tell you. What *he* did to get out was embark on a slaughtering rampage. He frightened people into leaving him alone. Is that what you and I are going to do? Go on a slaughtering rampage? No. Because I made an oath not to kill anyone."

She remembered the promise he made not to kill anymore.

"You and I made a negotiation with Saucedo," Chet continued, watching traffic stream by. "When we follow the plan, everything will work out smoothly. My men are trained well. We do this—we did this—all the time. I'll get Louie to talk. The money and drugs will be returned to Saucedo. You and I will get out. After tomorrow night, everything will change. We'll be free."

"Yeah, all three of us," Ayden muttered.

Chet pretended not to hear.

"Let's go home," he stated stiffly.

"I have no home. In case you haven't noticed."

"Let's go back to Nolan's cabin," he replied dryly.

"No."

"No?"

"I'm hungry."

"Then let's go get something to eat."

A car honked, and a hormonal, teenage boy driving it shouted something derrogatory at Chet who was moving toward the Mustang's driver's side. Chet gave the kid a friendly wave. The boys in the backseat of the passing car laughed, taking turns calling Chet out, making ridiculous offers to meet on the sidewalk and rumble.

"I'm not buying any girlscout cookies this evening," Chet responded as the kid took off in daddy's car.

If only that kid knew who Chet was...

22

"Not here," Ayden protested, but Chet drove into the parking stall and turned off the car.

They'd argued unsuccessfully about where it was safe, and the places Chet was comfortable being seen in public, until Ayden whacked the dashboard.

"No one dangerous will be here," was his explanation. "You said you wanted food. Here's food."

They stumbled into the bar and right into a cluster of beautiful people. The mid-twenty-something men were all looking up and down Ayden. They tilted their pints, full to the brim, in the air. It wasn't her fault her clothing was too tight. She hadn't purchased the outfit herself. A plain, gray shirt, form-fitting jeans, and a pair of antique cowboy boots. She hadn't gotten the opportunity to change, do her hair, make a phone call. Not even the decency to object as to where she was going. Now, the country clad ensmeble was garnering quite a bit of male attention.

But Ayden didn't care for that. She was glaring at the scantily clad women that were part of the bar crowd. All sparkly tops and stilettos, mid-drifts and daisy dukes, gaping openly at the blue-eyed specimen next to Ayden. Chet was regaining his composure at her side. Donning his usual black attire and nonchalance, his piercing eyes were magnificently bold against the dark of his hair. It didn't matter that he'd vaulted through the entrance of the bar with *her*. Every female in a ten mile radius was swooning.

The bravest of them touched Chet's sleeve, angling into his tattooed arm and making a suggestive remark. Ayden couldn't help herself.

"He has an STD," she scoffed.

Chet grabbed Ayden's elbow roughly, turning around and stepping away from the doorway.

"Have you met my schizophrenic sister?" he asked a spectating male, glancing at Ayden. "This is Ayden. Or is it Lucy today, sis? Please don't cut me."

Scornful, Ayden tried to wrestle free. Chet took hold of her other elbow. The pressure of his fingers was crushing. Forcing her ahead of him, he steered her further into the bar. Ayden was sputtering under her breath, struggling against Chet's grip, and kicking out at his heels. He wrapped his other arm tightly around her waist. After knocking into a few tables, he'd had enough of her antics. He released her and kicked an abandoned stool from the bar out into her path. She doubled over it with a grunt.

Growling, Ayden shoved the stool aside and flipped Chet the middle finger. He ignored her, grinning errantly as he searched for an empty table. Ayden jumped at the opportunity. She sidled over to the nearest eligible looking bachelor, grabbed the collar of his shirt, and wrenched his face toward hers.

"Hi, I'm Lucy. You are?"

Chet's head spun on his shoulders.

Ayden's admirer smiled slickly. He reached a hand out to rest his palm on her waist, gloating at his buddies. They were all drinking martinis. Chet rolled his eyes.

"Are you from around here?" the man asked.

She traced the rim of his martini glass. "I am."

"No, she isn't." Chet grabbed the front of Ayden's shirt. He ripped her clear of the ground, heaving her around and setting her down behind him, away from those high-class perverts.

"Careful, I'll cut you," Ayden told Chet.

Chet frowned down at her.

"Cut me," he said above the noise of the bar, "a deal. Truce?"

Ayden grabbed a full shot glass off a passing tray and tossed it at Chet's face. He gracefully dodged the flying ounce of liquid, stealing a shot for himself off the same tray before the cocktail waitress noticed.

"You've got it quite wrong," he told Ayden with a raise of his eyebrows that said, "See?" With a cock of his head, he drank the shot and produced the empty glass before Ayden's nose before slamming it down on the closest table. "Much more useful when ingested."

Ayden stared at Chet slit-eyed. "I thought you didn't drink?"

"You've reduced me to desperation."

Grasping her shoulder firmly, Chet dragged Ayden a few more feet and then plunked her down in a wobbly, wooden chair at an empty table near the karaoke stage. Someone was singing a very inebriated version of Margaritaville. Sitting across from her, Chet ran a hand down his hair and dared a conceited smile.

"Having fun yet?"

"I've learned to tolerate your company," Ayden quipped. "How hard can it be?"

"I know how hard it isn't," he mumbled.

"Oh, ouch!" She pretended to have a heart attack, groping her chest. "That one really hurt."

"Do you need me to make you feel better?" He slipped his fingers beneath the table to stroke her knee. "There's a bathroom just around the corner—"

"Sorry," Ayden sneered. "I choke on small bones."

Chet smiled slyly at her. She hadn't smacked his hand away.

Leaning forward so his elbows disappeared below the table, he let his hand skate up her thigh. Her cheeks darkened to a shade of dusted rose

"You're deliriously sensual when you're mad."

"I don't want to know what you find sensual," Ayden snapped, finally shoving his hand away. "It indicates you've had enough practice to know what you *don't* find sensual."

"And you don't?" he countered lazily.

"No."

"Mitchell?"

"Husband." Her expression held more contempt than he'd ever seen on her pretty face. She glanced at the bar. "The one and only."

"What about Craig?"

Ayden gritted her teeth as she replied, "Unlike *some people,* Craig wasn't into high-speed car chases and guns and sensuality. He was a proper gentleman. We didn't really get passed the classic, old-fashioned dating."

Chet allowed one of his eyebrows to arch. He sat back in his chair, linking his hands behind his head and muttering under his breath, "Point two for Chet."

"You're so infuriating!" Ayden squalled, but her shrillness was not heard above the clamor of the bar and karaoke singers.

"I offered to make it up to you," Chet grinned sideways as he kicked his chair back onto its hind legs. It gave her a teasing glimpse of his tongue ring.

Ayden crossed her arms over her chest and averted her gaze.

After a moment, Chet returned his chair to its natural position and asked, "What about me?"

A wave of hurt flared in her gaze before she squelched it.

"Our time together hardly qualifies as 'passed dating,'" she answered. "You've brought me into this catastrophe, with no way out. It's the single biggest mistake of my life."

He knew she was ticked off. Her feelings had been radically jarred. Her safety compromised. Her life in upheaval. *Good*, he thought to himself. His feelings were in disarray, too. It was about time she felt the weight of the situation the way he did. Her running to Craig was about the stupidest thing she could have ever done, and because of that they had a bigger mess on their hands.

Ayden was thinking back to several days before also. Her frown was downcast as she tried to force memories of being in Chet's arms from her mind. His lips, his body, his smell. Then, agony, tears, heartache. To think so much had transpired since then, she wasn't even sure it really happened. For a moment, the crowded room of social drunkards dissolved. The music diminished until numbness rang in her ears. She was back at the estate, on the ground. . . alone.

Chet was strumming his fingertips on the tabletop to the beat of the song being sung terribly on the karaoke stage. His thoughts had traveled a very similar course to Ayden's, though from his perspective things were much different. He remembered vividly the craze and panic he'd felt when he'd heard Craig's voice through his cell phone when he'd called her. If his Mustang hadn't been fine tuned for such hard driving, he probably would have rolled the vehicle well across the road with how sharply he'd cranked the wheel and started back down the street with a new destination in mind.

Ayden was alive—at least he knew that much—but for how much longer?

He'd never felt such crushing despair than when he'd

returned to the estate and found the house key. How could he have been so rash? She was gone. Captured.

Well, Ayden was the one who left. It was her fault she got lifted. Saucedo's men tailed Chet and found them at Craig's place.

Ayden was simmering as she watched Chet across the table, both because she was still upset about everything that had happened and because she wanted very badly to crawl in his lap and hug him. She wanted consolation. That's what she needed. Not a bar, not a drink, not even romance. Right now, she just wanted reassurance. In this establishment, there were too many masculine stares following her every move. She had no doubt each one of them would offer her some form of comfort. The comfort she was not going to get from the tattooed man across from her.

A smile lit Chet's face into a theif's expression as he leaned in and told her, "Every hound dog in this joint is sniffing around you."

"It takes one to know one," Ayden rebuffed.

The barb only invoked a roguish smile from him.

"You're in an awful mood," he jeered with a hint of a smirk. "For looking as good as you do."

"Really?" she murmured dryly. "I was feeling quite grand, actually."

"Don't call me Ashley."

Ayden kicked Chet beneath the table and he grimaced, laughing, "Don't be so pessimistic. Things could always be worse."

"Worse?" Ayden snorted. She looked away from him for fear that his smile was contagious, and stared hard at the casual drinkers amongst the bar. "What are you thinking, Chet? How should I be feeling right now?"

He let his eyes wander below her lips to her throat, to her bust, and back up to her face.

"You should be letting me make it up to you."

Ayden tried the best she could to stifle her smile, but Chet caught on and his grin broadened.

"Can't I just be mad for a minute?" she pouted.

"Sure," he shrugged.

Chet bent over the table, stealing one of Ayden's

hands and kissing her fingers. His lips did things to her head. Things she didn't trust. He was trying to manipulate her.

"I wish you'd leave me alone," she lied.

"Nah," Chet sighed. "You're just grumpy because you love me."

"I don't love you," she lied a second time. "I hate you."

"Hate is a strong emotion." He pointed a slender, skillful finger at her nose. "That's where it betrays you. Hate is still a sentiment. You wouldn't hate me if you didn't care at all."

Ayden rolled her eyes and grinned. Chet scooted his chair around the table so that he was sitting closer to her side. His eyes darkened to azure tones of the undiscovered ocean. He was serious now. Bending forward, he brushed his nose along her ear.

"How many times do I have to tell you?" he purred softly. "I love you. *You*, Ayden. You know I do. And you know you can't resist me."

A flush sent sparks through her core.

"This isn't a joke, Chet," she replied. "You said you love someone else. You love me, but you love Keeley."

He sat back and exhaled, resigned. "I don't want to talk about that right now."

"I don't want to talk about it ever," Ayden growled. "You think I want to hear the man I love say he loves another woman?"

"So you do love me. I knew it."

"Shut up." She flagged down a passing cocktail waitress. "Can I get a water?"

Ayden turned back to Chet who still had that exasperating sideways smirk on his face. He *had* to be handsome and dashing and ridiculously sexy. Even during the most perilous times he could make her laugh. Her heart was on fire, her face flamed with the aching flow of her blood. If she didn't get water soon, anything to quench the boiling emotions within her, she thought she might disintegrate to ash.

"You can't love two people at once," Ayden disputed, not meeting Chet's unblinking gaze.

"You are very wrong," he countered.

"Well, I certainly don't believe it. I don't believe in love triangles. If you loved the first, you wouldn't have fallen in love

174

with the second."

"Ah," Chet said lifting a finger. "Who said I was in love with two women? This isn't a love triangle—"

"But—"

"But nothing," he interjected. "You assumed. Just because I love two women doesn't mean I'm *in love* with two women."

Ayden skewered him with a glower. "That doesn't make any sense."

"That's the thing about hearts," Chet replied.

The waitress returned with Ayden's water, flashing Chet a flirtatious smile, before returning to the bar. Chet watched the girl leave and then spun back to Ayden with an expression that read, "So?"

"So, what are you saying?" Ayden asked, closing her eyes to try and think straight. The madness of the bar and horrid singing was mindboggling.

"I'm saying I am in love with you," Chet repeated, leaning in close to her again. He whispered quietly into her ear, "You are the only one I want to be with."

"I don't know if I can handle knowing you love another woman," Ayden sat back, lifting a hand to keep Chet from coming any closer. His minty breath was intoxicating, his lips against her cheek tantalizing. She forced herself not to kiss him. "I don't want you to *like* another woman. I don't want you to *love* another woman. I don't want you to *feel* for another woman. I don't like it."

"You don't have to," Chet stated. His brushed his lips along her jaw. "You should trust me more often." He kissed the skin by her chin. "You're the only one for me, toots. You have my heart. And I have yours."

"I don't know if I can trust you," Ayden replied.

He pulled back to look her deep in the eye. "You already do." And he kissed her lips once, quick and hard. Standing abruptly, he winked down at her. "Now, let me prove it to you."

23

Ayden hardly heard him. She was soaring, daydreaming, blissfully imagining his mouth still touched hers.

Coming back to her senses, Ayden lifted a finger to her lips where the sparkling kiss was still in effect. How she loved the feel of Chet's kisses. Why did they feel so right? How come she felt such peace with Chet, such calm and solace, at the same time feeling such fear and mania? Their lives together were so hectic. Just because she'd survived thus far didn't mean she would again.

Chet had moved over to the karaoke DJ and was speaking to him, as Ayden let her thoughts drift away once more to the moment he'd rescued her from all of life's threats. The waitress brought a basket of fries Chet had apparently ordered, and Ayden munched on them mechanically. Even after Chet retook his seat, they sat in silence. Ayden ate every last fry, licking the salt of her fingers. She sat across the table from Chet for twenty minutes, not paying attention to the crowded bar, but not necessarily paying attention to him either. There was too much on her mind.

She finished her water and was now just probing the ice cubes with her straw. Every so often, she would glimpse up at the blue eyes staring back at her. Chet was considering something, she deduced. His eyebrows were drawn together. His black hair was a little too long for a fauxhawk, but it was styled up regardless. His black shirt hugged his torso. There had to be a law somewhere that stated men couldn't look so good all the time.

Meanwhile, Chet was musing about her. There was only one way to do this, really. One way to convince Ayden he meant all the things he said. He wasn't a liar. And he did want to tell her everything. But she wasn't the only one hurting. She'd hurt him. By running to Craig, not waiting for him to come back to the estate and make sure she was safe, letting him worry like a panicked wreck well into the night because she wouldn't answer her phone.

How could Chet tell her the secret parts of his soul now? He wasn't even sure *he* could trust *her*.

His mind drited to Nolan. The man would recover. It filled Chet with inexplicable gratitude. He'd promised Nolan that he and Ayden wouldn't drag any drama from town into the cabin, but

Nolan's drama followed Chet all over the city. Haunted him. Chet was used to loss. He'd lost Nolan once, but it was easier when Chet was a kid and could blame himself for Nolan leaving. Chet couldn't fathom losing Nolan to an overdose.

One thing Chet was thankful for was the phone call he'd shared with Nogo Saucedo. The man might be the leader over the organization Chet worked for, but his boss still held some sentimentality toward Chet. That would bode well for Chet. He knew Saucedo didn't want to let him go, for more reasons than just the criminal "code of conduct". *You don't get out.* Saucedo wanted Chet around because he thought of Chet as a son. And that was the only reason Chet was still alive.

As Chet monitored Ayden, certain her temper was mellowing but not quite sure she wouldn't hiss and claw at his face like a feral cat if he moved to touch her, he thought back on the conversation with his boss. Chet had told Saucedo that Ayden would *never* be part of this business, and that Chet would go to any length to make sure anything that could put Ayden in danger never happened. In fact, the last six months Chet had spent doing more of Saucedo's ruthless deeds just in hopes that he could gain a favor. Chet wanted to use that favor to pardon himself of the business in case the meeting with Louie went awry.

Nogo Saucedo had been receptive to almost all of Chet's persuasions, until the part came where "she knows too much". Saucedo wouldn't let Ayden out into the world after being inside of the Saucedo's mafia web. The conversation was left to be dealt with later as Chet took over the current deal.

Chet was putting it all together now. Rocco, the one man who had always been jealous of Chet and Chet's relativity with their boss, framed Chet and made it look like he'd stolen the shipment that belonged to Saucedo, as if Chet planned to sell the drugs and keep the money for himself. This was punishable by death—if you were lucky—and brutal torture for you, your family, and your family's family, by Nogo Saucedo's assassins if you weren't. Chet wasn't about to find out which would ensue from his father figure. He also knew envy and greed drove a man to insanity.

Rocco had wanted Chet's position and credence in the organization for years. If Rocco took care of Ayden and Chet behind

Nogo Saucedo's back, Rocco would move up to be the boss's right hand man. It meant more money. More trust. More power.

Chet knew his boss was going to give him the chance to set straight what had gone wrong at the deal. Deep down, Nogo Saucedo trusted Chet enough to give him one opportunity to seek out the missing shipment. And Chet most definitely wanted to see for himself that the men who set him up paid dearly. After that, he and Ayden would vanish. He'd done crazy things.

He was doing crazier things for love.

24

The bar was obnoxious and loud, even for him. His thoughts were jumbled, his body fatigued, and his mind over-worked. Sitting mere inches from Ayden, Chet could see the tired-ness in her eyes. He thought she was probably annoyed that he'd brought her here, but it was a safe place, and he personally wanted to unwind. They could both relax in this environment…sort of. Chet basically ran Fresno, and none of Saucedo's men stepped foot in a country bar.

Mostly, Chet wanted to forget about the hours Ayden spent captured, everything that Rocco and Armando had done to her, and everything she was going to have to do. He wanted to see her smile.

"Hey," Chet said, seemingly breaking out of his own thoughts as well as lulling Ayden away from hers.

She looked up at him.

"Do you hear the song this guy is singing?" he asked with a tilt of his chin toward the stage.

Ayden looked down a moment, concentrating on the words.

'And I know what it means. To walk along the lonely street of dreams. Here I go again on my own…'

"Whitesnake," Ayden nodded.

Chet let a pleased grin split his face. "I think this song is about you and me."

She rolled her eyes and let out a sad laugh. "No joke. It's probably more about you, though."

"Probably," he agreed. Ayden's eyes flitted to his. Drawing attention to his mouth, he sang the lyrics boastfully, "'Goin' down the only road I've ever known. Like a drifter I was born to walk alone.'"

Ayden enjoyed the sound of his voice. If she was already blushing, she was in for a real show. He'd never had an ounce of shame when it came to singing. And the bigger the audience, the more fun it would be.

"You weren't born to walk alone," Ayden muttered.

Chet put a hand on hers. His fingers were lukewarm and soft, the creamy complexion of his forearms slightly tanned from his exercise at the cabin chopping wood.

"Who was I born to walk with?" he asked.

She didn't look up right away but shrugged.

"Ayden, Ayden, Ayden," he sighed and she slanted a gaze at him.

Just then, the guy she'd hit on earlier came sauntering over to their table.

"Lucy!" he called, waving his martini. His speech was induced with a slur as he clobbered over to her side. "Hey, Lucy."

Ayden blinked up at the sloshed, excuse of a man. "Give it a rest," she stated. "I'm not going home with you."

The man had the nerve to look affronted, though his eyes didn't open more than halfway. His gaze swayed over to Chet's prideful smirk and his upper lip curled. "This trash gonna take you home instead?" he garbled, nearly spilling his drink down the front of his shirt.

Chet was on his feet before Ayden could say, "Stop!" She grabbed hold of Chet's wrist, the right one inked with delicate tattoos, as his fingers balled into a tight fist. "Let it go, Chet," she said under her breath.

The guy who kept referring Ayden as Lucy gave Chet a mocking sneer. "Low life," he spit.

Chet twitched again, raising his other fist as the man flinched. The guy spilled half his drink and skittered away.

"And I'm the low life," Chet grumbled.

Ayden was still holding Chet's arm when he eventually turned back to her. They'd caught the attention of a few observers, but most of the bar was much too busy to care. After the bystanders went back to their carefree socializing, Ayden fluttered her eyelashes at Chet.

"It's your fault, really," she said.

Chet shook out the front of his shirt and gave his hair a toss.

"My fault?" he replied disgruntled.

He was scarcely heated. Martini Guy couldn't ruffle Chet if

all of Saucedo's men couldn't. Chet was merely entertaining himself.

"Yes," she replied, pulling him to his chair.

They both sat down, opposite one another. Chet glared a moment over her head and then looked back to her face.

"How is it my fault? Or is it always my fault?"

She grinned sideways. "You're the one who told everyone I was schizophrenic."

"I suppose I'm the one who hit on Scumbag Joe also?" Chet refuted.

"You might have influenced me."

He reached over to her and yanked her off the chair, sitting her in his lap. "There. I don't think I'll have any more problems tonight with men trying to hit on what is mine."

"Yours?" Ayden let the shock show on her face. "I'm yours, am I?"

Chet watched her for several long seconds before answering, "You were born to walk with me."

Ayden's heart did a little jump. She loved when he said things like that. Sweet nothings that came out of nowhere. It was stupid how hung up she was on him.

"Is this your metaphysical gesture of romance?"

"Si, mi amore. I suspect," Chet murmured into her ear while wrapping his arms tightly around her waist, "I've begun a descent into romanticism. What a change you've enthused in me."

Ayden thought immediately of Starla. The stripper that looked Ayden in the eye and said, "You must be the change in him." She turned around to face him nose-to-nose.

"You're a certified nuisance," she muttered.

Chet squeezed her tighter to him. He barely resisted kissing her senseless. Only their surroundings and the possibility of getting kicked out due to public impropriety kept him seated in his chair.

Taking a pleasurable moment for himself, Chet stared into Ayden's hazel eyes as if they were back in time, in the estate, far from danger. He could read her and her fears about intimacy easily. Her ex-husband had used physical affection as a weapon. If nothing else became of their relationship, Chet hoped Ayden would know how much their intimate moments really meant to him. That he treasured them above riches. Never again did he want to share such a closeness with another woman.

There was a softness, a gentleness, and a hesitancy to Ayden's touch that bound him to her. He could be so aggressive with desire, but she made him delicate. Sharing his love for her, spending his love on her, it was the only thing left in the world for him to do. He had given up everything, his life, his addictions, his business, and the men he'd called "family", all so he could be the man Ayden needed him to be.

His angel was snuggled in his lap, one arm draped leisurely around his shoulder, and the other hand tracing the lines of his tattoos. He knew she cared. He knew she loved him. They'd damaged each other, but there was hope for a future.

Was there not?

Chet's thoughts drifted involuntarily to Brandylynn, the girl that was his first real, romantic relationship, and whom he thought was the only woman he could ever love. Looking deep into Ayden's eyes, Chet knew he never loved Brandylynn. As a teenager, all he knew of love was addiction and dependency. He loved his drugs. Brandylynn had been a part of his world, a bigger part of his downfall. She'd gotten into the hard stuff long before he had, and when he'd begged Brandylynn to stop—for her sake and the sake of their future—he fell apart watching her reject his pleas. She destroyed her life, and relatively anyone else's around her, tearing Chet's heart right out of his chest in the process.

That was practically ten years ago. It still stung, thinking about her big betrayal and all the decisions that could have changed the path their lives took. Chet'd had a chance—he and Brandylynn—to flee and escape it all, before it was too late, before Chet was too deep, before men from the organization would come after them for abandoning the family business.

They didn't run. Brandylynn was dead to him. And Chet was sucked into a world that robbed him of his soul.

Chet prayed with all his might that Ayden saw a soul in him. He hoped he wasn't too far gone, that with her belief of forgiveness and religion he could seek some form of redemption. There may or may not be a God, but Chet would do whatever it took to prove to Ayden he was a changed man. He'd done the unthinkable weaning himself off the drugs that had consumed him for many years. Never before had he been able to do it, not even the three times he'd be forced into rehab. Then, he'd just stopped. He'd quit. No more would he commit the terrible crimes he did to satisfy his deplorable addiction.

There was nothing like Ayden Harper. Nothing like the girl who walked straight up to him in the dairy aisle and spoke of yogurt when she was merely a young teen. Chet had been a kid—it was so long ago he could hardly remember anything besides her face, her smile, the glow that surrounded her, and her hair bouncing as she skipped away and out of his life. Well, he hadn't let her get far. He'd been stalking her from a distance up until their encounter in Vegas.

Thinking of Ayden at the craps table brought a wry grin to Chet's face. Ayden quirked an eyebrow in response, shifting her weight in his lap. When he told her what he was reminiscing about, her cheeks colored. She hadn't expected anyone to come up behind her that way, let alone the boy she'd met at the beach seven years earlier. His heart had been pounding so hard in his chest he was sure she would see it vibrating through his shirt. His confidence came from the fact that he hadn't been using.

He was clean—as clean as he could get.

Eagerness stirred inside of Chet, and though he didn't want to cause Ayden any more grief, any more pain than she'd already endured, he decided the time was nearing when he would tell her everything. He loved her, unbearably, and with every bone in his body. If he expected her to trust him, and he wanted to trust her in return, there could not be secrets between them. It was time he shared his whole story with her.

It made Chet nervous. He felt anxious all of the sudden, and the only way to assuage his nerves was to pull Ayden tighter and bury his face in her neck. When she let him, not expressing any contempt or resistance, he felt the weight of his stress lighten. They were going to be okay. There was a way out of their dilemma. Tomorrow would come soon enough, then it would be over. They could leave town. They could make it. They would survive.

We're survivors, you and me. People like us survive.

"Mi ami?" Ayden whispered against Chet's shoulder.

It caught him unaware, and the tender words he held so close to his heart—literally—nearly ruined him. He let Ayden bring her face before his. He rested his forehead against hers, regarding her demurely as she said it again.

"Mi ami?"

Chet couldn't contain his relieved smile. "You know I do," he murmured, tracing her upper lip with a finger.

She took hold of his wrist, letting her gaze fall, before dragging it back up. "Tell me you love only me," she cooed.

His stomach clenched uncomfortably. It would be a lie to say he loved only her. But it wasn't a lie to tell her, "You are the love of my life, Ayden. I want only you."

She let out a short, curt breath, dropping her hands to her lap.

"Stop this," Chet snapped. Taking the side of her cheek in his hand, he lifted her face to his. "Don't start with that, okay? What more do you want me to say? I need you! I love *you*. I am *in love* with you only. We can be together. This is what I want." He ran a hand down her thigh and back up, giving her a squeeze to reinforce his vehemence. "I want this, right here. Forever."

Ayden's despair diminished slightly. They both repeated that word internally. Forever.

"Ayden, look at me," he demanded quietly.

She didn't, and instead picked at her nails.

"Do you trust me?" he asked.

Ayden gave a half-hearted shrug. Yes? No? As far as she could throw him? With her life?

"I think you do," Chet continued. He took both of her hands in his as if comparing their sizes. "You can trust me. I would never tell you something I thought you wanted to hear. When I say something, I mean it. Ask me anything, and you'll get an honest response that you'll absolutely hate. I know there are still a few hidden chambers left unexplored between us, but I mean to tell you everything—I really do—when we can find the right time. But first, I need to know that I can trust you, too."

Ayden's eyes flicked up to his. She didn't so much look upset as puzzled.

"Can I trust you?" Chet questioned.

She blinked a few times and her gaze strayed down to his lips. "I…I'm so scared, Chet. My fear overrules my entire source of rationality. I will be careless and foolish just to protect my heart. But I never…want to hurt…you." She met his eyes again with her own, looking frighteningly frail. "I've never been more afraid yet more starving for something at the same time."

Chet mirrored her wan smile. "Toots, I couldn't have said it better myself."

Ayden wasn't given the moment for a reply. The DJ got on the mic and called Chet to the stage. Chet wanted to kiss her, but instead slipped her off his lap and stood. She looked like she was about to say something, but it would have to wait. Now that he knew she would at least hear him out, he felt more confident about the situation. Indeed, things would work out between them. He'd strived too hard to give up and walk away. He didn't want to walk anywhere unless Ayden was walking with him.

Like a drifter I was born to walk alone.

Not anymore, Chet thought with a grin.

No matter how long it took, or how far he had to go, he'd find a way for he and Ayden to be together.

He shuffled her out of his arms and back into her own chair, and then he strolled up to the stage. With a final glance over his shoulder, he winked at her. This was going to be good. If she doubted his motives, doubted his words, his love, his trust, this would surely change her mind.

As the spotlight shone on Chet, he squinted out into the bar. It was a lively crowd this evening.

25

Chet looked as comfortable as ever. Calm, collected, poised. Delicious. Ayden was mentally preparing herself for some rendition of Elvis. A romantic, apologetic lullaby. Something to try and convince her not to be so concerned about everything. She pictured him singing Hound Dog the day he'd driven her to the beach. He sang well to The King. But the TV screen lit up, displaying the karaoke brand logo along with the title How About That in the style of Bad Company.

"Oh, great," Ayden mumbled.

Chet was taking his position behind the microphone, with one hand on the mic itself and the other on the microphone stand. His legs were spread just further than shoulder width apart, in an effortlessly seductive stance. He cleared his throat. Just standing there, he already looked like a rock God. Women hushed their tittering. It just wasn't fair. Every female in the room was drooling. Somewhere in the crowd, a woman whistled.

Then, the first strum of the electric guitar rang throughout the bar. The hi hat started ticking to the four count beat. Lyrics appeared on the TV screen, and everyone around the room quieted in anticipation. Who was this new guy, they wondered, and what sort of competition was he going to bring to the drunken karaoke contenders?

The guitar struck a few more chords for the intro.

Some of the locals were murmuring to one another how Chet was probably going to suck. Martini Guy and his nine-to-five buddies looked like they wanted to toss peanut shells. Ayden herself feared for Chet, having only ever heard him sing along in the privacy of his car. She'd enjoyed the sound of his voice, thinking it had a nice, raspy, baritone quality. He'd once quoted Aerosmith, which told her he was familiar with the whole eighties rock era. Clearly, with his choice of Bad Company, he was a fan of classic rock. The problem Ayden saw, was most of the singers throughout the eighties had fabulous anthem voices. Nearly impossible vocal ranges.

But then the first line of the song began to light up. And Chet started to sing.

"'Last night, when the moon was new, I couldn't sleep. I was thinkin' of you. And how much I need ya...How about that. '"

The entire bar erupted into applause. Ayden's jaw dropped almost to the table, and she looked around at the faces of men and women. The men were watching the women, who were gaping at Chet with wistful looks in their eyes. Ayden forced her jaw shut, turning her attention back to Chet, who had a face-splitting grin on his face as if he too just discovered he had Freddie's vocal skills. Although, it wouldn't have mattered if he sounded like a blow horn. Chet would sing to Ayden regardless.

Chet and his extremes.

He swaggered back into nonchalance, beginning on the second line of the song.

"'I act like I'm tougher than steal'"—He glanced away from the television display and directly at Ayden—*"'With a heart like a stone. But you know it ain't real. I need you, baby. How 'bout that. Hey!'"*

He grabbed the mic stand, dragging it with him as he started across the stage. The background vocalists on the track were singing, *"'OooOooOoo,'"* to which Chet finished, *"'How 'bout that?'"*

By now, he was off the stage, out of the illuminating spotlight, and pacing through the tables. Several women who'd been sitting at the bar hopped off their stools to dance and clap their hands.

"'I used to spend my life on the town,'" Chet sang to them. *"'It took your lovin' to turn me around. I'm crazy about you. How about that.'"*

Slipping the mic out of the stand so that he could wind through the chairs, Chet left the stand by the guffawing group of girls and continued on like he owned the place. Ayden was stunned speechless by how good he sounded, like a mixture of Brett Michaels and Steven Tyler. He wasn't great, but he wasn't crappy. He was perfect. He looked even better, resembling a black-haired David Bowie. The way Chet would sing and stick out his tongue, swivel his shoulders and hips, he looked like a cross between Gene Simmons and Axel Rose, and also like he'd never swiveled his hips in his whole existence. He had the time of his life figuring it out.

Chet grabbed a chair and whirled it around, straddling it while resting his elbows along the back. He was right beside Ayden, singing into her ear, as the other women looked on with envy.

"*'People used to tell ya, I'm a crazy fool, but you taught me more than I could learn in school. I say, I really need ya, baby. How 'bout that.'*"

Ayden felt her own mouth water at the sight of him, now standing up directly in front of her. She blushed as Chet kicked the chair aside and skirted around the table. Holding the microphone with one hand, he clasped the cord in his other. She peeked over her shoulder at him. Bending at the waist, he leaned forward and sang low and huskily into her ear.

"*'If ever you need time and space'*"—he twirled a long, index finger around in the air and then tousled a lock of her hair— "*'Don't run away, just tell me face to face. Yeah.'*" He straightened a bit, striding toward the stage until he stood under the spotlight. The chorus of the song began, with the background vocalists once again singing, "*'OooOooOoo'*" and Chet bellowed, "*'How about that!'*"

The crowded bar reciprocated by singing along to the lyrics, "*'How bout that. OooOooOoo.'*"

Chet completed the line, "*'How about that.'*" He tilted his head back, marching in place as he mimicked Brian Howe effortlessly, "*'Yeah. Alright. Oh, Baby.'*"

Ayden's face was hot. Yes, Chet looked too grand for words to describe. Yes, he could sing, and that made her melt like soft caramel. Yes, he was serenading only her. And yes, it was better than any movie she could've possibly compared it to.

The guitar solo kicked off. For several measures, Chet didn't have to sing. He moved stealthily through the congregation, passed the oogling blondes. One of them clawed at his shirt. He positioned his hands as if he were holding a guitar, strumming the air, making the female fans go wild. His black hair bounced. The girlish screaming was deafening. Then, he tossed the mic way up into the air, catching the cord when there was about five feet of slack. Spinning the mic in the air above his head like a lasso, he nearly whacked a couple of guys. Ayden giggled as Chet released the cord and caught the mic again. Everyone applauded.

Chet stepped back toward where Ayden sat at her chair and stopped at her feet. He squatted down, thrusting Ayden's knees apart while he inched his way between them. The mic was pressed against his lips, while his free hand slid up her knee. He had an arrogant smirk on his face, holding her gaze with his magnetic eyes. As the guitar solo neared it's end, he didn't even have to look at the lyrics displayed on the TV.

" *'When I think back of how it used to be, before we met it's just a mystery.'*" Ayden grinned despite her best efforts. Chet was a natural born aphrodisiac. And he continued, " *'I can't live without you, no. How about that?'*"

He spun away again, turning his charms on the group of bedazzled blondes.

" *'And you've got my heart, and you've got my soul!'*"

One of the blonde girls groped at Chet's black T. Her fingers slid beneath the v-neck, caressing the velvety skin Ayden loved so much. And he let the girl for a few jealous moments on Ayden's behalf, until she was ready to stand up and scream, "He's mine!"

But then Chet gracefully stepped aside, moving further into the bar as he sang. Once again, he flashed Ayden a roguish smile that made her heart stop. " *'Ooh you got my whole life under control. Looks like we made it. How about that.'*"

He leapt up onto a vacated chair, perching himself for everyone to see. His heel tapped to the rhythm. He really had no shame, no qualms whatsoever. He wasn't an erotic dancer, but neither was he tone-deaf and drunk. It was beautiful. Rocking to the music, he pointed a finger across the bar at Ayden.

" *'Every time I see your face, it lightens up the whole damn place. Yeah, I wanna see this whole thing through. Yeah, there's nothing I won't do for you. Oh, yeah.'*"

The audience chanted the chorus, " *'OooOooOoo.'*"

" *'How about that,'*" Chet sang, hopping off the chair. His eyes never left Ayden's face. " *'How 'bout it, baby.'*"

" *'OooOooOoo.'*"

His smile broadened, " *'How 'bout that.'*"

Chet danced his way back to Ayden, placing one hand down on the table, looming over her with the mic held up to his lips. She smirked with delight, staring hypnotically at the tiny, silver piercing. It was working, whatever spell he'd cast.

The music quieted, and he sang eloquently.

"*'Last night, when the moon was new, I couldn't sleep. I was there—'*" Ayden had had just about enough of his enchantment—"*'looking at you.'*"

She stole the mic out of Chet's hands, halting his charade. Holding it up to her own lips, she finished the line, "*'Yeah, I'm glad that I found you.'*" She stood up and marched toward the stage, batting her eyelashes while stating into the mic pretentiously, "How about that?!"

She was familiar with Bad Company.

The entire bar roared with enthusiasm. Chet's stare was fastened to Ayden. He watched her hungrily, his tongue pressed against the inside of his cheek, as she continued singing the bridge, "*'Every time I see your face, it lightens up the whole dang place. Yeah, I wanna see this whole thing through.'*"

Chet stood tantalizingly slow, but in two long strides he was next to Ayden. He wrapped his fingers around hers holding the mic and leaned in so that they were sharing it. And they sang together, "*'I wanna spend my life with you. Oh, yeah.'*"

The crowded room cheered and chanted, "*'OooOooOoo.'*"

"*'How about that,'*" Ayden sang.

Chet reached out and seized her waist, yanking her against him. Bending his knees, he pressed his nose into her cheek and groaned into the mic, "*'How 'bout it, baby.'*"

"*'OooOooOoo.'*"

Ayden giggled, singing into the mic while throwing Chet's wandering hand aside, "*'How about that!'*"

The audience continued with a chorus of, "*'OooOooOoo.'*"

Chet wrenched the microphone from Ayden's lips to his, belting out, "*'How 'bout that!'*"

"*'OooOooOoo.'*"

"*'Tell me,* baby'" he sang.

Ayden smiled as Chet slithered a hand up her back, into her hair. They finished the rest of the song in unison, "*'Tell me.*

OooOooOoo. How about that. How 'bout it, baby. How about that. How about it, baby. Yeah, how about that."'

The music died down, and the people of the bar whistled and hollered their appreciation. The song ended. Chet and Ayden didn't. Ayden was breathing heavily, her lungs aching from singing her heart out. Chet gazd at her with a blue-flame stare. He was still holding her, splaying his hand against her lower back so that her hips were forced up on his. They were smiling at each other like they were the only two people in the room. None of it was for show.

At the same time Ayden released the microphone, Chet pulled it aside and kissed her. Ayden pushed against him, embarrassed at first, and then liquified into his chest and forgot who she was for a moment. After a second, Chet pulled back and nipped at her cheek. She grinned. The DJ came through the speakers, announcing the next singer.

Chet slipped the mic back into the mic stand, keeping an arm locked around Ayden's waste, and then led her off the stage. The bar mob parted, and Chet pulled Ayden through the chairs, passed the swooning blondes who glared at her through their resentment, toward a back hallway.

"Where are we going?" Ayden laughed.

Another song started playing, someone else took the stage and dragged the attention off them. The second they were out of sight in the hall, Chet pushed Ayden up against the wall and sunk his lips into her neck.

"Chet—"

"Let's go into the bathroom," he murmured.

She smiled at the ludicrousness. "No."

"Let's go home," he rasped, moving his lips to her collar bone.

"Okay." Ayden couldn't form more words than that. She was halfway laughing. The other half of her had missed the physical contact with Chet. After all they'd been through, it felt well-deserved to share some affection. They could go no further, however.

Chet took Ayden's face in his hands, holding her steady as he kissed her lips once, twice, and then a third time that Ayden was sure would last the entire evening. Her hands gripped the neckline of his shirt, stretching it out as he pinned her to the wall.

"Let's go into the bathroom," he begged a second time.

"No," Ayden chuckled.

"Why not?"

Her mirthful smile made his heart swell. Even her cherry brown eyes gleamed at him the way they had at Pismo Beach. With one hand, he gripped her jaw. Ayden captured his wrist with both her hands.

"Chet!"

"Yes, toots?"

"Let's go home."

He pushed off of her. "Fine."

Stealing her hand and interlacing his fingers with hers, he blew through the crowded bar, and in a manner of seconds they were in the parking lot. Ayden struggled to keep up with Chet's lengthy stride, skipping to match his swift pace. He kept glimpsing down at her out of the corner of his eye, his lips stretching into a breathtaking smile. She smiled back, bounding through the dark next to her knight in black armor. Passing a few cars, Ayden felt his grip on her hand tighten. They were nearing the Mustang. When they reached the car, Chet threw her up against the driver's side door.

He kissed her. And kissed her. And kissed her.

Ayden wove her fingers into Chet's hair.

"Are we going home?" she wheezed.

"Un-uh," Chet grunted, trying to catch his breath.

"I thought we were going home."

"You'll be lucky if I make it inside the car," he declared coarsely.

Ayden gave him a playful shove. "You know that's not happening."

He gave a wolfish grin and asked innocently, "You don't wanna makeout in the backseat of my car?"

She wagged a finger at him. "I don't think you want to makeout in the backseat of your car, either."

Chet dug for his car keys. "I would, if you would."

Her head angled crookedly. "Mmhm. We're going straight home, Chet. To the cabin!"

"To the cabin," he grumbled under his breath. He gave her a wry glance. "How 'bout that?"

Ayden skirted around the hood and let herself in the passenger's side. Chet took a little longer situating himself into the driver's seat. He shut his car door and put the keys in the ignition.

"Just once more kiss?" he plead.

Ayden gave a shake of her head, but obliged. She leaned across the stick shift, resting her hand on it for support. As her lips met Chet's, he grabbed her and started to pull. Her elbow hit the steering wheel, and the horn sounded with a loud blurt of noise.

Chet laughed out loud, and then she did, too.

"Point taken," he mumbled, letting Ayden return to her side of the car.

He turned the key, and the car roared to life. Ayden felt like nothing was roaring as fiercely as her heart. How she loved this man. How hard it was to have to wait. *Wait for what?* she then asked herself. Would there ever be more? Did Chet know she reserved herself for marriage? Did she dare even dream about that with him? It wasn't something people who were members of her faith did often, marry outside their faith, let alone to...to...guys like Chet.

They started down the road. Ayden felt a smirk tug at her lips. She watched Chet's profile.

"I'm sorry I couldn't fool around in the back seat of your car."

He grinned at the street. "Another time. There's a first for everything."

"You mean you haven't fooled around in the back of your car before?"

His tongue wet his lower lip. "No, I have not. Why, have you?"

His teasing eyes darted to hers.

"Fooled around in the back of your car?" she asked. His mockingly stern warning made her smile grow. He deserved it. "Of course not, Chet."

He shifted gears, his errant smile an absolute dream. "Let's go home."

"Home," Ayden sighed thoughtfully. She reached over and

laced her fingers with his. "I am home."

Chet looked down at her. "I'd do anything for you."

Ayden felt time slow and then stop completely. It would be a miracle to wish for this forever, to have this love between them without a hint of danger. Miracles happened. She would've stayed in the warmth his gaze forever, and he would have held her there just as long, but he directed his focus to the freeway entrance.

"Can we stop at the estate?" he asked. It pleased her that he requested her permission. "I have a few more things to grab."

"Sure," she yawned. Resting her head back, she closed her eyes. "Whatever. Whenever. Wherever."

The night was quiet, the streets empty and clear of traffic. Ayden didn't realize she'd fallen asleep until Chet woke her with a soft kiss on her lips. Her eyes fluttered open groggily, and she peered out the windshield. They were not surrounded by trees and darkness so all-consuming. The car was parked in the circular driveway of the estate. Chet's inherited home. The porch light illuminated the front door, but everywhere else the yard was unlit. This was where he'd left her. Unwanted feelings began surfacing.

Ayden wanted to go back to sleep, and she really wasn't fond of this place anymore, but Chet nudged her cheek with his nose, telling her to wake up.

"Why?" she moaned.

"Come on," he demanded. He got out of the car and moved to the passenger's side. "You can sleep in the bed for a bit while I gather some stuff."

He carried her out of the car, kicking the door shut with his heel, and then walked up to the front of the house. She was dozing off again on his shoulder, and he wrestled with his key ring to get the house key separated. Finally, the door was unlocked. He stepped over the threshold, cradling her and kissing her forehead. His throat hummed a tune, his lips parting as he whispered into the dark house.

"How 'bout it, baby."

26

Chet navigated the halls by memory, pacing through the shadows of the house until he reached the bedroom. Only then did he flick on the lamp. A pale, yellow light strengthened across the walls, revealing the furniture. The bed. The dresser. The bathroom door. Ayden sighed as he laid her down on the bedspread.

"Don't leave."

"I'm not," he answered.

She turned her face into the pillow and yawned. He pulled a blanket up to her shoulders and patted her hair.

"I'll be right back."

Chet circled the perimeter of the house externally, searched the rooms internally, and scoured the garage. The kitchen was dark, but he stepped around the center island and checked the hidden compartment below the sink for the loaded magazines he had stashed there. He grabbed a bottle of water from the refrigerator and padded back down the hall when he suddenly froze. The air conditioning kicked on.

Chet spun slowly, careful not to make a sound. The estate was so large, the house so enormous, any noise echoed throughout the vast interior. He listened keenly, even as the AC system thrummed overhead. There was a thermostat down the hall, by the master bedroom door. He knew Ayden would never have turned cool air on. In fact, no intruder would. Why would they? Someone had been in his house. Who?

Treading lightly, Chet crept to the first room on the left, darting inside. Dashing around the bed, he opened the top dresser drawer, wincing at the slight creak of wood. Reaching into the very back, he retrieved a hidden knife. It was small and practically useless, but it would have to suffice until he could reach another firearm. Besides his collection in the master closet, there were several located around the house. Unfortunately, his main worry was sleeping peacefully unaware of any hazards.

Moving stealthily back into the hallway, Chet glanced right and left. Seeing no one, and nothing incriminating, he stepped toward the master bedroom. A few feet. That's all he had left to travel. Adjusting the knife in his hands, he licked his lips. He paused just outside the doorway, sucked in a long breath, and blew it out as he peered into the room. The lamp light still shone around the room, lengthening tall shadows in all the corners. The bed was empty.

Chet bent his knees. His eyes swept to the back windows that ran almost the entire length of the wall. He couldn't see anything beyond the glass, but at least it wasn't broken. Taking a few steps into the room, he flattened his back against the wall and sidled closer to the bathroom. The door was ajar, but no light was on. His fingers twitched around the knife in his grasp. He closed his eyes for only a moment, and then burst into the bathroom.

Two silhouettes stood on the far side of the room, near the bathtub, one significantly taller than the other. Chet was prepared to lunge, his arm outstretched, the blade pointing at the two figures. The air conditioning clicked off, and in the silence he could hear Ayden's muffled breathing.

Ayden.

Her mouth was covered. She was stiff, which meant her captor likely had a gun shoved into her back. Chet analyzed it all within seconds.

"Stay where you are," a male spoke.

Chet recognized Rocco's voice.

"Leave her out of this," Chet demanded.

He teetered onto his tip-toes, clenching the knife tighter. Ayden gave a violent wriggle, to which her adversary struggled. It was too dark to see either of their faces clearly, but as Chet's eyes adjusted with the tiny stream of lamplight entering from the bedroom, he saw a better glimpse of Rocco.

"Drop your weapon," the man ordered. "Back away with your hands above your head."

Chet did neither.

"I hear you've got a big deal going down with Louie," Rocco hissed. "Seems like Nogo Saucedo isn't going to get his money back from you. You're no good for this buisness, Chet. Not when you're hung up on your muchachas."

Ayden gave a little whimper. Chet knew he could throw his knife with perfect aim at Rocco's face.

"You think you know everything, Chet. But what you don't

know is Nogo Saucedo is going down."

Chet was hyper-analyzing. "You think you're going to be the one to do it?"

Rocco gave a silent laugh. "Not me. Not you."

Rocco wouldn't have turned on the AC either.

"We're taking down Louie to get back Saucedo's shipment," Chet stated.

Rocco shook his head. "Louie? Nobody cares about Louie, Chet. You've missed the whole thing. So distracted, you've been." Ayden wriggled in his grasp. "Louie's just another Saucedo. But my new Brazilian contact...he's bigger than Saucedo. Bigger than you, the great, big, Chet. You're all done for."

Chet swallowed, his head swimming.

Who had Rocco come for?

"You know what else, Chet? I think after I'm done here with you, I'll take this one to Vlad. Keep Keeley for myself."

Chet launched the knife through the air. It struck the shower door, shattering the glass. Rocco flinched. Something heavy and metal clattered to the ground. Ayden screamed. Chet used the momentary disorder to pounce on Rocco. The darkness worked in his favor as he sped forward, bent at the waist, and snatched Ayden's flailing arm. He tugged her aside. Rocco was fumbling on the ground in dire search for his lost firearm. Chet reeled around and kicked Rocco's arm aside as the man's fingers closed around the handle of the gun. Rocco's raised arm was flung aside. A bullet discharged into the mirror on the wall.

"Ayden, run!" Chet barked.

The chamber clicked a second time, and a bullet flew over Chet's head.

"Chet!" Ayden screeched.

"Go!" was all he could manage, tackling Rocco to the ground.

The man's hands were big and sweaty, groping Chet's wrists as the two battled over a target. Chet did not have influence over the trigger, though he fought to maintain possession over aim. With several more cracks, the gun fired into the shower wall. Tile and glass fell like crystals onto the bathroom floor. Chet released one hand from his enemy's weapon and swung a fist into Rocco's full head of hair. The man fell backward, crashing into the sink. Chet grabbed a porcelain soap dispenser from the counter and smashed it over Rocco's head. He kicked the gun free, advancing on the body with every intention of ripping it limb for limb, when something stopped him.

The man was unconscious.

Ayden scrambled toward Chet from where she'd been hunkeed down by the door. Chet stood, taking her in one arm while examining Rocco's breathing body.

"What do we do, Chet?" Ayden gasped.

"Let's go," Chet demanded, not bothering to turn on any lights.

No one from the organization had ever dared mess with Chet's estate. If Rocco had the nerve to, he must really feel confident that Chet's downfall was nigh at hand. Who was this Brazilian contact he spoke of? Could a man more powerful than Saucedo and Louie really exist?

Chet led the way out of the bathroom to the closet where he dropped to his knees. Removing a panel of wall, he gazed at his collection. As he suspcted, one of his .22 caliber pistols was absent. He withdrew two small handguns and handed one to Ayden.

"Here."

For once she didn't feel repulsed at the idea of holding a weapon. Nonetheless, she had no desires to use it. The sleek design brought back memories of the haunting shootout in Chet's other home when she'd killed two men. She shivered, still feeling the cold barrel of Rocco's firearm that was held against her spine just minutes ago.

Chet had just straightened to his full height when two hairy arms came around his shoulders from behind. Rocco had awoken, and the two men slammed into the bedroom wall with a thunk. Ayden yelped, raised her gun, lowered it, raised it again. Chet elbowed the man in the nose, and it broke with a crunch. He then bent in half and tore Rocco off the ground, propelling him forward into the dresser. Chet stood erect and spun toward Ayden.

"Don't shoot!"

Rocco staggered to his feet, but Chet launched into attack. He soared toward his assailant, catching him around his waist.

Ayden could see why Chet had not fought Rocco at the nightclub even though Chet appeared to have wanted to. Rocco was a skillful fighter, proficient in hand-to-hand boxing. He actually looked like he might have been professional at it at one point. He landed a few rough blows against Chet, one of which split Chet's lip. Chet had street-fighting on his side, and although it was dirty, and not as clean as Rocco's, Chet's skill gained him the upper hand. Throwing a right hook, Chet knocked Rocco in the side of the head with his gun barrel. Rocco slumped to one knee, then yanked an empty drawer from the dresser and swung it at Chet. Chet raised an arm to deflect the blow, but the thick wood cracked against his bone. Ayden grimaced, her hands shaking on the firearm Chet handed her.

Rocco began to pitch the drawer a second time, but Chet ducked and punched him in the ribs. As Rocco doubled over, Chet hit him in the side of the face. A third strike to the temple and the man went limp. His head fell to the floor and the drawer clattered aside. Chet was breathing rapidly as he squatted beside Rocco's head. Tucking his gun into his belt, Chet turned the man's cheek, searched his pockets. Finding nothing, he wiped a hand across his mouth.

Ayden followed Chet through the bedroom and down the hallway. Chet paced swiftly, his footsteps scarcely heard. She tried to mimic his covertness but found it difficult. At the front door, Chet scanned the porch and yard. His mind was racing. The estate was compromised. By who, he still had no idea. None of Saucedo's men were allowed near Chet's place. None had the guts, and Chet doubted Saucedo would ever order someone onto Chet's land. Rocco had gone rogue, or perhaps joined forces with whomever the Brazilian contact was. And that was more disconcerting than ever.

It was late, after midnight. Chet felt chilled inside, his eyes flitting around the vicinity. He hadn't seen another vehicle, but was not about to rule out the possibility of multiple enemies. Hurrying straight to the Mustang, he helped Ayden inside and then rushed to the driver's seat. Revving the engine, he punched the gas and the car chirped. They were down the driveway and cruising toward the freeway before one of them spoke.

"Thank you for not killing him," Ayden whispered.

Chet glanced at her out of the corner of his eye. He'd had other reasons for not ending Rocco's life, but he'd kept her promise in mind.

"Did he hurt you?" Chet asked.

Ayden shook her head, rubbed her bare arms.

"Where are we going now?" she asked him.

"The motel," he answered. "I'd drive to the cabin, but I need cell service. I need to make a few phone calls."

Carefully, she placed her gun on the ground by her feet.

Only a couple cars passed by them on the freeway. Chet accelerated up the onramp, cruising toward downtown Fresno and the cheap motel. Ayden remembered lying in that flat bed, suffering drug withdrawals.

"I'm just not sure about tomorrow," Chet muttered.

He was chewing the inside of his cheek, his thumb on his chin. It was rare to see him question himself, his own plans.

"It will be fine," Ayden fibbed.

"Something isn't right," he continued. "Rocco. He acted out of line. I think he's left Saucedo's assocation. But I don't think he's working for Louie. I don't know who he was talking about, but I know he'd never dare go near my estate before today. This isn't the first time I've ticked him off. Believe me."

"Then what would he want?"

Chet shook his head side to side, pushing his lower lip in between his teeth. "He wanted you."

"And Keeley?"

Chet didn't answer. Ayden scooted closer to him, wanting to crawl into his lap like she'd been at the karaoke bar. How wonderful that moment had been. Neither said anything until they reached the motel. It was two in the morning when Chet parked in front of door 12. There were a few cars in the lot, but nobody nearby. Ayden unbuckled her seatbelt and opened her car door, but paused when Chet didn't move. His hands were on the steering wheel, his eyes dropped to his lap. He looked beautiful in the moonlight. Beautiful and deadly.

"Should we go inside?" Ayden asked.

Chet nodded, but remained stagnant.

"Come on," she urged gently.

He finally glanced up. "Stay here."

He got out of the car and walked around the area. Ayden knew he was doing his Chet Reconnaissance. When he felt safe, he beckoned for Ayden to get out of the car.

Ayden took her gun and set it on the nightstand beside the bed, next to Chet's. He was standing at the window, peeking through a gap in the curtains. She examined his tall frame, his rounded shoulders, slim torso, lean legs. His posture spoke of anxiety, although his face held little expression. It's what he did best. Hide everything.

A few hours from now, the sun would rise, and Chet would leave to solidify his plans with Pasquale. They'd have to fill Saucedo in on Rocco's betrayal. Who knew what they would make of that? Their entire scheme to lift Louie was already daunting. All of California's most dangerous criminals would all be gathered under one roof. Ayden would be on stage, dancing around a pole for all of them. Her duty was crucial. She was to be the beautiful entertainment. Chet hadn't said so out loud, but Pasquale had, and Ayden had overheard. None of the ladies that worked at the nightclub were as attractive as Ayden. None were as clean, either. Ayden would be a jewel among theives. She kept telling herself, over and over, that Chet and Nogo Saucedo would succeed in their plan. Louie would be taken, questioned, or whatever, Nogo would have his money, and Chet would gain his freedom.

Ayden would be safe to escape.

"Hey," she said quietly.

Chet turned his shoulders half an inch, keeping his eyes locked outside. Ayden stepped up to his shoulder, taking his hand into both of hers.

"Hey," she mumbled into his shirt, nuzzling his bicep with her cheek.

Lifting his arm, she wrapped it around her neck and snuggled close to his side. Tucking one arm around his waist, she lifted the other to the back of his head.

"Should I sing to you?"

Chet's eyes slid down to hers, glistening like the ocean. She wished he would smile.

Instead, he asked, "Mi ami?"

"Yes," she answered.

"Why do you love me, Ayden?"

She raked her fingers through the front of his hair and watched his eyelids flutter closed. The tension in his back eased, and he drew closer. Combing the hair behind his ears with her fingertips, she let her fingers trickle down his nape. One by one, his hands slipped to her hips. She lifted her elbows to his shoulders and traced circles around his sideburns. His eyes were still closed, but he began to rock slightly one way, then the other.

"'*Baby*,'" Ayden sang in a whisper, "'*I get chills when I'm with you. Whoa-oh. Baby. My world stands still when I'm with you.*'"

"A one hit wonder," Chet murmured, swaying to the melody.

Ayden grinned. "You've heard of Sheriff?"

"I've heard of everything."

"That can't possibly be true," she teased.

She knew it was.

Chet opened his eyes. "Logorrhea."

"Lo-what?"

"An excessive flow of words," he explained. "That's the definition."

"You're weird," Ayden said through a smile.

His eyes crinkled and his lips almost turned upwards. "I have exactly three point five credits from Fresno State to my name."

"You went to college?" she asked dubiously.

"I sold the English teacher dope," he responded flatly. "I got an A."

She laughed aloud, not totally sure if he was kidding. His heart was thrumming against hers. She could see desire warming in his eyes.

"We have a big day tomorrow," she stated as confidently as possible.

Chet's arms tightened around her middle, and he rolled his back against the wall. "We should get some rest."

Ayden reminded him to behave, and gave him a kiss goodnight. Stretching onto her toes, her lips conformed to his. One of his hands surged into her hair while the other splayed against her back. Her fingers skimmed the three scars on his abdomen beneath his shirt, ones just below his ribcage. There were identical ones on his back, which led her to believe they were some kind of puncture wound. Was he stabbed? The thought of Chet bleeding, knifed down in a back alley, caused her more discomfort than she knew how to bear.

Chet watched Ayden tuck herself into bed, and then he took his gun, tucked it into his pants, and stepped outside to make a call.

***

The next morning, Chet drove them back to the cabin to check on Nolan. Several times throughout the drive, Chet checked his cell phone. Ayden didn't want to be nosy or self-conscious, but she was. And once, she looked down when he had his phone in his hand and saw that he was scrolling through his call log. The number of outgoing calls to and incoming calls from Keeley was startling. She forced her eyes to the window, feeling like she was being crushed beneath an enormous Redwood tree.

They reached the cabin at late morning. Nolan was out. Chet searched the cabinets and drawers and found several other prescription pill bottles that he confiscated. There was something about confronting the issue of Nolan's overdose a second time that set Chet offf. He was obsessing over his phone. He mentioned his estate a few times, and said he was expecting a call but that cell service at the cabin was bad.

When Nolan didn't come back after an hour, Chet's agitation grew. A second hour passed, and still Nolan didn't return. Ayden could sense Chet's distress. Everything from the confrontation with Rocco to the impending confrontation with Louie was compounding. He marched into the kitchen and pressed his palms into the counter, head lowered, motivation thwarted. All of the possible outcomes were interweaving before his eyes, and she was powerless to stop it.

27

It was as close to "losing it" as she'd ever seen Chet. His eyes were an ice storm. Emotion that had been caged permeated his self-possessed exterior. It made his release of anger against Grayson at the club seem like a toddler's fit.

"Come on," Ayden demanded.

Chet's gaze pierced Ayden's soul with icicles. She took it.

Reaching across the counter, she grabbed his car keys. "Come on, Chet."

He didn't respond, but he didn't protest. When she moved to the front door, he followed. She walked outside. He moved down the porch toward his car. She opened his driver's side door. After he was seated, she got in the passenger's side. Leaning across the gear shift, she stuck the keys in the ignition and turned the car on. A deep growl reverberated against the sky.

Chet's door was still open. The mountain breeze whispered between them. It smelled of pine and crisp oxygen. Ayden flipped on the stereo. The custom dash had a fancy CD player. She knew the artist that would play. Skipping through the tracks, she settled on number six. The King immediately started belting.

The warden threw a party in the county jail.

Chet's foot hit the clutch. He thrust the car into gear and peeled out. The Mustang spun a hundred and eighty degrees. Switching gears, he yanked his door shut and tore down the dirt road.

Chet sped away his worries, his right hand tightly clasping the stick shift, his left commanding the steering wheel. The roads had little traffic. It wouldn't have mattered if they did. Traffic laws had little impact on him as he worked through his feelings. Ayden let him. She rolled her window down, leaned her head against the side of the door, and let the wind blast her face. The vroom captivated her spirit.

Closing her eyes, Ayden stuck her right hand out of the win

dow and let her palm ride the air. The muscle car purred, hugging the apex of every curve. Eight cylinder-echoes ricocheted off the mountains, howling their presence to the world. Sunshine flickered against her eyelids. She didn't care where they drove, how fast they got there, or what they would do when they arrived. For a moment, she just wanted to drive.

Elvis sang all twelve of his top hits. The stereo fell quiet. They ended up in a foreign part of the Sierra's. Chet pulled off to the side of the road and pushed in the parking brake. Ayden opened her eyes. She got out of the car as he did, and they moved to the passenger's side where they faced an open valley. Chet leaned back against his car, gazing out into the scenery. The metal rumbled against Ayden's legs as she copied him, taking in the majestic troposphere.

Chet pulled his cell phone out of his pocket and lifted it up against the horizon. Ayden heard the camera shutter notification. He then nodded his chin at her.

"Me?" she asked.

"Get out there," he said, holding his phone up again.

Ayden felt bashful. "You want a picture of me?"

He good-humoredly shoved her. She stepped in front of him, her back to the picturesque outdoors. Chet looked at her, not his phone.

"I would take a thousand pictures of you," he said, snapping the photo.

Ayden brushed her hair away from her face.

He lowered his hand holding the cell. "None of them would capture you properly."

"I'm not very photogenic," she agreed.

Chet shook his head. "Your magic cannot be captured in 2D."

Their eyes met. Ayden was relieved his demeanor had pacified. She was timid, however, that he now had a picture of her on his phone—one she was pretty sure she'd blinked in.

"Let me see," she said, reaching for his phone.

Chet kept it out of her reach. "Why?"

Ayden tried again. "Let me see."

He grinned. "No. Why?"

"Because I wasn't ready," she laughed. "You can't have a hideous picture of me on there."

"I'll photoshop it," he replied, grabbing her arm and keeping her at a distance.

She struggled a few more seconds before relenting. Chet kept his grasp on her arm, pulling her into his chest. He spun her around so her back was to his front, then lifted up his cell phone and took a picture of the two of them.

"Let's see how it turned out," Chet exhaled, tugging Ayden into his embrace.

With his free hand, he showed her the picture he took. Ayden's face broke into a smile. On Chet's phone she saw an image of a girl and a boy. A girl with cinnamon brown hair. A boy with black messy hair. A girl with hazel eyes. A boy with wide, strikingly blue eyes. A girl with a giddy smile on her face. A boy pretending to be shocked. He looked frivolous. It was Ayden's favorite picture ever.

"I have to have a copy of this!" she giggled.

Chet stared at it a little longer, too. His lungs inflated against her spine, his one arm wrapped around her torso. She clasped his forearm with both her hands, staring at Chet's face. She saw a magic captured in that 2D picture she feared she'd never see again in real life. Chet's fake "surprised" expression, her very real smile. The way he held her. The way the image was at an angle that demonstrated he'd taken it himself with only his arm's length. A corner of his car's hood could be seen in the background. The red paint glistened in the sun. It could've been a movie poster.

It was so ordinary.

Sometimes Ayden forgot Chet was just a guy in his late twenties. If she erased everything she knew about him, and just had this picture, she'd think he was a typical, normal boy. One she'd date. Fall in love with. Marry.

Then again, Ayden wanted all of those things knowing precisely everything about Chet. She wanted to know more. She loved all of him. She longed to take thousands of goofy pictures together and set one as the wallpaper on her own phone. Taking one last glimpse at the picture of them two, Chet put his phone back in his pocket. He wrapped his arms around Ayden's shoulders. They both felt the magic. And for their next act...

"Where would you disappear to?" she asked him. "Right now? If you could go anywhere this instant?"

"This instant?" he breathed out. "Putting pressure on me."

"No pressure," she countered. "Just think. Where would you go?"

He bit his bottom lip. "Where would we go?"

He'd said "we." It made her heart flutter.

"Puerto Rico?"

"Is that a question?" Ayden asked.

He smiled against her hair. "Don't pressure me. I'd go anywhere you want to go."

"I'd go to Puerto Rico," she assented. "I've never been. Have you?"

"No. I've seen pictures."

"Professional ones, I hope. I don't know if I trust your judgement on photographs."

Chet squeezed her. "Ayden."

"Chet."

He released her. "You drive."

She gasped, watching him climb into the passenger's seat. "You mean, I get to race the beast?"

Chet grinned at her through the open window as he shut the car door. "Get crazy."

Ayden adjusted the seat and integrated herself into the driver's side. She became one with the car. Chet pushed play on the stereo again. Elvis's rich voice crooned Little Sister through the speakers. Chet turned the volume up. Ayden revved the engine against the bass. Her foot barely reached the pedal, but there was a true respect between man and machine. A serpentine smile split her lips. Subwoofers were a gift from above.

28

Chet hadn't been the same after the incident with Rocco at his estate. Ayden was itching to ask Chet how he was feeling, and why he thought Rocco would come after them. She paid attention to how frequently Chet glanced at his phone. He appeared to be texting back and forth. He strode around the motel room pensively, checking his cell each time it lit up. Punching a reply, he'd move to the window and check outside. This continued all morning until he told Ayden it was time to go to the club.

They drove by a church on their way, taking a few back streets. Chet monitored the rearview mirror, causing Ayden to check the side mirrors occasionally. She wanted to know if they were being followed, too. When they drove by her religious place of worship, she pondered how plain and simple the exterior of the building was. All people were welcome to her congregation, even people like Chet. What she wouldn't give to know what a bishop would say to Chet's confessional.

Ayden's spirit glimmered with hope as she thought about their future, and the end of dealing with Nogo Saucedo. It was a lot to hope Chet would want to change, and almost too much to hope he would want anything to do with her religion. She saw glimpses of faith in his eyes, and she felt like she could live by example and possibly influence him. However, no one could survive on the testimony of somene else. He would have to figure out for himself what was truth and error. He'd need to build his own testimony, and then work on strengthening it. Ayden knew well a spiritual strength was just like a physical strength. The more one exercised it, the stronger it became. On the other hand, the less one exercised it, the weaker it became. Many times the gospel rug had been pulled out from underneath Ayden's feet. Without a firm foundation, she'd have been lost herself.

Chet had plenty of reasons to doubt God's existence. He knew disappointment and sorrow unlike any person Ayden had met. Yet, she believed God saved his toughest battles for his toughest soldiers. If Chet joined God's army, he would be unstoppable.

***

Hank was in front of the bar, arranging the stools. The lights were flickering in different hues, changing intermittently to the music. Starla was on stage with Ayden, walking through her routine. The veteran dancer had all kinds of ideas about the performance, from the colors of the lights, to which way Ayden would face during particular spins. It was irritating.

The men were gathered near the front door, conversing in their business jargon. It reminded Ayden of the dress rehearsals she used to attend before every dance competition in her teens. So many rules. So much attention to detail. So much adrenaline. The coach would have all the dancers line up and mark the dance with partial movements, so they wouldn't burn up any energy. Chet had already made his team walk through their evening. Then, all the dancers would all sit together and have a meditative pow-wow, playing their competition song on a radio while visualizing a perfect performance in their minds. That's probably not what Pasquale was doing at the bar with Carter and Benecio.

Ayden's favorite dance in high school was the jazz routine. The technique was challenging, the formation changes intricate, the song hip and catchy. Everywhere her team went, they swept the podium. Judges always gave her team's jazz dance high scores, and the spectators would rave. It was different dancing on a team, though. You had less of an opportunity for self-expression. Less individual attention. On the other hand, you had to be unerringly precise with your actions. Each dancer had to replicate the other so that the whole team moved as one body. In that aspect, if you were the one to mess up, it was blatantly obvious. The whole team would suffer.

Only once did Ayden thoroughly botch a performance. Luckily, it wasn't at a qualifying competition.

Here, in this nightclub, Ayden would not be dancing with a team. Nonetheless, she knew she could not botch it. The whole team would suffer if she did. If she screwed up the dance performance, the men wouldn't know, but there would not be anyone else on stage to draw attention away from Chet and Saucedo. This was *her* recital. Even though Starla was aptly making herself a certified Dance Mom, Ayden could care less about how "gorgeous" she looked on stage. She was afraid of what would happen if the men couldn't get Louie.

Ayden was not a spring chicken.

Spectators weren't allowed to interact physically with the dancers. Ayden knew that much. Ayden would be up on a stage, several feet higher than her viewers. There wasn't much risk of being groped, nor did anyone know she was working with Chet and Saucedo. The nightclub would be open for business just like it would any other night. Hometown natives would have no clue what kind of deal was going down. She'd just stick to her arrangement, follow the performance step by step, and it would all be fine. If she thought of it that way, of just a performance, it helped keep her nerves at bay.

Night was only a few hours away. With it, would come regular attendees as well as Louie and his associates. Ayden had been given descriptions and photographs of them all. She knew who she was meant to entertain. She had all her rules memorized systematically. Chet snuck glimpses of her throughout the evening, his efforts to reassure her he was well aware of her precise safety at all times. But she wasn't sure how reassured *he* was. He had a wrinkle between his brows constantly. Whatever he'd discussed with Saucedo concerning Rocco, he'd strictly forbidden the others discuss with Ayden. In fact, only Pasquale and Saucedo knew what had happened at the estate.

At nine in the evening, people started filtering into the club. Ayden was in the dressing room with Starla, and other female employees were currently dancing on the individual podiums. Louie's men were set to arrive shortly after eleven. Chet's team was stationed around the area, Benecio at the front entrance, and Sebastian and Carter seated at the bar. They blended into the crowd, appearing your average lonely male. They weren't part of Nogo Saucdo's organization, which helped them fly under Louie's radar. Pasquale was somewhere with Chet, possibly outside with Nogo Saucedo.

Saucedo.

Ayden shuddered at the thought of encountering Chet's boss again. The last time she saw the man was when she was being tortured and drugged.

At ten, she dressed into the glitzy leotard thing Starla had for her. Her costume. She'd become accustomed to wearing less clothing when dancing on stage as a teen, but tonight she felt over-exposed. She wasn't a little girl anymore. This wasn't a high school dance competition. Even though the leotard was as modet as a one-piece bathing suit, she knew what the spectators would be thinking. What if she messed up? What if one of the strings came untied? For just that reason, she tied them all in double knots.

Starla was primping her hair in the mirror and seemed to read Ayden's thoughts.

"You're going to do great," the woman remarked, lining her lips with lipstick. "Besides, even Vlad's girls forget their moves once and awhile. Marybeth fell down flat, one time." Starla laughed at her reflection. "Smoked it to the filter, that one. If you freeze up, improvise. Give a flirty smile and shake your booty."

Ayden didn't pretend to play nice and be friends. She wasn't at all very happy with the woman, nor how silly she treated Ayden because of Ayden's preferred modesty..

Starla stood and donned her robe. She was wearing less than Ayden. Tassels and a g-string. Her flaming red hair was teased mountain high. It was Starla's job to get on stage prior to Louie's arrival. From her view of the audience, Starla would assess the men and confirm that all was going according to plan. At eleven, with a signal from Sebastian, Starla would exit the stage and meet Ayden in the dressing room. As soon as Louie was seated at the podium, it would be Ayden's turn to dance.

Ayden's stomach rumbled with unease. The music was pounding through the walls. Voices grew louder as the club attracted more customers. She slipped her feet into her heels and ran through her routine in her head. Several times her mind drew a blank, and she'd chastise herself. In fifteen minutes, Starla would leave her alone in the back room. The thought of standing by herself in this filthy establishment, surrounded by villainous mobsters, caused Ayden to perspire. If her hands got too slippery, she would not be able to grip the pole. Muttering, she grabbed a towel and blotted her palms.

In the mirror, Ayden saw a pretty girl. She wore dense

makeup, and her hair was curled. Her figure was enviable, not even close to the other dancers' bodies. Vlad's women were mostly strung out single moms, strung out middle-aged divorcees, or strung out junkies needing cash for a fix. As long as it kept the focus of Louie and his comrades on her, Ayden wouldn't complain about the leotard. Not tonight. Tonight, she would have to bite her tongue when men wagged money at her and treated her like a low-life. Shaking her arms out to her sides, she warmed up her muscles. Starla checked the time and then glanced over.

"I'll be back," she stated through a smile. "Show time."

Ayden could tell Starla was nervous too, but Starla's eyes were bloodshot and glassy. Starla had numbed *her* worry.

It made Ayden recoil. She already thought little of Starla, and hated to imagine what had ever transpired between the dancer and Chet. Starla didn't express any amount of contest toward Ayden when it came to him, as if Starla knew him first and owned the rights to his friendship. However, that moment when Starla had touched Chet's leg and laughed like they shared a life-long camaraderie made Ayden prickle with spite.

Starla was busying herself by the mirror before heading out. She bent forward and sniffed the counter, running a finger over the front of her gums. Adjusting her cleavage, she turned to Ayden and jerked her head.

"You want a bump?" she asked.

Ayden didn't ask what it meant. She shook her head forcefully and glanced away. Starla patted her eyes and lips a final time, and then left the dressing room.

The woman had a favorite song, and when the beat strummed loudly beyond the curtain, Ayden forced herself to take a seat. If she kept pacing, her feet would tire. The bass was booming. Rowdy cheers and glasses clanking sounded on the other side of the curtain. Some of the other females with less seniority than Starla took over the dressing room.

At ten forty-five, Ayden dabbed some perfumed glitter on her chest. She longed to see Chet, to feel his arms around her, hear his voice whisper in her ear. It had been several hours since their last interaction. He had been curt, not out of anger, but necessity. After relaying his orders, he then moved on to instruct Pasquale.

Ayden was left in Starla's company. She knew things had to be going smoothly. If something went awry, Chet said either Sebastian or Carter would notify her. She was to exit the building immediately, go down the block, and wait for Chet at the bus stop.

Ayden hoped, if that happened, she'd have time to throw on some appropriate clothes.

Precisely at eleven, the music dimmed and Starla reentered the dressing room. Ayden had been resting in a plastic chair, but got up.

"Let loose," Starla encouraged, a thick wad of single in her palm. "It's just like we practiced."

Ayden gulped and nodded, but her feet felt like lead. She clomped rather clumsily to the curtain, flexing her feet beneath the straps of her heels. Starla held the curtain back for Ayden. The bar was jammed full of both men and women, though the ratio greatly favored the male gender. Cigarette smoke wafted in thick puffs, hovering near the ceiling in a fog. Cocktail waitresses in skimpy dresses maneuvered through tables and chairs, collecting cash for drinks. An overweight man near an empty podium received a lap dance from one of the club's employees.

Ayden searched for the faces she knew. Benecio. Sebastian. Carter. The lights were so bright in places, and so dim in others, she had a hard time deciphering any of them. Everything was going according to plans thus far. It wasn 't time to panic. Her throat seemed to close up, but Starla was there with a motivating nudge.

"Go on," Starla urged, and Ayden stepped into the room.

Nobody looked at her at first. She wasn't wearing a robe, like Starla, but then again she was more modest than the rest of the dancers. Ayden's leotard felt clownish now. Chancing a glance at the bar, she thought she saw Hank watching her. She was supposed to make her way to the stage. Some of Louie's men were probably already seated around her pole. Did the club allow men to carry weapons in here? Were they all on drugs? Ayden's thoughts spun wildly.

Moving of their own accord, Ayden's feet led her to the stair case. Lights strobed around her. Her heart thundered. She pranced delicately, reaching the stage, as a spotlight danced around her body. Beyond the stage, the faces of her audience were dulled by shadows. Men, dangerous men, druglords and criminals, sat in those shadows. There would be no way to recognize them from Chet's pictures until the spotlight dimmed. She strutted to the pole and gave her hair a shake. The song cut off, and the tune she'd trained to blared through the speakers.

Ayden counted to the rhythm.

Five, six, seven, eight.

29

Halfway through her routine, when Ayden was on her knees on the podium, a man seated just below the stage leaned forward to stuff a wad of cash into the strap of her heel. She momentarily froze, her choreography not timed for the acceptance of money. The men were permitted to do that. Starla even joked that Ayden could keep whatever funds she collected tonight. It was horrendous to Ayden. She didn't look at the man's face and tried to keep an impassive expression.

Keeping time with the music, she quickly picked up where she'd left off in the dance. Her eyes scanned the man's attire. He was an expansive man in a business suit. She twirled around. His coat was draped over the back of his chair, but his tie hung slackly around his neck. The top three buttons were undone, and Ayden saw a glimmering gold chain. He had darker complexion, so she guessed Italian. Another turn, and she caught a glimpse of his face. His prominent features suggested he was handsome, but she did not find him attractive. Especially with the way he sneered at her.

Ayden returned to the pole, elated that the song was almost over. Twirling around and around, she disregarded the bar a moment to prepare herself for what was to come next. In the dressing room, she had a bag packed. It held her cell phone, a change of clothes, and a loaded firearm. Chet would enter the club from the back at any moment, at which point Ayden was to dismount the stage and head immediately out of sight. With her belongings, she was then to drive the Mustang to the hotel and wait for a verification call from Chet.

She would not see the showdown between Saucedo and Louie. She would not be a part of anything. Chet made sure of it.

Ayden realized, about the moment she spotted Rocco emerge from the back hall, carrying an automatic assault rifle, that the scene was about to get bloody. Behind him, a shorter male appeared with an identical weapon. Benecio ventured toward the center of the room, removing a pistol from his jacket pocket. Concurrently, Sebastian and Carter abandoned their stools at the bar and marched toward Ayden's podium. Ayden froze. She improvised, striking a pose, something that allowed her to gape at the terrifying scene.

Nogo Saucedo flew in from a side entrance, his pin-stripedd suit and kerchief identical to the last one she'd seen him wear. Her heart lurched. Chet entered last, a massive shotgun in his grip. Together, he and Saucedo observed the entire room, including Rocco and the rogue personnel heading for Louie, Pasquale, and Carter and Sebastion moving toward the podium. Chet's eye met Ayden's. Rocco was aiming his semi-automatic weapon right at the group of men sitting in front of her. She was directly in the line of fire.

None of the club's citizen patrons saw Rocco's gun. It was dark. Ayden was doing her job by demanding attetnion. She paused. It was only for two seconds, but it felt like forever under the strobing lights. Chet's face morphed as he tore his eyes off her. His black shirt was tight against his muscles. They flexed ominously as he raised his weapon and fired it toward the ceiling.

"Everyone, get down!" he shouted.

Screams erupted everywhere.

Glass bottles splintered on the floor as gunfire ruptured. Three men seated around the stage jumped to their feet, each reaching into their suit coats. One of them had been puffing on a large cigar. His hair was mocha brown, slicked back, and tapered short around his hairline. His ears were pierced. He looked to be around thirty to thirty-five years old. With a gesture of his hands, the two men on either side of him opened fire on the club. A couple innocent bystanders dropped to the floor, including a female dancer girl. Rocco was blasting the stage with bullets. The room was in absolute mayhem.

Ayden sunk to the ground, kicking of her heels. She shimmied beneath shrapnel to the edge of the stage. The lights above her were struck. Glass and plastic rained down on her, many of the bulbs going dark. The music pounded on. People ran for the doors.

Nogo Saucedo and his team retaliated, but against whom was uncertain. Bullets were flying in every direction. A new song began pumping through the speakers, even as one exploded into electric fragments. Chet leapt over a few chairs, cocking his shotgun and aiming toward Louie and his associates. He fired at a chair purposefully. The Italians ducked in time as pieces of wood blew across the stage. The splinters stung Ayden's bare legs as she shrieked and dove for the stairs.

As Chet ordered, Ayden did not look back. She ran. Into the dressing room, she ran. Her feet now felt lighter than air as she flung the curtain back. Starla was almost passed out in front of the mirror, her eyes drooping so heavy she could barely focus on Ayden. White powder lined her nostrils and dusted the top of the counter. Other dancers were running in and out of the dressing area.

Ayden didn't hesitate. She grabbed her bag. Promptly, she took out her flat shoes and stuffed her feet in them. But as she began pulling out the long pair of pants, the echoes of gunfire rang louder and more frequent. She'd have to dress elsewhere.

"Come on," Ayden yelled at Starla, jamming the clothing back into her back and zipping it up. "We have to get out of here."

Starla was in a daze. Her eyes rolled and her jaw dropped open. ,

"Just…go, honey," the woman commented with a lazy wave of her hand.

Ayden had no patience for this. So she did.

Peering out of the dressing room, Ayden saw an all-out brawl that would put any old, Western film to shame. She looped the bag onto her back and hustled out into the club. The room was in turmoil. Bodies lay at odd angles over chairs, on top of the bar and stage, in the walkway. Survivors were fleeing out the front door. The pop of gunpowder illuminated the gloomy atmosphere in orange sparks. Ayden barely caught a glimpse of a black-haired bandit sprinting from one upturned table to the next, firing toward a cluster of heads hiding behind one of the podiums. If it was Chet, she didn't have time to holler at him.

Ayden darted around the corner and into the back hall. his exit would lead her to an alley behind the club, which opened up onto a fairly busy downtown street. With any luck, she could duck behind a dumpster to throw on her clothes and shoes, then fish out the cell phone as she made her way to the Mustang. It was not parked in the club parking lot, but half a block away. The keys were in her bag.

The back door came into view just as a bullet ruptured the wall near Ayden's head. She whirled around at her incoming assailant, recognizing him as one of the men who'd watched her podium display. He leveled his gun at her and pulled the trigger as she tumbled to the ground. The bullet missed. She fumbled with her pack, tugging at the zipper, struggling to retrieve her own weapon. Chet had insisted she not pull it out unless she had to, since it would label her a threat. This man was not on Chet's team. She didn't know if he was part of Louie's group, or Rocco's rogue assailants, but she wasn't going to make polite introductions.

"Where do you think you're going?" the man hollered as he stormed down the hall toward her.

Ayden scrambled to her feet, failing to secure the gun in her hands. The man was too close now. He grabbed the color of his shirt and spoke into it.

"Down the back hall. She's making a run for it."

Ayden tightened her grasp on the bag, ready to use it as a projectile, when Pasquale materialized behind her aggressor. Lifting his pistol, Pasquale shot the man once in the back. The man wailed and fell forward, turning frantically to shoot at Pasquale. Both emptied the rounds from their guns. Chunks of drywall sprayed out at Ayden. She wasn't sure who had been hit, or how many times, but she bolted out the back door and into the night without waiting to see.

The alley stunk of putrid waste. Still in the sparky leotard, Ayden jogged to the closest dumpster and hunched down behind it. She could hear the sounds of guns popping within the walls of the club. Crowds of people were still exiting the building, yelling frenzied at one another. Cars were burning rubber as they sped out of the parking lot. Sirens rang in the distance.

Setting the bag on the ground, Ayden tugged out the pants and shirt, pulling them on over the leotard. Her hand shook. Her pulse skipped. At the bottom of the bag, she found her cell phone. Holding it in her teeth, she finally withdrew the small gun and tucked it into the back of her jeans. She then moved rapidly toward the busy street. The sirens grew louder. Nervously, she covered the sparkly leotard and wiped her lipstick off on the sleeve of her shirt as she paced to the corner of the building. She tried not to let her mind wander to what was happening inside the club. Who was alive? Who was dead? How long would she have to wait to find out?

Once on the sidewalk, with the flash of headlights and streetlights to comfort her, Ayden strode to the nearest crosswalk. Cop cars materialized and sped toward the nighclub. Crying voices mixed with the sounds of the approaching ambulance. The gunfire seemed to be slowing. She couldn't be sure. The loud, distinct *crack-crack* of a shotgun noised.

Chet's Mustang was only half a block away. The hard part was going to be waiting at the motel, until she heard from him and he told her everything was fine. In fact, Ayden had a hard time caring if everything was fine, so long as Chet was uninjured. She feared his safety above him getting arrested. They didn't have a second chance to escape Chet's enslavement to Nogo Saucedo. Not even jail could protect Chet from the wrath of Saucedo. There were men from Saucedo's organization permantnetly incarcerated. Chet's boss would not let him live, let alone out of the organization, if Louie was not brought down tonight, and the stolen money returned.

Ayden thought about Starla, incoherent in the dressing room. She didn't feel hatred for the woman, but pity. That lifestyle brought nothing but sorrow or death.

Crossing the street, Ayden glanced over her shoulder at the club. It wasn't obvious to the outside world what was taking place inside. Now that most of the innocent socialites had vacated the warzone, and the building was surrounded by policemen, it looked like any other criminal occasion that made the Fresno City news. Only faint sounds that could be passed off as a car backfiring told Ayden the shootout was not over. It had almost gone smoothly. Up until Rocco burst on the scene, Ayden had hoped the evening would go according to Chet's plans.

She lowered her chin and continued on until she reached the Mustang. It was parked conveniently under a steet lamp. Her heart was pounding against her ribs, and only when she was seated inside, digging into her bag for the keys, did she realize her lungs were aching. She'd been holdng her breath. Her hands were shaking so badly she could scarcely get the right key in the ignition.

When the engine rumbled to life, she drove straight to room 12.

30

Ayden slammed the door shut and locked it behind her. She'd driven around the area, checking her rearview mirror sporadically for a tail, before finally pulling into the motel lot. Positive she'd not had a follower, she'd gone inside the dark room alone. Chet instructed her to keep the lights off, but she turned the TV on for peace of mind. She immediatley put on the news. Cameras were rolling on the nightclub. Gnawing her lip, she took out her cell phone and checked the time. It was 11:59pm.

12:00am.

12:01am.

She ambled into the bathroom to wash her face, desperate to get the makeup off. The bathroom door was still crooked on its hinges. She thought about taking a shower to wash away the entire evening, but she decided against it. Instead, she changed out of the leotard and shoved it into the waste bakset before putting her clothes back on. Back in the room, she settled onto the bed and stared at the reporter standing across the street from the nightclub interviewing an eye witness.

An hour later, Ayden's eyelids began to droop. She was tired. And famished. Chet had forbade her from leaving the motel room until he arrived, which meant she couldn't even walk down to the gas station and get some sleep aids and snacks. She had one-hundred dollars for emergency cash, but she had to save it in case she needed to take a cab to the airport. There was no activity on her phone, which heightened apprehension.

Ayden jolted out of a dream to Elvis singing in her ear. Alarmed, she squinted around the dark room. The TV was on mute, and a brighter square of light was blinding her. Her cell phone was ringing Burnin' Love. She fumbled to free her hands from the blankets, catching and dropping the phone several times before her eyes focused on the screen. The time read 4:43am. Chet was calling.

"Hello?" Ayden gasped. "Hello?"

"Cops," Chet coughed.

There was a pause in which she could hear the high-pitched sirens. Two bullets popped off. Someone in the distance shouted,

"Over here!"

"Chet?" Ayden asked, sitting upright in bed.

He was breathing harshly. The sound carried through the receiver like sandpaper scratching across slate. She jerked the blankets back and hopped off the bed, searching for her shoes. When he spoke again, she could hear the tightness of pain in his voice.

"Do you remember how to get to the cabin?"

"Yes—no—I don't know. Chet, what—"

"Go there. Now. Drive as far as you can with the headlights off. Make no stops."

"Where will you be?"

"Ayden," he whispered hoarsely. A firearm discharged. "Nolan will be waiting for you. He knows what to do. Get out of town. Take my car. Go anywhere you want, but dump the cell along the way. You'll have enough money in your account to disappear."

Between each sentence he took in a harsh, ragged breath. Ayden was starting to suspect something dismal. She was jamming her feet into her shoes as fast as she could, trembling so much that she almost let go of the phone.

"Where are you?" she demanded.

"I'm—" Chet gasped and the blast of a gunshot thundered closer than before –"I'm stuck. Stupid cops. They ruin everything. Go without me."

"I'm coming to get you," Ayden interjected. She swiped the car keys off the nightstand, repacked her bag, and ran outside. "Tell me where you are."

"No, Ayden. Don't."

She started the Mustang, backing out of the stall, and tore off down the street. There was very little traffic, so she paid very little attention to traffic regulations. Speeding through every red light, and every stop sign, she crammed the gear into third and raced on. She knew Chet would be able to hear her driving. He was still on the phone she held by her ear.

"Are you at the club?" she asked.

Chet grunted. "Toots, you are going to get us both killed."

"If I haven't already," she grumbled.

"I'm around the corner from the club, hiding down one of

those manholes."

"Like the Ninja Turtles?"

"That's exactly what I was thinking," Chet wheezed. "And I was equally as agile and adroit as they were. One problem. There are police on every corner, and armed thugs everywhere in between. Nogo is gone. I'm pretty sure Louie is gone, too. Rocco's working for someone else, and they all...came to play. It's a battlefield."

Ayden grimaced. "What do you suggest?"

His breath shuddered. "Pepperoni."

"Chet!"

"I want you to drive to the mountains, Ayden. Nolan will help you get on your way safely."

"Ain't gonna happen," she retorted. "You've risked so much for me already. I owe it to you."

"You've never owed me anything."

"Chet, that will never be true."

"Then what do *you* suggest?"

Ayden pondered it a moment, recalling the streets in her mind. "Is there a long stretch of road I can ride into? If I don't stop, you can run out from the shadows and leap into the moving vehicle."

"Just like that, huh?" he replied dryly.

She rolled her eyes. "You're the ninja. Figure it out."

"There's one more problem."

"As in?"

Chet grunted. The sound of a police car zoomed by.

"*If* you manage to make it through the barricades," he groaned, "and *if* you manage not to get gunned down by lunatic mobsters, and *if* you manage to drive deftly enough that I can seize the opportunity to Donatello my way into the automobile without getting run over..."

"Yes?"

"I've been shot."

Ayden's heart lurched. She swerved, narrowly missing a lamppost as she regained control.

"What?" she shrieked.

Chet gave a frustrated moan. "You see, there's no point

coming after me. Go to Nolan, Ayden. You have your freedom. Saucedo is gone. I'm finished with him. What you've wanted is yours. It's done."

His breath was becoming shallower.

Ayden hit the break and the clutch at the same time, cranking the steering wheel as she drifted through a right turn.

"What about Rocco and this new Brazilian contact?"

He coughed. "I don't know yet."

"Where are you shot? How severe is it? Is the bleeding staunched? We can go to the hospital."

"We cannot go to the hospital," Chet countered. "They'll be looking for me. I'll be—I'll be fine. I'll vanish, like you. I just have to do a few things first."

Ayden was nearing her destination. She could see the glow of blue and red lights flickering against the buildings. Asking Chet for his precise location, she deccelerated to the speed limit. Chet gave her the coordinates.

"I'm telling you," he continued, rasping in and out, "if you want to get out, if you want to start today to live the rest of your life, free of this pandemonium, leave now. This is your best chance. Ayden, just go. I'll be alright."

"And I'm telling you," she fought back, "to shut up."

"Please, just listen to me. Rocco's still out there. He'll come for me, but he'll leave you out of this now that Saucedo's dead, and he doesn't have to pressure me for power."

"Chet, if you didn't want me to come get you, you wouldn't have told me where you were. I'm just down the block. You'll hear me coming. Door is unlocked. Window is down."

Chet sighed his resignation.

Gratified, Ayden punched the throttle and squealed down the street. Several cop cars were blocking an intersection. She could see more down the street, creating a cordon. Two residential citizens had pulled over to the side of the road, sticking their heads out their windows to guffaw at the hoard of policemen. News vans were parked on the curb. The majority of people had been cleared from the scene, but a handful of nosy observers skittered from wall to wall, trying to catch a glimpse of the excitement.

Ayden jarred the wheel sideways until the Mustang scaled

the sidewalk. She flew passed the first set of police vehicles, smashing her right side mirror off in the process.

"Eek," she muttered as the car clobbered back onto the road.

She took a hard right down an alley, crashing into several garbage cans, and burst out onto another side road. Cranking the wheel left, she straightened and hit the gas. Chet would be just up ahead. Any moment now.

Sirens wailed behind Ayden, and she glanced in the rearview mirror to see a cop car chasing after her. Shifting gears, she ignored the voice on the loud speaker.

"Stop the car! Get out and put your hands in the air! We have you surrounded!"

She almost drove right into Chet. He'd jumped out from behind a dumpster, raising his hands in the air. It wasn't even dawn yet, and his body was silhouetted in moonlight. He stood hunched a bit to one side, hindered by the injuries he'd sustained. Ayden hit the brakes just enough that when she glided by him, he reached out to hook his hands into the open window. Dragging his feet a few seconds, he began wrestling his way into the car through the window. Ayden then accelerated, keeping an eye on the pursuing vehicle.

"Don't look back," Chet rasped.

She obeyed, gazing forward as the speedometer climbed. She wanted to glance over at him, to see his face, read his eyes. His voice was soft and hampered. Though he tried to hold back any signs of trouble, she knew he was hurt. He slouched back in his seat, clutching his right side. She could smell the tang of blood on him. He'd been shot. How bad? Where?

"I want to take you to a hospital," Ayden stated.

"No," Chet responded through a wooden expression.

A second cop car materialized behind them.

"Great," she mumbled.

Chet exhaled. "We're not going to get caught."

"We're not?"

He shook his head.

Ayden snuck a glimpse at him, and instantly regretted it. Even obscured by the darkness, she could see his face covered in red residue. His hair was messy and matted. She let her gaze flick to his hands that were balled into fists in his shirt. They were wet with fluid. She met his stare and saw her horror reflected in his eyes. They looked like precious stones, blinking methodically at her.

"I don't know what to do," Ayden told him.

"You mean you don't have a plan?" Chet asked. He hissed through his teeth and pinched his eyes shut. "Yet here you are, coming to my rescue. Just drive. You know what you're doing."

"But we're being followed." She tried to outrun them. The Mustang had some extra advantages under its hood. "What if they call for backup? What if we get caught and arrested and…"

Just as she said it, an enormous brown truck surged through an intersection and smacked into the front police car. The truck was boxy and old, rusted around the edges. Both cars slid sideways, into the oncoming second policeman. It successfully delayed the cops' advance, and Ayden was able to drive the Mustang onto the freeway without crossfire. Once in the fast lane, she stomped on the pedal until they were cruising well above the speed limit. She didn't care. There wasn't any about at this hour, and all of Fresno's authorities were heading up the criminal investigaion surrounding the nightclub. Driving in the direction of Nolan's cabin, she finally let out a puff of air in relief.

"Nice one, toots," Chet whispered.

They'd gone a few miles. Ayden peered over at him, shocked at how pale he looked. His skin was ashen. Circles hovered beneath his eyes. He tried to smile at her.

"Chet, you're not alright," she stated.

"Don't be dramatic. I've been shot before. This is just—ah!"

"What? What is it?"

"Nothing," he moaned, shifting in his seat. "Just drive. There will be medical supplies at the cabin. Or, at least, hunting supplies. Same thing, right?"

"Right," she murmured, and she abruptly changed lanes. Exiting the freeway, she sped down the off ramp. Tires chirped as she pulled into the nearest gas station and slammed the car in park. "Stay here."

"Yes, ma'am," Chet uttered.

Ayden took her emergency cash and ran into the gas station. The attendant was an elderly fellow, watching some boring game show on the miniature television. He didn't look up upon her entering, so she disregarded him, too. Pacing hurriedly toward the pharmaceuticals, she clutched anything she could find that might be useful. Band-Aids, gauze, OTC painkillers, tape, tweezers, sanitizer, Neosporin. On the way to the register, she snatched two packages of donuts and a bag of licorice.

Back inside the Mustang, Chet was panting. Ayden was winded from all the running and panicking.

"Take your shirt off," she commanded.

"Here?" Chet questioned. "First you refuse to get in the backseat of my car, now you're commanding me to. I know I'm irresistible, but couldn't it wait? I'm in an awful lot of pain and a bed sounds so much more pleasant."

"Chet!" Ayden barked.

He removed his shirt and tossed it in the backseat. There was too much blood for her to see the puncture wound. He was still clasping his right side.

"Let me see," she said.

He angled his body toward her, lifting his palm so she could view the smattering of perforations. It wasn't a single bullet. He'd been struck by the wreckage of a shotgun shell.

"It's really not as bad as it looks," Chet commentated.

"What did I say about shutting up?" Ayden snapped.

"Yes, ma'am," he replied dutifully.

She was digging through her bag of purchases. First, she pulled out the tweezers. If there were any remains in Chet's skin, they would have to be detached. While she set to work examining his skin, he fingered a package of donuts.

"Are these to curtail the bleeding?" he asked.

"They're because I'm starving," she replied.

He ripped it open with his teeth and took a huge bite of the first donut. He hummed in appreciation. Then he held it up to her lips. Without taking her eyes of his abdomen, she opened her mouth. He pressed the package to her lips and she took the second donut from the package, chewing. A minute later, she decided

228

Chet's skin was salvageable. She slathered some sanitizer on her hands and started cleaning his wounds. It was almost useless, as he was still bleeding, but it didn't appear to have resulted in internal damage.

Using the gauze, Ayden started wrapping the bandages around Chet's middle. He would lean forward an inch, groaning every time, as she reached around his back to tighten the strips. Next, she took the tape and secured it all into place. He had eaten the whole package of donuts and was opening the second. Again, he offered Ayden a bite. She complied, feeling her hunger abate as she tended him. When she was almost complete, she looked up.

"This is going to scar."

He shrugged.

Ayden finished and sat back to wipe her hands on her pants. Her hair was everywhere, she just noticed, and she brushed it out of her face. Chet was lying in an awkward position, obviously trying to alleviate some of the pain from his middle. He was facing her, and the light from the gas station poured in through the windshield, illuminating his bare chest and face. He was here. His heart was beating. He was going to live. She felt like she could breathe again.

Her eyes dropped to the bandages that covered the three raised scars he had below his ribcage.

"You've been shot before," she stated. "Were you also stabbed?"

Chet chuckled lightly and grimaced. "Uh, yeah. All of the above."

"What haven't you been?"

"Me?" he asked nonchalantly. "Hung from a bridge."

Ayden laughed. Her head fell back onto the headrest and she sighed.

"Is it over?" she asked after a moment.

A smile spread across his face as he nodded. He closed his eyes, still nodding.

"You were…impeccable tonight," he whispered through the dark.

The dance on the pole felt like years ago.

She took hold of his forearm and squeezed it. Several hours

drive did not sound appealing, but she wanted to rest. Good grief, she wanted rest.

"How many…" Her voice caught, and she cleared her throat. "How many men did you have to kill?"

Chet's eyes snapped open. He had the audacity to look offended.

"I didn't break my promise."

"How is that possible?" Ayden questioned.

He gave a lift of one shoulder, touching his wound with a crusty palm. "You know. I shot *at* them. Near them. Made them tap like puppets."

"You made it out of there without killing a single soul?"

"Not a single one. But—" he interrupted when she started to express reprieve –"my team. I don't know who is left."

Ayden made a face.

"I know," Chet drawled. "But it is all over for you now. Once we get back to the cabin, you're free to go where you please. You don't *please* to stick around in Fresno, do you?"

"Not at all," she responded through a yawn.

He covered her hand with his, apologizing about the mess. She waved him off, interlacing their fingers. When he stayed silent a few more minutes, she glanced up at him worried.

"What about you?" Ayden asked.

"Hm?"

"What will you do?"

Chet held her gaze, a gentleness lining his eyes that she hadn't seen nearly enough. For several long minutes, he just watched her. He looked truly liberated. It was the truth. They were really done with Saucedo and the business.

"I plan on taking a vacation. Indefinitely," he told her.

Ayden knew he was skirting around her question. What she really wanted to know was who he would be vacationing with. If he was hesitant to tell her, she already knew the answer.

Ayden murmured, "Will I…be able to contact you? Ever?"

"If you want," Chet replied cautiously.

"What do *you* want?" she asked tentatively.

"Ayden," he said. His hand constricted on hers. "I wonder, if maybe, you wouldn't be better off without any connection to me whatsoever. Trust me—I do want to stay in contact with you. I really want...us."

Us.

The one little word made her float and sink at the same time.

Ayden forced the words out of her mouth. "What about Keeley?"

"I'll take her with me," was Chet's brisk reply. "I guess. I mean, I could take her wherever she wanted to go, but—"

"But you want to be with her?"

"Not like I want to be with you."

She kept her eyes away from his jewel ones.

"If I recall," Chet stated, "yesterday you said, and I quote, 'after midnight tomorrow I'm gone.'"

Ayden remembered those feelings. She *did* want to get out of town and never see these people again. But she wanted...*us* too.

"It doesn't give me a lot of expectation," he said under his breath. "Or hope. I wish there was some way to help you understand. Keeley and I...we need to spend some time together. I think it would be good for her. She's suffered—"

"Emotional trauma?" Ayden said, repeating his reason for why Keeley'd been in rehab with him.

"More than that," Chet elaborated. "I'm responsible for her, and I just know it would help her—to—build a stronger relationship. With me." He pinched his eyes shut and squirmed against his painful stomach. "I never really thought I'd be given this opportunity. I don't think I tried hard enough for it. Before. But now that it's here, my freedom..."

"Chet, please stop trying to put it in plain words."

"If you gave it some time," he carried on, "maybe you'd find it easier to accept. She and I." He seemed frustrated with himself, so he grunted and tried again. "I need time. Just while Keeley and I...make up for lost time. I only want what is best for you. Just because I do not work for Saucedo anymore does not mean my life is spotless. I'll always have—this tarnished history—these ugly wolves of my past. Don't you think you ought to try and find some...thing better?"

"I honestly don't know," Ayden exhaled.

She was so unbelievably tired, she couldn't think accurately. It was hard to hate his motives. What he was doing for Keeley sounded reasonably noble. Especially if Keeley was ensnared in Saucedo's business also. Chet wanted to help the poor girl, whoever she was. They'd all be free of the underworld of crime. Chet had told Ayden that he wanted only her. Nevertheless, she was insanely jealous of Keeley.

Chet gave Ayden's hand another compression and tilted his chin toward the steering wheel.

"Let's get back to the cabin," he suggested. "We can talk more in the morning. Right now, I need what you need."

She gave him a cynical glare. "A bath and a nap by a log fire?"

"Precisely."

"Licorice?"

"Coming right up."

31

Ayden dragged her feet up the porch steps to the cabin. It was early in the morning, and the air was crisp and cool. The sky was a pale shade of blue. Birds were chirping around in the thicket of trees. Chet hobbled behind her, still shirtless with a hand supporting his wounded side. Goosebumps sprouted up across his bare chest and arms, and Ayden had the sudden desire to brush them with her fingertips. She paused at the front door, examining the red splotches on his skin. Her own hands were filthy.

Nolan was out. The note on the kitchen counter said so, in that one word message. Chet eased his way into the bathroom and drew a bath for Ayden. He would have to wash himself in the sink, since he couldn't submerge his injuries in water yet. Ayden left the bathroom door unlcoked as she sunk below the steaming water. It made her feel safer. She smiled when she heard a radio crackle to life outside in the living room, and Elvis began enchanting their countryside abode with Are You Lonesome Tonight.

When she was finished, Ayden put on some clean clolthes and wrapped her hair in a towel. She was still in the bathroom when Chet entered carrying a bundle of towels and shaving gear. She hadn't paid attention to the scruff growing on his cheeks. It was so blonde one wouldn't see it from afar. His hair was still dyed black, which she preferred. She loved the way it made his blue eyes glint.

Chet set to work at the sink, dabbing shaving cream on his cheeks and throat. The razor glided across his skin. His back muscles contorted with his movements, pulling against the gauze Ayden taped to his side. She surveyed him and the way he was humming to the music. A moment later, his eyes flicked up to the mirror and caught her staring back. He gave her a modest smile.

"What would you like to do today?" he asked, tucking his upper lip under to shave off the whiskers there.

Ayden shrugged. They had options now? Could she appropriately repsond, "I want to go miniature golfing?"

"I don't have much to pack," she said. "I just want to sleep and sleep and sleep. When I wake up, then I can decide where to go."

"Sounds good," Chet replied, lifting his chin for an upward stroke.

When he was done, he rinsed his face and used the towel to wash his torso. He left the bathroom a moment, and returned wearing the long johns he'd borrowed from Nolan. A flannel shirt was draped over his shoulders, hanging open in the front. He set a second flannel shirt on the counter for Ayden, along with her fuzzy socks. His hair was damp and he gave it a shake, running his fingers through the ends until they stuck up.

"I need a trim," he muttered. "Are you up for the task?"

"Nap first," she yawned. "Haircut later."

He chuckled.

"I've got the fire going," he said. "There's a mound of blankets on the couch. You can sleep all day. All week if you want."

"You'll be here?"

"In and out."

"Hm."

Chet stepped to the bathroom door. Glancing back, he pointed his index finger at the front window and said, "I'll be out front working on my car."

Ayden smirked. "Sorry for the cosmetic damage."

He coiled that index finger toward his abdomen. "I'm used to it." And then he left.

Ayden was hibernating two feet deep in blankets. The fire was cracking, warming the room pleasantly with fragment fumes. The interior of the cabin glowed under the flash of flames. There was nary a sound except The King singing softly from the radio. It was so cozy and peaceful, she slept for four hours straight. She was awake now, just listening to embers sizzle, watching the orange coals flare and dim. The last twenty-four hours were a distant confusion. She wasn't sure what time it was, and had no desire to find out. Nolan's concept of light and dark made a lot more sense. She was just glad her dealings with Fresno druglords were finished.

Chet walked through the front door still wearing pajamas, although the flannel shirt was tied around his waist. Sweat dotted his breastbone and forehead. His hands were blackened with engine grease. He was carrying some kind of car part in a dirty cloth. Leaning down, he peeked into the heap of blankets to see if Ayden was awake. Her eyes darted to his. She grinned. He'd probably never understand how devastatingly sexy she found him, especially covered in oil.

"Its two-o-clock," he remarked, moving into the kitchen. "Want something to eat?"

"Sure," she mumbled. "Where's Nolan?"

"Hunting," Chet answered, washing his hands in the sink. "He'll be back tonight."

"Nice of him to give us some space," Ayden murmured.

"Yeah. Nolan is a caring guy. Lina, his wife, was probably the most charitable woman I've ever met. She's the one who encouraged and sponsored my first trip to rehab. I thought—Lina would be there when I got out."

Ayden sat up on the couch and gazed across the room at Chet. He was speaking about his past. Openly. The way he mentioned Lina's involvment in Chet's attending rehab made it sound like he wanted to get clean. Perhaps for her. Or she and Nolan. It was a rare occasion that Chet opened up to Ayden about his younger years. She hoped that meant he trusted her more and more.

"What happened to Lina?"

"I'm not sure," Chet replied. "Addictions, demons, depression. We're not the most lucid clan, if you haven't noticed."

Ayden kind of wished he wouldn't drift into sarcasm when she really wanted to know the truth, but she didn't pry further. Plenty of free time awaited them. Nolan didn't have much by way of groceries. They snacked on popcorn and grilled-cheese sandwiches.

"Luxury dining," Chet called it.

He had a soda, which reminded Ayden of the days they spent at the estate. He'd go through several a day.

When Ayden asked him why he was fond of sugared pop drinks, he told her, "Actually, it's kind of a substitute. People who quit hard drugs, they often find other forms of stimulants. Lots of people pick soda, coffee. Caffeine, sugar, sex."

Ayden glanced at him stoically. "Don't call me Ashley."

Chet smacked her socked foot. They were sitting opposite one another on the couch. Her feet were poking out of the blankets, and Chet had propped them in his lap. She was pretty sure she'd never looked less appealing, but somehow not having to care so much about her physical appearance around Chet made her adore him even more. He enjoyed being with her for her. "Which one is your favorite? Ayden inquired, blushing afterward.

Chet lambasted her with a crooked grin. "I'll give you one guess."

"Sugar?"

"Wrong!" He captured one of her feet. His fingers trickled up her calf. Then he wrenched her leg forward so that her body scooted toward him. Adjusting her legs in his lap, he answered, "It's caffeine."

She giggled. "Speaking of caffeine. You look like you could use some."

Chet raised one eyebrow. He rubbed his freshly shaven jaw as if he'd spent hours preparing for a beauty pageant.

"You've got indents the size of Mars under your eyes," she remarked.

"I've been shot," he argued playfully. "What's your excuse?"

"I'm sleep deprived, stressed, been up all night, picked up a Ninja Turtle in an alleyway, and been forced to endure the company of a lumberjack outlaw who has the uncanny ability to make tiny, brown longjohns look more stylish than I can."

"Thank you, toots," Chet teased. "While we're being complimentary, might I just say that your hair looks like a witch's broom in all its divinity."

Ayden kicked out at him, but he dodged her heel, slumping back against the armrest with a lazy smirk. She grabbed an armful of blankets and scowled. He looked younger and happier. Every time he opened his mouth to talk, she'd catch fleeting glimpses of his tongue ring. Amazing, she thought, how they'd morphed from strangers in a motel room into the closest of friends at a Lake Tahoe resort.

Raking her fingers through some of her tangles, Ayden cocked her head to one side. She wasn't a virgin, and most of intimacy had lost its value while she was married to Mitchell, who robbed her soul of the precious parts of intimacy with his abuse. However, Ayden allowed herself to imagine being intimate with

Chet. Under moral circumstances, of course. It was pleasing to feel like she could enjoy a man's touch after all. Even a snoozing, lumberjack outlaw.

"You know what would be fun?" she asked.

Chet's chest rumbled in response. He was still affectionately holding one of her feet, toying with the fuzzy sock.

"Going for a ride on your bike," she finished.

His eyes lit up with boyish excitement. "In the woods? That could be dangerous."

His gaze slid sideways to hers. She raised her eyebrows.

"Let's go!" he whispered, and he hopped up off the couch so quickly Ayden nearly fell over.

They changed into jeans and boots, Chet in his all black, and met outside near where his motorcycle was stored beneath a tarp. He checked the motor, the oil, the tire pressure. It had been a while since he'd started it. He turned the key and gassed the throttle, revving it a few times. The engine echoed across the mountains like the howl of a lion. Ayden loved it.

Chet walked the bike toward the lake, and Ayden followed. Pine needles crunched under her feet. She kicked a pinecone in front of her. Tied to the dock was Nolan's small canoe. She still longed to take it around the lake before she left. Who knew when she'd come back to the cabin? If ever? Maybe she'd leave Lake Tahoe, move out of the state, and never return to California.

"We'll take the path around the lake," Chet explained.

"Will the motorcycle fit through the trees?" Ayden asked skeptical.

He shrugged. "We'll make it work. Over there, you see that ridge? You can get cell service up there."

"Because I have so many people I need to call."

He grinned. "There's a great view, too. Hop on."

They straddled the bike, Ayden snuggled tightly into Chet's back, carefully wrapping her ams around his bandaged middle. She smiled when he tore through the trees, the front wheel popping into a wheelie before the bike cruised onto the skinny, dirt trail. Ayden yelped, clinging to Chet for dear life. Tree branches hung low and scraped against their arms as he drove. The path was lumpy, and

Chet had to stick his foot out on the sharper turns to keep the bike from tipping. They jumped over logs, rocks, veered close to the lake shoreline, and back into the forest. When they reached an uphill path, Chet stopped and rested his foot on the ground to balance them. He teased the clutch and glanced over his shoulder.

"Hang on tight. I'm gonna go fast."

Ayden nodded.

His left foot shifted, and they sped up the mountainside. The bike caught a little air as they mounted the incline. Ayden fell into Chet's back as he hit the brakes and slowed the bike. Blowing a strand of hair out of her eyes, she clutched his shoulders, delighting in the round firmness. After killing the engine, he tousled his own hair and swung his leg off the seat. He helped her dismount and flipped down the kickstand. Lifting the hem of his black shirt, he checked the bandages on his abdomen. They looked alright. He was moving stiffly, so she suspected it still pained him.

"Sorry. Did I hurt you?" Ayden questioned.

"Nah," he replied, patting his navel. "Come over here."

They strode through the foliage, emerging at a huge boulder overlooking the lake. A fish jumped, causing an orbit of ripples in the water below. Ayden breathed in the mountain air, in awe of the sight before her. The sun was sinking toward the horizon—a jagged line of cresting peaks—and the sunshine twinkled off the waves below. It was still a few hours before sunset, and she was tempted to sit on the rock until then just to garnish this memory with a bit more beauty.

Chet sidled up to her side, nudging her shoulder with his elbow. Together, they stared out over the Sierras, somehow hearing the unspoken message between them. This was a goodbye. Temporary, but the length of time was unknown. Tonight, they would pack their meager belongings into separate bags, and drive away to separate places. Ayden was set to disappear. Chet had a life to live, with Keeley.

"Are you cold?" Chet asked.

The breeze was nippy, but Ayden had worn a jacket as a precaution. She shook her head.

"Do you want to sit?"

She grinned. "Yes."

So they sat down on the ledge of the boulder, letting their legs dangle over the rim. There was a long drop before a canopy of evergreens. It was the least dangerous thing she'd ever done, but it would be the most dangerous thing she'd do for the rest of the year, she mused. Chet scratched at his sleeve of tattoos, and then stretched, relaxing into his laissez-faire persona.

"What do you think?" he asked, breaking the silence. "Cabin or cabana?"

"Cabana," she replied hastily.

"Ditto."

"I would like to live somewhere with a view like this," she observed. "Part of the year. Somewhere so quiet and calm. Far away from civilization and crowds. It would be a fun summer home, to escape from the heat."

"Sounds dreamy," he murmured. "It could be pleasant. In the winter. I bet you could sled down these moutains in a toboggan."

She quirked her brow. "Did you just say toboggan?"

"Yes. Toboggan. What? Why are you looking at me like that?"

Ayden smiled dopily. "'Cause normal people don't say toboggan."

Chet smiled back insecurely. He shook his arms out in front of him. Cool guys said tobaggon.

"You've been sledding before..."

"Yes, on a sled," she responded. "I've seen snow, also. White fluffy stuff. Freakishly cold."

"Ha ha."

She shook her head and muttered under her breath. "Tobaggon." Then, "You have a lot of money, Chet. I imagine it won't be difficult for you to get yourself a place up here. *And* a fancy toboggan."

"Have you checked your savings account recently?" he asked, not looking her in the eye. His left hand panned across the horizon. "You've complelty cleaned me out. The tabloids read: Chet and Ayden go through multi-million dollar break-up."

He smirked at himself.

Ayden tossed her hair over one shoulder. "Multi-million

dollar?"

He gave her a sinner's smile. "We just broke up, and you want to know numbers?"

"We didn't break up." She rolled her eyes. "And I didn't clean you out." She'd never permit it.

"Did we split everything, 50/50?" he asked.

"Even the cars."

"Ouch."

"I'm going to take the Yenko Chevelle to a car auction," she decided.

Chet's eyes widened. "You're going to do what?"

"I want to donate the proceeds to a charity that focuses on struggling youth." His head shook. To his smile, she added, "Maybe even those addicted to drugs."

"You'll have to repent for giving away such a beautiful creation," he muttered, disappointed, she knew, that it wouldn't remain part of his automobile collection.

"I think God will look past the indiscretion," Ayden teased. "For what it's worth, I'm giving ten percent of the profits to my church's charity."

She rubbed his back as he moaned, "I'll pretend that makes it easier to accept."

"I'll keep the fuzzy, flamingo keychain. For old time's sake." He dropped his head and mourned the loss. "From there. I don't know. I'll probably end up in a studio apartment in the midwest, developing a southern accent."

Chet liked the sound of that.

"It would suit your Justins," he mentioned.

She kicked up a booted foot. "They've grown on me."

His gaze slid over her, envisioning the black bikini he'd first seen her wear at Pismo. "You still miss the ocean?"

"Every day."

"There are some fabulous beaches in South Carolina I hear."

She glanced up at him then, and although he was smiling his tantalizing smile, the mask he wore at "work" had been removed. His eyes harbored a hidden grief. While his laugh was genuine, so was his mourning. She didn't know how to feel about the fact that he was dreading being separated from her.

They indulged both their fantasies, Ayden's desire to stay a few hours and watch the sunset over the magnificent mountain range, and Chet's desire to remain as close to Ayden as possible for as long as possible. He promised not to be a creepy stalker. She called him a liar. He called her a renegade diva. The sky transitioned from blue to peach. Simmering rays lengthened across the lake where a few people where enjoying the view from rowboats. She'd never take Nolan's canoe out.

Ayden watched a pair of birds flirting in the distance. Their wings flapped rapidly as they fluttered into a tree. Some birds mate for life. Some mammals do, too.

"Time," she sighed. "'*Goes by. So slowly. And time can do so much.*'"

There was a long moment of quiet. It surprised her when Chet leaned closer and rested his chin in the hollow of her neck.

He whispered, "'*Are you...still mine?*'"

His voice held a raw ache. It made her heart miss him. He was familiar with The Righteous Brothers, then? He knew everything. It was stupidly unfair. He was a freaking, walking almanac of random information. And she loved each and every part of him. Every page. Every chapter. The sequel...

She turned her face to his just as he kissed her. It was the sweetest of kisses. A treaty.

Ayden's fingertips grazed Chet's jaw, down his neck, to the back of his head. He wrapped an arm around her, drawing her close to his side. She tucked her knees into his lap, linking her arms around him until there was no more space to diminish. The wind swept around them, tossing leaves, carrying the scent of pine up into the clouds, as the sun set on an uncharted future.

Epilogue

Ayden hoisted the bag of groceries against her hip, kicked the car door shut, and took the house keys from her mouth. She glanced up and saw a man standing on her porch. He was tall and broad, with silver-flecked, cocoa-colored hair. His suit was of the finest quality, right down to his shiny dress shoes. There was an ease in his stance as he rocked from one foot to the other. His hands were clasped behind his back. She wondered how long he'd been standing there, so sure of himself.

Door salesmen were annoying.

Stepping up the sidewalk, Ayden cleared her throat loudly. "Can I help you?"

The man turned, displaying a face mangled by an abundance of scars. He smiled, and the features that must have been handsome at some point puckered.

"Hello, Ayden."

The bag of groceries slipped from her grasp and dropped to the ground.

"Mitchell."

About the Author

Brittany Shannon is the author of the Conquest of Canaan trilogy. Book one, Og, Book two, Rahab, and book three, Jael are part of a historical fiction, adventure saga detailing the story of Joshua who crusaded across Canaan, mixing fact and fiction, for sensitive biblical enthusiasts and ancient dreamers alike. She has worked for a marketing agency as a creative content writer and currently evaluates manuscripts for a local publishing company. Her hobbies include anything within the realm of the performance arts, cooking, fitness, and cosmetology--which has been her career of choice for over a decade. She volunteers for The Addiction Recovery Program and has a special place in her heart for the beautifully broken. She thanks her husband and children for being her favorite people in the whole world, and allowing her to pursue many of her ambitions in between scooping up poop, wiping up poop, and scrubbing poop out of clothes, bedsheets, and the carpet. Although she spent some years in the past inactive, she is a loyal Latter Day Saint, and has a strong testimony of her Savior, Jesus Christ, whom she hopes to please with how she spends her time and talents. For more about Brittany visit BrittanyShannon.com.

www.ingramcontent.com/pod-product-compliance
Lightning Source LLC
Chambersburg PA
CBHW020638260626
47157CB00008B/2812